Go To Sleep, Tully!

Available in the Tales of Tully series

Tully's Life
This heart-warming story follows the journey of Tully from street dog to much-loved family pet, teaching young readers about the importance of kindness, understanding and hope.

Tully Takes Off!
Tully has arrived in her new home with her new grown-up, but she does not like it one bit! When Tully sees an opportunity to go back to her old life on the streets - the only life she has known up to now - she takes it with both paws. With a search underway, it is up to her new grown-up to work out what Tully needs and help get her safely home.

Tully and the Sad Day
Tully has woken up feeling grey and cloudy inside and she does not know what to do. She cannot help her big feeling because she does not know what it is. As her different feelings begin to work together in the wrong way, it is up to Tully's grown-up to help her to understand what she needs.

Go To Sleep Tully!
It is night time and Tully is tired, but she does not want to go to sleep. Her new grown-up knows that Tully is trying every trick she can to avoid going go to bed! With lots of adventures planned and Tully needing her rest, Tully's grown-up needs to find a way to help Tully learn to not be so worried about bedtime.

Tully and the Midnight Feast
Tully is a newly-adopted dog settling in with her new grown-up. Since her arrival, her snacks have started mysteriously disappearing from the cupboard and appearing under her bed, she seems to have forgotten her manners, and there are days when she just cannot stop eating! Tully and her grown-up need to work together to help Tully with her worries about food.

Tully and the Scary Day
Tully has woken up feeling scared. She isn't really sure why, but today feels like a very scary day, and she just wants to hide. Tully's grown-up is thankfully there to help Tully manage her big feelings and see that the day is not so scary after all.

Don't Touch Tully!
Tully is settling in with her new grown-up She has learned that the new grown-up is a safe person and she enjoys strokes and cuddles with them. Then Tully starts to meet new people, who want to show her how loved she is. Unfortunately, Tully doesn't feel the same about people she does not know and trust. It is up to Tully's grown-up to find a way to help Tully with her big feelings and to be Tully's voice, when she can't use hers.

Tully and the Tummy Ache
Tully has a tummy ache and it's making her feel quite grumpy. She doesn't want to eat or drink, and she can't get comfortable. Her tummy is sore and it's getting worse! Tully is in a toilet muddle. So, Tully and her grown-up work together to sort the muddle out and help Tully to cure her tummy ache.

Tully's Birthday
It's Tully's birthday, and her grown-up has planned a special day for her, but Tully doesn't feel like celebrating. As the day begins to unfold, so do Tully's big feelings. Tully doesn't know what to do about the big feelings, so she does a bad thing. Luckily, Tully's grown-up is there to help her feel better about herself, and enjoy the rest of her birthday.

Listen, Tully!
Tully does not always like to listen, especially when her grown-up is trying to stop her having fun. Tully decides that instead of listening, she can be in charge. But when things start to go wrong, Tully and her grown-up need to work out how Tully can begin to find listening a little bit easier.

Tully and the Makeover
Tully has been having lots of fun playing in the mud, but now her grown-up says she has to have a bath. Oh dear! Tully is not sure she wants one of those. She is feeling a bit nervous about what is going to happen to her, but Tully's grown-up shows her that there is nothing to worry about. Having a bath is a good thing after all.

Tully and Vera
Tully has moved in with her new grown-up but she is missing her foster carer, Vera. Tully is struggling to understand why she had to leave, and whether it is okay to have big feelings about Vera. It is up to Tully's grown-up to try and help her to understand loss and endings and why, sometimes, they have to happen to make space for new beginnings.

Tully and the Chase
Tully loves to be chased. It gives her a feeling of excitement which starts off as being fun, but one day the excited feeling suddenly and very quickly becomes a feeling which is too big. Instead of feeling excited, Tully starts to feel scared. Tully and her grown-up need to work out how they can play Tully's exciting game without it becoming a bit too much for her, and causing a muddle.

Tully at Christmas
Things are starting to feel a bit different in Tully's house and all around outside. Tully's grown-up looks different, strange lights are appearing everywhere and people have started putting their gardens indoors! Tully is not sure what to make of this thing called Christmas – she just wants everything to stay the same. What can Tully's grown-up do to make Christmas-time a nicer time for both of them?

Tully Goes on Holiday
Tully has gone on a holiday with her grown-up. After a difficult start, things seem to be going well. But when the fairground opens up, with all its flashing lights, loud music and food smells, Tully's big feelings get the better of her, making her want to run. And she does! Tully's grown-up needs to find her in time to show her that holidays can be fun after all.

Tully and the New Rules
Tully likes lots of things about living in a house with her grown-up, but one thing she really doesn't like is all the rules! Tully thinks the rules are all very boring and her grown-up must want to stop her from having fun. One day Tully breaks her least favourite rule, and something bad happens. Tully doesn't know what to do! Can Tully's grown-up get to the bottom of this muddle so it doesn't happen again?

Go To Sleep, Tully!

TALES OF TULLY

Jess van der Hoech

JV Trauma Tools & Training

ISBN-13 978-1-83-81987-8-7
Editing by Sarah Ogden
www.jvtraumatools.co.uk

Acknowledgements

As always, to my trusted editor Sarah Ogden for all that you do to make these books come to life. I will never fully know what goes on behind the scenes, but it is a joy to work alongside you on these projects. Thank you.

Thank you to my supervisor Linda Hoggan for your continued support, encouragement, discussion and much-welcomed feedback on this series. I learn so much from you and the knowledge I have gained form our conversations has been invaluable across my practice, the books and now this series. Thank you.

Thank you to Laura Benham, for your support in giving me feedback, the searching questions, your friendship and of course, the countless conversations about dogs, the content of which has become quite useful! Thank you.

To the children and families who I meet in my therapy room, from whom I have learned more about hope and healing than any course could ever teach me. Your input, ideas, questions and answers are so valuable to me and I will be forever grateful. Thank you.

Preface

The Tales of Tully Series is based on the adoption of an ex street dog from Bosnia who came to live with me in September 2023. Watching her try to settle and adapt from everything she had previously known to fit in with a new way of life began to present a number of ideas as to how to communicate such difficulties that can be experienced, to others who are in the process of adopting or who have adopted children. The aim of the series is to provide an opportunity to explore different situations, circumstances, feelings and experiences, finding new ways of communicating and understanding each other, through the voice of Tully.

Bedtimes can be a tricky experience for children and parents for multiple reasons. Bedrooms are decorated to perfection, blackout blinds in place to counteract the effects of the light summer nights, fans for the warm weather and heaters when it's cold are all measures put in place to create the perfect ambiance for a good night's rest, but still, some children find it hard to sleep.

For children who have been adopted, night time can be the most complex time of day. Fears of the dark itself, or fear of the unknown that the morning might bring, can create huge worries for the child. With a mind full of worries and big feelings, conscious or not, sleep can be difficult.

When Tully first arrived in the UK, she attempted to stay awake for days, such was her high level of fear, angst and confusion. The smallest noise woke her and I would often witness her body attempting to give in to the need for sleep, her eyes gently beginning to close, before she remembered that sleep was not a safe state and so she would fight it once again. Similarly, I hear descriptions of bedtimes in my therapy room; the child needing to check the parent is still there or trying to stay awake for as long as possible, the list of tactics to stay awake becoming more bizarre the later it gets!

Through the story of Tully, the children were able to give me significant information about their experiences of bedtime and night time in general. Once the information was in the room, parents and children could begin to work together to find ways of alleviating the fears, making bedtime and night time routines a more comfortable experience for everyone.

How to use this book

First and foremost, ensure that both you and the child are well-regulated and comfortable when you begin to read Tully's story. Make sure you choose a time when you are unlikely to be interrupted. The child may like a soother, a favourite or fidget toy, a drink or something to suck or chew to help them to stay regulated.

If the child is calm, then begins to try and distract or move away from the reading, make a note of what they have just heard in the text. It is very likely that they will have just provided you with some valuable information about something that they cannot tolerate or want to avoid for now.

The questions have been designed not only to explore the internal world of the child, but to help to develop a common language between the child and adult who are using this book together. The child cannot get the answers to the questions incorrect. Their interpretation of the thoughts and feelings Tully is having may provide some very significant information about the child's own thoughts and feelings. The child may want to expand the answers to talk about themselves and may even be able to make comparisons between Tully's feelings and their own.

Go To Sleep, Tully!

Tully lay on the sofa, gazing out of the window, watching as the sun started to set. It looked very beautiful, but Tully could only think about one thing. Soon, it would be bedtime.

How might Tully feel about bedtime?

How do you feel about bedtime?

Tully started to get a big feeling in her tummy. She did not like bedtime one bit.

What things might Tully not like about bedtime?

There were lots of reasons Tully did not like bedtime. When Tully had been a street dog in Bosnia, night time was very scary for her. It was so scary, that Tully often tried to stay awake all night. Now, the dark reminded Tully of the scary feeling and she felt like she still had to stay awake, just in case.

Can you draw Tully in the dark?

How do you feel about the dark?

When Tully had lived with her foster carer in the shelter in Bosnia, she had felt safer there and she liked it.

One morning, Tully had been woken up and then taken on a bus to the UK and had moved in with her adoptive family.

How might Tully have felt about moving to her adoptive family?

Tully sometimes worried that when morning came round, her new grown-up would be gone too.

Why might Tully have this worry?

When it was dark outside, the noises in the house sounded very loud. Sometimes, Tully did not know what the noises were. She did not like this at all!

What noises might Tully hear in the house at night?

Tully had a very comfortable bed with a blanket, but she had to stay on her own in the bed and this gave Tully a big feeling.

What feelings might Tully have about being on her own?

What could help Tully with these feelings?

Tully could hear her grown-up calling her to get into bed. Tully stood at the door to be let out for the toilet. "You've been to the toilet Tully, you don't need to go again" her grown-up said.

Tully scratched on the door to let her grown-up know that she definitely did need to go to the toilet again, even though she didn't!

Why is Tully pretending to need the toilet again?

When Tully came back inside after her walk in the garden, she crept upstairs and hid next to her grown-up's bed. Tully could hear her grown-up calling her, but she decided to ignore her grown-up, even though she knew she should be listening.

How might Tully be feeling now?

Tully's grown-up came and found her and sat beside her, stroking her head.

"I know you find bedtime scary Tully and I don't think you like the dark very much. I am going to leave a little light on for you so you don't have to worry about the dark anymore."

How does Tully feel about this?

"I am keeping you safe now," Tully's grown-up told her. "We live in a safe house and I am your safe grown-up. We have busy days ahead and it's important that you get enough sleep for when we go on our adventures. I don't want you to not enjoy our days together because you're tired!"

"I am going to leave my t-shirt in your bed because it smells of me and it will remind you of where you are and that I will be here when you wake in the morning."

How does Tully feel about this?

Tully and her grown-up went together to Tully's bed.

The light was left on and the t-shirt was in Tully's bed. The grown-up tucked her in and stroked her head as she began to fall asleep.

Every evening, Tully and her grown up completed the same routine. Tully and her grown-up sat together to have a snack and a small drink. Tully went out to the toilet and when she came back in, she got into her bed with her grown-up's t-shirt in it. Her grown-up sat beside her and stroked her head until she began to fall asleep.

How does Tully feel about her night time routine?

What is your night time routine?

One evening, after completing the night time routine, Tully noticed a feeling she had not had before at night time. She felt tired, relaxed and comfortable. At last, Tully felt safe.

"Have sweet dreams Tully" her grown-up told her.

And she did.

What dreams might Tully have?

How do you feel about bedtime?

Is there anything that would make bedtime even better for you?

About the author

Jess van der Hoech is a qualified therapist who has spent the last ten years studying and working with the impact of developmental trauma and, in particular, the assessment and treatment of children and adolescents with complex trauma and dissociation.

As well as supporting birth families, Jess works with looked-after and adopted children and families, using skills in attachment-focused therapy and therapeutic parenting techniques.

Jess is a supervisor, trainer and motivational speaker with a passion for writing therapeutic books that are accessible to children and families to help with the healing process and to increase awareness in the impact of trauma.

Also by Jess van der Hoech

What A Muddle (2016) ISBN 978 18381987 0 1 (Co-authored with Renée Potgieter Marks)
An interactive, practical workbook designed to help children who have difficulties with emotional regulation to begin to understand what is happening in their bodies. A variety of activities throughout the book enable the child to start to explore these ideas through the story of Sam, while gently encouraging them to begin to verbalise their own experiences. Carrying out the physical exercises in the book can promote changes in emotional regulation. The text is written in a child-friendly, gender-neutral style, and is easy to understand for parents, carers and practitioners alike. For children aged 4-12.

These Three Words (2018) ISBN 978 18381987 5 6
Also available as an e-book. A unique therapeutic novel for teenagers with the aim of linking together the feelings, emotions and behaviours connected to anxiety, with some of the therapeutic tools that can be used in order to enable better self-regulation, increased confidence and different ways of thinking. The book is equally valuable to parents of teenagers with anxiety, giving them an insight and understanding into some of the issues that may be affecting their child, and potentially opening up a line of communication and a way forward between parent and teen.

These Three Words: The Journal (2019) ISBN 978 18381987 2 5
A thought-provoking and hands-on workbook, combining a series of practical exercises and tools designed to assist teenagers who are struggling with the symptoms of anxiety. Addressing the anxious responses in both brain and body, this journal provides the reader with the opportunity to discover therapeutic coping techniques and learn how to apply them to their own personal problem areas, before committing to a twenty-eight-day practice to promote good emotional regulation and reduced anxiety. The journal can be used alongside the therapeutic novel These Three Words, or as a standalone workbook, and it is suitable for use by the teenage reader on their own, with a parent, or in a group.

Beastie, Baby and the Brand-New Mummy (2022) ISBN 978 18381987 3 2 and *Beastie, Baby and the Brand-New Daddy (2022) ISBN 978 18381987 4 9*
A therapeutic story that looks at the external signs of pathological dissociation in a child. Dolly's story helps children who have experienced early trauma to begin to understand, in a very simple way, what dissociation is and why it has happened in their internal world. Tools and techniques are included within the story that parents and caregivers can use to assist the child in the first stages of their healing process. Beautiful illustrations on every page enhance the story of Dolly, and help the reader to relate to the events that happen, to notice the methods Dolly has developed to manage her feelings, and to think about what is happening in their own internal world. For children aged 4-12

Printed in Great Britain
by Amazon

BEYOND REDEMPTION

THIEVES' GUILD ORIGINS
LC BOOK TWO

BEYOND REDEMPTION

THIEVES' GUILD ORIGINS
LC BOOK TWO

C.G. HATTON

First published in paperback in 2017
by Sixth Element Publishing
Arthur Robinson House
13-14 The Green
Billingham TS23 1EU
www.6epublishing.net

ISBN 9798411061666

British Library Cataloguing in Publication Data. A catalogue record for this book is available from the British Library.

For Hatt

And with a big thank you to everyone who has put up with me, helped, supported and encouraged me throughout these slightly bonkers times...

1

I don't see the blood until we stop. Until Luka hands me his rifle and I can see in the flickering light of the lantern that it's slick with red.

He squeezes my shoulder and says, "Keep watch."

He's pale. He has a scar across his cheekbone that someone said was from a machete. From a Bhenykhn machete. I know he was on Erica. And I know the intricate pattern branded into his chest is from when he was caught by them. Hilyer told me. Luka doesn't talk about it.

I stare at him as he sinks to the floor and pulls out a field dressing that he pushes against his side. He's hurt really badly and I don't know what to do. I don't think rescue will be coming so easily this time.

"Tell me about the guild," I blurt out.

It worked before. He kept a whole basement full of kids quiet as he told us about Kheris. This time, it's just him and me. Separated from everyone else. In a tunnel I'm scared is a dead end.

He doesn't answer. I glance back. He's closed his eyes and leaned his head back against the wall. I can tell he's in pain.

"I just need a minute," he mutters.

I go and sit opposite him, positioning myself so I can see the way we've just come, the rifle in my lap and my finger on the trigger. "I want to know what happened after you met Hil."

"No, you don't," he says, voice so quiet I can hardly hear. "He was an idiot. He hated me. And the first tab we were sent on almost got both of us killed."

A combat booted foot crashed down into the space where my head had been only a fraction of a second earlier. I kept the momentum of the move going and rolled up onto one knee but he was fast. A vicious, straight kick was aimed right at my head. I raised both arms in a blocking move that Benjie had taught me and grabbed his leg to twist and throw him off balance but he was ready for it, he went with the move and spun. A roundhouse kick from his other foot caught me on the shoulder.

I flinched away but he was on me again. His fist punched into the side of my head as I ducked, senses rattled. I couldn't beat him. My right hand was still in a cast, left knee in a brace. And I was being clumsy as hell because the gravity on board the Alsatia was lighter than I was used to. He was faster than me, stronger than me, and he knew what he was doing.

His other fist pummelled into my kidneys, a low punch right into my back that almost sent me to my knees. I staggered and twisted round, catching his leg with my foot and kicking out enough to throw him off balance and away from me.

The reprieve was short lived. He twisted, grabbed hold of my shirt and dragged me close, driving his fist into my face and connecting just above my eye, again. The pain that exploded in my head was about as bad as anything I'd ever felt, and I'd been stabbed, shoved off a roof and shot not so long ago.

I felt my knees going.

If I ended up on the floor, I figured I was done.

He still had a fistful of my shirt. He spun me around and slammed me into the wall, catching my right arm and twisting it behind my back. Pain shot through my hand. He hissed, "You need to learn when to give up, kid," and shoved me hard into the cold metal surface, head bouncing with another rattle. I almost blacked out, vision narrowed to a dark blur. Blood was pouring down the side of my face, hot and sticking up one eye. I couldn't see, couldn't get free and couldn't stop myself as my legs turned to jelly and I crumpled.

He helped me on my way down with another blow to the kidneys that took my breath away. The floor came up fast, cold and hard. There was an instant of lull, a moment of calm. I could hear the blood pounding in my ears, and his breathing, controlled and calm as he stood over me.

I could feel the others watching and I didn't care. I could see his boots, feet apart, fighting stance. He shifted his weight and I tensed, trying to curl up against the kicks I knew would follow but I could hardly move.

The kicks didn't come.

There was a sharp clap and a different voice said, "Again."

I sagged.

"Anderton, get your sorry ass off the floor and show me some goddamned effort this time."

A huge figure knelt close and leaned in, grabbing me by the scruff of the neck as I sprawled there on the floor and whispering harshly into my ear. "You're Thieves' Guild now. Get the hell up."

He leaned closer. "Understand this… you do not get to quit. You do not get to flunk out. No one leaves the Thieves' Guild. You make it or you die. And you earn your damned keep. I don't care that you are only thirteen goddamned years old, son. You have a tab. You want to survive it? Show me you can fight."

He shoved me and stood back, giving me room to gather myself and push, inch by inch, to my knees.

I left a bloody mess on the floor but I got upright, a warm trickle still dripping down my face, and my hands shaking but I got upright and stood there, weight on my right leg, raising my head slowly and trying to calm my breathing.

Zach Hilyer was staring at me, standing at ease, hardly looking like he'd been fighting at all. The big guy who'd just given me the inspirational pep talk was the Chief, our big boss, head of Acquisitions, and he was standing, arms folded, looking less than impressed and more like he was tempted to throw me out of the nearest airlock into deep space.

4

"Understand this, gentlemen," he said, "you fight for your life or this tab is going to be your first and your last." He shook his head. "Now stop messing about and show me what you can do."

Hilyer came at me again, using the same opening attack as the two previous times. He wasn't expecting anything to be different and I started to respond in exactly the same way, using the same block that had failed me twice already. He had no reason to think this was anything but a rerun. He almost grinned but this time I knew what was coming, he fell for it and I did the one thing, the only thing, I had left. At the last possible moment, I lashed out with my left leg, throwing the full weight of the exo-brace behind it and drove my foot up into his groin with all the force I could muster.

Hilyer collapsed to the floor clutching himself.

There were a couple of incredulous gasps, a faint cheer from somewhere.

"Now that's more like it," the Chief said. "Anderton, get back to Medical and get that eye seen to. Hilyer, stop lying around making my gym look untidy. You just got decked by a child. Get cleaned up. Then both of you, get your asses over to Ops. Mendhel is waiting for you."

He turned and walked away.

Another guy, one of the instructors, clapped his hands together and shouted, "Kowalski, Lewis, you're up next and, for Christ's sake, don't be as embarrassing as these two."

Hilyer didn't say another word to me and he didn't wait for me to get fixed up. He took off once he'd showered and I was left on my own to get up to Medical, get sorted and make my way back to Ops. The deep spacer we were on, the Alsatia, was huge. An enormous wandering star ship that was the guild's base of operations, masquerading as a corporate-owned cruise liner, shuttling between Earth and Winter or just hanging out in deep space at jump points close to wherever the guild needed to be. It was awesome. Totally self-contained with four main sections – Acquisitions, Legal, Media and Science – and that was just the guild side of things. The cruiser itself had a load of other stuff going on that we never even saw. We were in Acquisitions. And even from the outset, it felt like that was something special.

It had hardly been a week since Mendhel had taken me from Kheris. When he'd brought us on board, they'd kept us both in quarantine for forty eight hours, running a barrage of medical and physical tests, then they'd let Hil loose and told me I wasn't going anywhere, not until they sorted out my knee and my hand. After three more days of surgery, meds and physio, and rapid heal sessions in medical iso-pods, they'd shown me a deckplan, told me where I could and couldn't go – made it clear I wasn't being discharged from their care yet – and kicked me out to go train in Acquisitions with strict instructions to be back within two hours.

It had been five. I doubted they were going to be impressed. It felt like no one was impressed with me.

It was strange walking through the ship those first few weeks. There were no other kids on board. Hilyer was only a year or so older than me and we stood out a mile. Everyone I passed looked at me weird, like I was some alien curiosity that had got lost or some stray cat that had wandered into a house belonging to a dog and was daring to make itself at home.

There was an air of tension in every corridor, raised voices, open arguments. I didn't know whether something was kicking off or whether it was like that all the time. It was unnerving. I almost missed the streets of Kheris, with its bomb craters and tanks on every corner. At least there I could escape it all and run out into the desert anytime I wanted. On the Alsatia, there was no way out. Nowhere to go.

As I got closer to Medical, it got worse. I flattened myself against the bulkhead as a squad of troops in lightweight combat armour pushed past, covered in dirt and blood, nursing recently dressed wounds and grumbling, not bothering to keep their voices low as they complained. About shit happening, empty seats in the damned mess, again, and what the hell had gone wrong this time?

I was limping, holding a cold pack against my eye, and looking pathetic enough that everyone pointed me in the right direction. I didn't need directions, I knew the entire deck plan of that enormous cruise ship by heart, but it didn't hurt to look a bit lost.

And to be honest, not all of it was an act.

Medical was busy. They didn't waste much time in checking me over and cleaning me up. They already knew I had to get back to Ops for a briefing. That was the other thing about the Alsatia and the guild. Everyone knew everything, all the time. The way it was run was slick and efficient, certainly like nothing I'd ever seen before.

They weren't watching too closely so I snuck a handful of extra painkillers into my pocket as I slouched out.

I got back to Ops and stood at the door to the briefing room I was directed to. My first briefing, and I was standing there like an idiot, a fresh dressing taped above my eye, feeling like shit, not sure if I should knock and wait or just go in, and fairly sure that whatever I did, it wouldn't be right.

I was about to walk off, go find someone and check I was in the right place when the door opened.

Hilyer was sitting in there already, slouched back in a chair across a table from Mendhel, arms folded, looking like this was all second nature to him. He didn't give me any acknowledgement at all as I went in.

I sat down next to him and scratched at my hand, around the edges of the cast that was immobilising it, wrist to fingers. It was itching like hell. Getting shot sucks, trust me. They reckoned I'd get full use of it back eventually but right then I still couldn't move two of my fingers properly.

"How's the knee?" Mendhel said.

It was a mess, ligament damage they'd said. And it was hurting even though the brace had an auto-med feedback injector that was supposed to keep me up to date with pain medication.

"It's fine," I said.

He nodded and gave me a slight smile like he knew I was lying. He looked at us both. "You think we're going hard on you?"

I was sitting there with sore ribs, an aching back and a black eye that was almost swollen shut. I just stared at him.

He pushed a data board each across the table towards us. "We are. Because this is the job you're going to do for us."

2

I glanced at it. They couldn't seriously be talking about sending us into that.

Hilyer sat upright and reached to scroll through a few screens. He had a tattoo inked on the inside of his wrist, this weird black symbol. I was naïve enough to think it looked cool. If I'd known back then what it was, I might not have screwed up so badly.

He tensed, looking at the data. I could feel the unease building in him. It was setting me on edge just sitting next to him.

"We don't have long to get you ready," Mendhel said. "The Chief is going hard on both of you because he doesn't agree that we should be using you for this tab. He thinks we shouldn't even be running this tab, and he thinks I'm going to get you both killed." He let that sink in then added, "He's trying to break you now to prove he's right. It might not seem like it but he's trying to save your life."

I didn't trust myself to speak so I didn't. I usually get in trouble because I can't keep my mouth shut but something about Mendhel made me nervous. In a weird way. Not like I was afraid of him but more like I didn't want to disappoint him.

"I believe you can do it," he said. He tapped his own board and the wall behind him lit up to show a three dimensional schematic, spinning slowly. "This is where you're going. Fort Redemption. It's a high security juvenile correctional facility."

I glanced sideways at Hilyer. He was steadfastly avoiding looking at me.

"It's part of a maximum security Imperial prison complex used as a draft facility for the Imperial military. It's tough, bleak, harsh. This is not going to be easy, for either of you."

My heart was in my stomach, beating with a steady thud.

Mendhel brought up a profile of the facility, stats, blueprints and satellite images appearing on the display. "We've had a deep cover agent embedded in the teaching staff there for a long time. Markus is one of our best talent spotters. Redemption has always been one of our best recruiting grounds. But, as I told you already, we don't recruit minors." He stared at us, sitting there underage as we were. He'd already told us how much his ass was on the line for taking us in.

"Normally," he said, "we tag anyone we believe could be a potential and if they're underage, we watch them until they're ready. Wherever they go afterwards. Even if that takes years. Some of them never are. But recently, five of Markus' latest potentials have vanished. He doesn't know what's going on, we don't know what's going on. But five kids that he tagged as high priority have disappeared from the entire system within the last three months. And that's from either side of the line. Officially, they were transferred out of Redemption and then they simply disappeared. And trust me, we don't just lose people."

The screen went black.

"These kids were exceptional. They have to be to get our attention. Thing is, the number of kids turning up at Redemption who'd normally score higher on every pointer we look for has increased. We don't know how or why but someone with similar interests to ours is funnelling these kids through. That's why we've brought you in. Way earlier than we normally would have. We want you to go in there and work with Markus to find out what's going on. Security has also been increased, way beyond any normal correctional facility, and we can't feed any more experienced operatives into the system at this short notice because we don't know who's behind it and Markus can't crack the new protections they've thrown up at the facility." He looked at me. "That's where you come in, LC." He just stared at me for a couple of heartbeats like he was fixing his resolve. "Markus will be able to provide you with the necessary equipment and get you access to the system controlling the base. We want you to hack into it. Your brief is to infiltrate, observe, gather intelligence. That's it. Stay under the radar. Don't stand out. Don't get noticed. Hil will be there to watch your back when Markus isn't around." He turned his head to look at Hilyer. "And as well as that, you have your own objective."

Hilyer looked like he could guess what that was going to be. I could guess what that was going to be.

"You get their attention," Mendhel said. "Whatever happens, we'll be there to track you and we'll get you out but we want to know where those kids are ending up. If there's someone else there recruiting them, we want to know who the hell that is and what they want them for."

Compared to Hilyer's, my task sounded easy. He was going into the lion's den but it seemed like they thought I was still too much of a kid to play with the big boys.

"When we get you into this facility, you do not know each other, you do not discuss the tab with each other. Markus will make contact with you when he's ready. You will follow his lead. Do you understand?"

I nodded but I only had the vaguest idea of what we were being sent in to. Hilyer was sitting there bolt upright.

Mendhel looked at us both in turn. "There's a lot riding on this. Everyone thinks I'm taking a huge gamble here, relying on a couple of kids with barely any training, and they're right. I am, but you need to understand, you can not ever reveal that you are Thieves' Guild. To anyone. Ever."

We both nodded.

"We have enemies who wouldn't hesitate to pull the trigger on a kid, or worse, if they thought you were linked to us. Do you understand?"

More nods. But it didn't feel real. None of it felt real.

"Okay, now pay attention," he said and started going through the plans of the facility, training rotas and briefing schedules we had to attend on the Alsatia. A lot of the training was going to be physical, some of it was for both of us, hand to hand fighting, disabling security systems, stealth training and intelligence gathering. There was a session on psychological conditioning and techniques for resisting interrogation. Some of it was just for me, interpreting how AI logic strings were constructed, how they could be manipulated, how to get in and out of data streams without being detected.

It was cool but it was like being back at school. I started getting ahead of them as they were working through the intel on the boards, skipped too far and got distracted.

I didn't realise I'd zoned out and I didn't know I was kicking my feet against the legs of the chair until Mendhel tapped at the table, with a curt, "Enough."

I looked up.

No idea what he'd been saying or what we were supposed to be doing.

My screen was open, displaying a load of old records. I was about to wipe it clear when he reached for it.

"Where the hell did you find this?"

It was a list of names, field-ops, Mendhel Halligan included, and points. He'd been a field operative. A good one judging by his position in the list.

"Who's Andreyev?" I said. That name was top, a leap ahead of the next one down.

"Ask the Chief."

"Do we get to go on this list?"

"It's called the standings board and yes, you will."

Hilyer was watching, scowling, but I couldn't help asking, "How do we get points?"

Like it was a game. I needed it to be a game. Losing Maisie and Latia meant that reality was still too painful. I desperately needed it to be a game so I didn't have to think about what was really happening.

Mendhel held one finger out, hovering poised over the list, staring at it with half a smile creasing his mouth, then he wiped it clear and pushed it back to me. "Why don't we leave that for another day and get back to what we're supposed to be doing?"

Just like school. They never let you near the cool stuff, like you had to log a million hours of tedium before they could trust you to go anywhere near anything actually interesting. I sat there trying to listen, trying my best to concentrate, but not well enough apparently, and it wasn't long before Mendhel tapped at the table again to get my attention. He didn't look impressed. "That's enough. LC."

I still wasn't totally used to them calling me that.

He sounded exasperated. "You can access the data back in Medical. You're due for another check up. Go get some rest. I need to talk to Hil anyway."

I didn't argue.

As I got up, Hilyer still didn't look at me. I didn't know what his problem with me was but I'd dealt with worse so I didn't really care.

Mendhel walked me to the door and stopped me there. "LC," he said quietly. "I brought you in early to run this tab for us. We didn't bring you in because of what happened.

I was coming for you anyway. Do you understand? We've been watching you for a long time."

Charlie.

I got a lump in my throat. I bit my lip to stop it, a pulse of adrenaline hitting my chest.

Mendhel drew in a deep breath. "I'm just sorry we didn't get there before…"

I shut it down. Sucked it up and shut it down.

He nodded, doing the same. "Go, get some sleep. And don't argue with the medics."

I was also not used to everyone knowing everything I did and being watched every second of the day. I hadn't realised I'd been such a pain that they'd report it.

He gave me a stare. "They know what they're doing. Don't fight them. We need that knee to be healed. We have a lot to get through. And trust me, I believe you can do this."

He looked up, something or someone behind me catching his eye. I turned. The Chief was approaching, and I don't know why but I knew there was something wrong, and it wasn't about us.

The Chief was big and I'd not seen him anything other than angry whenever we were around, but he took Mendhel by the arm and said softly, "Mend, you need to come with me, buddy. Now. Quinn can sort these two out."

Quinn was another handler. He was standing further down the corridor, watching. I had a horrible feeling that something bad had happened.

Mendhel was listening to someone else. Everyone at the guild had tiny devices implanted beneath the skin just below their ear, high end comms kit. Sensons. You just have to think to speak through them. They'd told us we'd get them but not yet, not considering where we were about to be sent. But I could tell Mendhel was talking to someone and it wasn't good.

He nodded, vague, turned to me and said, "Luka, listen to Quinn. I'll catch up with you later, okay?" and he went.

Quinn was looking at me as if he'd been dumped with the children and he had other places he'd rather be. He was another big guy, tall, not massive like the Chief, but intimidating like the kind of soldiers I'd always avoided on Kheris.

He walked up, said without ceremony, "Anderton, Medical. Hilyer, sit your ass down, we need to talk," and he disappeared into the briefing room, closing the door and leaving me stranded in the corridor.

I felt cold suddenly, like I wasn't going to see Mendhel ever again. Everyone was ignoring me so I made my way back to Medical and did my best to do what they wanted. It didn't go well. I came round with a shock, didn't know where I was, tried to sit, tore the line out of my arm and banged my head.

Waking up in an iso-pod really sucks.

I couldn't remember the nightmare but I was hot, shivering and I couldn't get it to stop. An alarm was screaming. I slammed my fist sideways into the release button, instinctive, desperate. Nothing happened. I couldn't move my left leg. I lay back, heart pounding, and banged at the side of the pod, biting my lip until it started to bleed, until there was a soft hiss and the clear cover slid open. I was struggling to breathe. It was stupid. I'd never been claustrophobic. Never had trouble with enclosed spaces. I'd learned that when I was five. On Kheris I used to crawl backwards through dark conduits that would have given a mouse trouble. Being stuck in that iso-pod in that first week on the Alsatia was something else. I still don't understand what.

The medic leaned in and placed a mask over my face. That made me flip out but I breathed through it. I wanted to recall the nightmare, raking through my memory to find any wisp of it that was left but it was all just beyond my grasp, no idea where I'd been or who'd been there with me just a sickening feeling that I needed to know, that it was critical to something or someone that I remember. And I couldn't.

I needed to get out. I thought I heard Mendhel, heard another voice saying, "No. You want that knee fixed? We have to put him under," and I panicked, lashed out, felt more wires break free, and the alarm screeched to a new high. The sting of a needle jabbed into the side of my neck and I went out like a light.

When I woke again, I was in a bunk with my leg trapped in some contraption, a machine beeping in time with my heartbeat and voices outside the door.

Someone I didn't recognise said, "But can he do it?"

It was Mendhel who replied. "I believe he can," he said, sounding restrained.

I tried to sit up. I wanted to talk to Mendhel. I wanted to see him. I wanted him to come into the room and make everything okay.

He didn't.

He added to whoever he was talking to, "Come on, NG, you've seen the reports. This kid is hypermobile and agile as hell. He's small but strong – he grew up on Kheris, for Christ's sake. His reactions are off the scale and he's fearless. Never mind what he can do with the logic strings. You want a perfect field-op? This kid is it, trust me. It's just going to take some time."

My heart was thumping so fast, I could hear it in my ears.

"What about Hilyer?" the other guy said.

"He has as much potential," Mendhel said.

"If…?"

"If he can keep out of trouble."

"Where is he?"

"Right now? In the Maze. Running off a temper. He just floored two of the grunts. Landed them in here."

"He's a fifteen year old kid… how the hell did he put two trained men into Medical?"

Mendhel lowered his voice but I could still hear what he was saying. "Hil's survived on the streets since he was able to walk. You do that, you learn stuff, you know that. He fights dirty. Really dirty."

"Does LC know where Hil was before we brought him in?"

"No."

"Does Hil know what LC did on Kheris?"

I sagged back onto the pillows, dreading what was coming next, but I heard Mendhel say, "No, no one does."

"Keep it that way. You've got two months to get them ready. We can't wait any longer than that. Media's picking up intel that's making her uneasy. Nothing they can put their finger on, but enough to make her think that something is going on. We need to know."

3

They kept me incapacitated, to accelerate healing they said, for another two days then kicked me out of Medical with a lighter brace on my knee, a box of meds, a schedule for physio and psych evaluations, and a kit bag of the clothes they'd given me. I had Charlie's knife in my pocket and his dog tags round my neck. That was all I owned.

I was escorted down to Acquisitions and taken to the barracks, to a door labelled 'Hilyer' and 'Anderton'. Guess we were sharing. Hilyer didn't have much either from the look of it but there was a kit bag under one bunk and stuff on a shelf next to it. The other bunk was made up, neat, no personal stuff so I guessed that was mine and dumped my bag on it. I put the drugs on the shelf and waited until my escort had left me alone before I put the knife under the pillow.

No one had told me what to do next so I stood there like an idiot for a minute then wandered out.

Acquisitions was huge. The barracks was only part of it. There was a mess hall and rec room, gym, then the Operations Centre that had a conference room and loads of smaller briefing rooms. It was weird being on board a ship. Time didn't mean much. People seemed to come and go randomly. There was no day or night. Everything went on all the time and people seemed to sleep when they wanted.

I must have looked like a lost child. I was about to go back to our quarters when someone yelled, "Hey, kid," and came over, throwing her arm around my shoulder and leading me into the mess. She stopped by the servery and grabbed a couple of bottles. That's one thing I never really got used to on the Alsatia. Even after I'd been there for years. There was food and drink available all the time, help yourself, no limits, nothing logged. We didn't have to pay for anything. It felt too good to be true. And it was so far from what I was used to, it didn't feel right. Like there was a catch and I was just waiting for it to hit me.

The woman steered me across the room. She smelled like the Imperial soldiers, gun oil and sweat. She was wearing black fatigues. The guild's Security division. Her other arm was in a sling, recent injury from the way she was holding it.

"Don't look so scared," she said with a laugh. "We don't bite."

I wasn't scared. I was trying to not flash back to Kheris. The heat. The dust. Soldiers that smelled just like her throwing me to my knees and holding a gun to my head.

I shook it off, digging my fingernails into my palm. It was not the same. The Alsatia was clean, the air fresh. I was clean. Light years from the kid scuzzing about the streets of that dirtball colony. That wasn't me anymore and I was never going back. Ever.

22

She took me to a long table where three other guys were sitting, stripping weapons, a couple further down playing cards, beer bottles lined up in rows.

She nudged me onto a bench and sat next to me. "It's Anderton, yeah?"

I nodded.

"Can I call you LC?"

I nodded again. She didn't ask what it stood for. I didn't know what I'd say if anyone did ask.

She gave me one of the bottles, water, and opened her own, beer. I took it and muttered a thanks.

She grinned. "How the hell old are you, LC?"

"Thirteen."

"No shit." She downed a mouthful of beer. "No one told me we'd started recruiting kids."

A guy with a split lip and a gash on his forehead sitting opposite us muttered something about damned babysitting. Someone else joined in, saying louder that at least it didn't look like I was in a fit enough state to kick anyone's ass like the other kid. Everyone laughed, at his expense from the look of it.

The woman next to me grinned again and leaned in to clink her bottle against mine. "Don't mind him, he's just a sore loser."

Someone said loudly, "Just a loser," and there was more laughing.

I didn't know what to do, shifted my weight awkwardly and opened the water.

He grunted, wiping oil off the last few parts from

the handgun he was cleaning. The rest of it was laid out in perfect lines on a cloth in front of him. There was another, fully disassembled, in front of me, not so neat. I guessed it was hers.

He raised his eyes to glare at me, and muttered, "Children shouldn't be allowed in here."

I watched him pick up one of the components and slot it slowly into place, starting to assemble the weapon, still glowering at me as he did it. I shouldn't have done but I couldn't resist. I reached for the gun housing in front of me and picked up the Aiden's tube, snapping it into place and going for the next piece, and the next, fast and efficient, becoming more and more aware that a hush was descending around me. It was a complicated weapon, intricate components, not one I'd ever handled before, but similar to one Charlie had shown me one time, and I'd seen the manual for this exact spec.

The guy opposite was speeding up, trying to match me. He had no chance. Even with one hand pretty much out of action, I beat him, clicking in the holding pin and the mag, and placing the assembled gun gently back onto the cloth.

He still had a couple of parts to go. He slowed and slotted in the next piece with exaggerated deliberation. There was a moment of still silence then someone swore and laughed.

The woman next to me slapped me on the shoulder and muttered, "Holy shit."

There was more laughing, the noise picking back up,

and he finished slowly, staring at me over the gun as he did it.

It was probably not the smartest thing to have done and I don't know why I did it. He slotted the mag into place and put it down, picked up the gun I'd assembled and made a show of checking the mechanism. He nodded slowly, probably about as much approval as I was going to get.

The woman laughed, squeezed my knee and whispered, "Nice one, buddy."

Around us, the conversation was getting rowdy and I was about to make my excuses and disappear, but a hand landed on my shoulder and I felt someone lean down behind me, saying, "Get your ass up to Twelve, Anderton. NG wants to see you."

NG was head of operations of the whole guild. Mendhel had told us that. I got the feeling that being summoned to NG's office wasn't run of the mill.

It wasn't.

Walking out onto Deck Twelve felt strange, soft carpet underfoot and a cast to the lighting that was softer than anywhere else I'd been on board. It felt expensive.

NG didn't keep me waiting. The door was open and his staff told me to go straight in. He was sitting at a large round table off to one side of his office, not at his desk, shuffling a deck of cards. There was something about NG. He didn't look old enough to be in charge, for one thing.

I stopped just inside the door, hesitating. NG looked up and beckoned me over. He pushed across a data board as I sat down. He had his sleeves rolled up, an intricate web of feint scars cutting across the tanned skin of his arm. He might have been head of operations but he obviously wasn't a pen-pusher.

He didn't waste any time with pleasantries, didn't introduce himself and didn't bother with any preamble.

"The report we got from Kheris," he said, "was that you can crack AI logic strings. You want to show me how?"

He had a black band around his wrist. Same as Charlie. Same as the guy in Dayton's crew, the one who'd given me the exact same puzzles. He'd been Thieves' Guild. They'd both been Thieves' Guild.

I looked up into NG's eyes.

"Loic was Charlie's contact in the resistance," he said softly. "They were two of our best." He tapped on the board. "C'mon, show me how you do it."

I swallowed against the lump in my throat and couldn't help the memories that surfaced, a small cell deep underground, blood pooling on the floor. A pulse of adrenaline hit my chest but NG started playing with the codes, solving the logic strings himself, fast. Way faster than I could. It was hypnotic. He nudged the board towards me and I took over, absorbed in it before I realised, and moving on to tougher and tougher puzzles. I completed the last one and the board went black.

I looked up.

NG was just sitting there, watching me. "You have an eidetic memory," he said.

I shrugged. I'd looked it up once when someone said I was weird. I didn't know if that's what it was or not. I could remember stuff. I didn't care how.

"Do you realise that less than one in a billion people can see through AI strings? And even fewer than that can actually manipulate them."

I didn't know what to say. I'd just thought they were cool puzzles.

"They control AI thought processes and logic procedures. How did you learn to solve them?"

I shrugged again. No one had taught me. I could just see it. I always had.

NG grinned.

"You need to learn how to use this to break into systems that are protected by AIs," he said. "Most of the places we go into are loaded with traps and tripwires that will kill you if you don't bypass them in the right way." He nudged the board again and it lit up, the display full of slowly spinning wire frame plans. "Redemption is run by an AI."

I almost choked when he said 'run by an AI', feeling my breath catch in my chest. My hands were burning, conduits exploding in shards around me, electrobes flaring...

"It's relatively high end," he said. "Smarter than anything you've seen before. Certainly smarter than the AI on Kheris."

Just hearing him say that made a cold spot twist inside. He pronounced Kheris the same way the locals did. Like he knew the place. Like he'd been there.

"We need you to hack it and get the intel we need. You have to know all the possible system protections you could encounter."

I shivered, feeling trapped.

"Don't get me wrong," he warned, softly, breaking the spell. He was looking at me as if he knew exactly what I was thinking and he brought me back in exactly the right way to bring out the best in me. "This tab is not gonna be a walk in the park. You've seen the brief. Mendhel thinks you can do it. The Chief isn't convinced. I'm not convinced." He leaned forward intently. "You want to prove to us you can do it? Get your fitness back up to speed. Do the physio. I'm giving you a training schedule. As much as Redemption is a feeder for the Imperial military, the juvie facility there is also a school. You'll have library time. That'll be your way in. Nice and easy. Markus will get you access. Keep your nose clean. Don't get in trouble and you'll be fine. We'll show you how to hack a terminal so no one can see what you're doing. Practise bypassing those protections until you can do it with your eyes closed. Do you understand?"

I nodded.

"And get some sleep. You having nightmares?"

I didn't want to talk about it but NG didn't push it. He just said, "Whatever meds they gave you, use them."

I nodded again.

He nudged the board towards me. "There are more puzzles on here. Work your way through them."

I took it but I hesitated. I wanted to ask him about Mendhel. As far as I knew from what I'd heard anyone say, NG didn't handle field-ops. I didn't know why I was even in there, why he was talking to me, when I was just a chump kid who didn't really know why I was there on the Alsatia at all.

NG looked at me and rubbed a hand across the back of his neck, like he was tired. He looked like he was trying to figure out whether he should be shouting at me to scram or sitting me down to explain the workings of the entire galaxy.

"I know it's not easy," he said carefully, "but trust us. Work hard, do what we say and you can do well here. Charlie believed in you, Mendhel believes in you. Show the rest of us why."

I sat there, staring at him, frozen like an alpaca pinned in headlights. I wanted to know what was going on with Mendhel. If he was okay and where he was, and why it wasn't him going through this with me. I wanted to ask if he knew why Hilyer had such a problem with me. I wanted to ask about Redemption.

He gave me that look again. "And know when to ask questions and when to shut the hell up and just do what we say."

I wished it were that easy.

He stood. "Come with me."

He took me through the cruiser without a word, until we reached a security door. It opened as we approached and he nodded me through.

It was some kind of locker room. Dark. Soft lighting. And it was warm. NG showed me to a locker and told me to open it while he went to another and started pulling out kit.

"Anything in there is yours," he said, shrugging out of his shirt. "Get changed."

The clothes were all black. Softer than anything I'd ever worn before. Woven like it was some kind of armoured fabric but supple and light. And it all fit perfectly, right down to the soft, lace up friction boots. There was also a small kit with basic medical supplies, tape, sprays, painkillers and a box of injectors. That didn't bode well.

I closed the locker and turned.

NG had changed into identical gear. He was waiting by another door and took me through to an anteroom, almost an airlock. There was a panel on the far wall next to the exit.

"This controls environmentals," NG said. "There are presets... and there are extremes. In between, you can set whatever conditions you want. Be careful with the electrobe settings." He looked back at me. He didn't ask if I knew what electrobes were. I knew he'd seen the report from Kheris. It made my stomach cold to think that everyone here knew everything about me.

I nodded. That explained the vials of antidote in the locker.

"Temperature, gravity, you can set as high or low as you want. Scenarios you can choose. Or if you want to go for a record…" He flashed up a screen of data, names and times, "…you set it as M1 or M3. Don't bother with any of the others. You understand?"

I nodded again. It was a list of accomplishments, personal bests and overall record times for different tests. One name stood out a mile, and I couldn't help asking again, "Who's Andreyev?"

NG set the screen at M3. "Ask Mendhel," he said.

There was also a standings board lit up there on the panel, same as the one I'd seen in the briefing room but with different names at the top. And my name at the bottom, next to Hilyer's. NG turned to look at me as I was staring at it.

"What?" he said.

"It's different."

"To what?"

"The other list, the one with Andreyev at the top."

NG laughed. "You've seen the old standings board? Christ. I thought that got wiped. We've started again. You want to make it here? You run tabs, you earn points and you make your way up that list." He had his hand poised on the door release. "Timer starts as soon as the door opens. It logs when you cross the threshold coming back out." He hit the release. "Welcome to the Maze."

4

The next four days were intense. Whenever I was kicked loose from whatever they had us doing, I went to the Maze. I loved the Maze on the Alsatia. It was our training ground, our playground. Right from that first week, NG gave me open access to it, as often as I wanted. I worked my butt off, running through it so I didn't need to think about anything, pushing beyond the point of exhaustion just so I could fall asleep.

Then I screwed up.

I was goosed, best run in the Maze yet, and I made my way back to the barracks, intending to just curl up and work on the puzzles, but our door was open and Hilyer was in there, sitting on his bunk tossing a knife tumbling up into the air, catching it and throwing it again. It took me a second to recognise it as Charlie's pocketknife.

I couldn't help yelling out, "Hey, that's mine."

He looked at me, the knife in his hand, blade out, and he threw it at me.

I ducked and caught it by the handle.

Hilyer gave a laugh like he didn't care, stood and walked out without a word.

I scowled after him for a minute then followed him towards the mess. I stopped by the door, as freaking awkward as ever. It was noisier in there than I'd seen before, way more people, a music vid playing on a far wall and some kind of game in play on another.

Hilyer grabbed a beer and wandered in like he belonged. He headed straight to a table in the corner where Kowalski and Lewis were sitting playing cards. They looked just like us, older but not by that much, eighteen, nineteen maybe. Hilyer looked like he fitted right in. I was the new kid, standing there like I didn't dare go in, and I almost turned and ran. I'd been there as long as he had but I hadn't realised how isolated I'd been keeping myself. My knee was throbbing. I felt like crawling back to Medical or going to hide in the Maze again.

I started to back away but I glanced round and the woman I'd talked to days earlier was in there. I hadn't seen her or any of her buddies since that first time. But then, like I said, I'd been avoiding everyone.

She caught my eye and waved, yelling, "Hey LC."

She beckoned me over and I was stuck even more. Hilyer was watching me, laughing with the others, joining in their game and downing his beer. The woman yelled again and I couldn't not go over. I sidled onto the bench next to her. There were no guns out that time, just bowls of snacks and more bottles, beer and stronger stuff, spirits and shot glasses.

She grinned and leaned over, saying loudly, "I heard you're from Kheris. No wonder you know how to assemble a weapon like that. Christ, kid, that place is a shit-hole."

I didn't want to talk about it but she said louder, "At least it was when I was there years ago. What the hell is it like now? That where you hurt your hand?" She didn't wait for me to answer. She yelled to someone further down the bench. "Hey, Jensonn, you did a tour on Kheris, didn't you? This kid is from Kheris."

I squirmed, wanting to sink into the floor.

"No way! That place is a shit-hole!" he yelled back and there was more laughter.

She turned back to me. "I heard your buddy is one hell of a fighter."

I wanted to protest that Hilyer wasn't my buddy but I just shrugged.

She laughed, stood and slapped me on the shoulder. "Excuse me, gentlemen, I am being summoned for a debrief. Won't be long. We kicked ass. What else do they wanna know? Take care of this kid for me."

I looked around as she left, tempted to follow her and leave but someone else appeared and sat next to me, nudging me along. More fatigues and that lingering smell of gun oil. I could hear them talking about all the shit-holes they'd spent time fighting in, and how badly wrong their latest tab had gone. I didn't want to hear it.

Someone pushed a beer across to me. I took it but I didn't open it. I didn't think alcohol was a good idea with all the pain meds I was taking.

Until someone started talking about Kheris and what had happened, hadn't some serious shit just happened out there?

They all looked at me. Someone asked me outright what I knew. I didn't want to answer so I opened the beer and drank more than I intended to, just so I didn't need to speak. It tasted as bad as the last time I'd been given one and I felt my stomach turn even as I was drinking it.

The guy with the split lip was there. He pulled out a pack of cards and everyone around me hustled into a game, the table stacked high with multi-coloured disks. It wasn't poker or mean queen they were playing, but it didn't take long to figure out the rules. They saw me watching and laughed.

One of them offered me a stack of disks. "Chips," he said to me, holding one up and explaining it like I was five, "and this is a loan. I wannit back with interest, you hear."

They all laughed again and dealt me in on the next round. When Charlie and his crew had taught me poker, they'd used bullets to bet with. Lined up in neat rows. It was like he'd been getting me ready for this. For everything.

Five beers later, my pile of chips was bigger than anyone else's and everyone was watching. I kept my stacks of tokens neat, obsessively, concentrating on the bright colours to keep me there and not flashing back to a cold wet outpost with thunder rumbling amidst the explosions outside.

Someone shoved a shot glass into my hand and filled it with ice cold liquid that was giving off a weird green-tinged vapour. He nudged the glass in my hand and clinked it with his own. I downed it in one, no idea what it was and coughing as it hit my chest. He laughed and someone else topped up my glass. I should probably have admitted I was on meds but I was beyond caring. For the first time in as long as I could remember, I felt warm and fuzzy.

I drank it and pushed my glass into the line for a top up as another bottle was opened and another round of cards was dealt.

Someone asked me again about Kheris but I just mumbled, "It was shit," and everyone laughed and started bitching about someone or other and what had happened on their last mission, who had screwed up and how it had all gone to hell.

"What you've gotta understand, kid," someone said, leaning too close, "is it's us on the surface that makes it possible for the ETs to get to you."

I didn't understand. I eyed the liquor in my glass, it seemed to have turned bright blue, and muttered, "What's an ET?" I'd lost track of time and I could hardly see straight.

The woman from earlier pushed in to sit next to me and said right into my ear, "The extraction teams. They're the ones that take all the damned glory but believe me…" She took the glass out of my hand. "…we're the ones that keep you alive, sweetheart."

It seemed to me that the field-ops were the ones that got all the glory but I didn't say it.

She drank what was left in the glass and turned to the others. "What the hell have you guys been giving this kid?

He's thirteen, for Christ's sake. Jesus. Someone throw me a bottle of water." She nudged my arm. "You've been assigned a tab already?"

I nodded.

"What's your call sign?"

I yawned. "Felix."

She nodded, knowingly as if she was storing the information. "Don't you worry, I'll look out for you."

I was struggling to keep my eyes open. "Who in here are extraction teams?"

She laughed, harsh. "They're the ones that just got three of our people killed." She pointed. "Smart asses over on that side…" Then she pointed to Hilyer and his buddies next and said, "Field-ops. At least you guys earn your bragging rights. And the guys with grey flashes…" She pointed to the door where one of the guys in armour had appeared. "…are the Watch. Don't mess with them."

I knew that much. "And you're Security?"

She squeezed my knee. "Damn right we are."

Someone pushed between us. "You're the damn grunts, Sienna, and you know it." A hand landed on my shoulder. "This kid shouldn't be drinking." The way he said it, the insinuation was clear, that I shouldn't be sitting there with them, drinking. "You turd monkeys want to land him back in Medical? Christ, he just got out. Come on, Anderton."

Someone grabbed my arm. The woman shoved them aside, protesting that she wasn't going to let me have any more, and there was shouting, scraping as chairs were pushed back.

I ducked out of the way, lost my balance and was yanked round by someone. Cards and coloured disks went flying. The room was spinning. An elbow from a wild swing by one of the grunts hammered against my eye and I went down. My head cracked against the deck and it was a blur after that. I curled up as boots thumped against my back. Someone stepped on my knee and that did it.

I came round as I was being hauled upright, blood streaming down one side of my face and my vision swimming. The mess was quiet except for sharp, snapped commands from the Watch as they hustled to get everyone out of there.

Whoever had hold of me set me down in a chair. A cold cloth was pressed against my eye, someone saying, "Hold this," and I just sat there, holding it. I heard someone that sounded like Hilyer saying, "Way to go, Anderton," sullen and kicking at my feet as he walked past. I opened one eye. He was being pushed forward by one of the Watch, some of the other field-ops and some of the grunts, Sienna included, being marched out. She winked at me as she passed. I got the impression that stuff like this happened a lot.

I closed my eyes and felt more than heard someone sit down in front of me. I blinked. The Chief, as usual, looked less than impressed. He held up two fingers. They blurred into three and back into one. He pulled the cloth from my eye and prodded. I flinched away, balance wavering. He cursed, took hold of my wrist and turned it, swore again and called for a medic. A cold sting hit my neck, warmth spreading.

I woke up in Medical. My second week in Acquisitions and somehow I'd got five field-ops and three grunts sent to the lock-up. Stunning.

They let me go after twenty-four hours, once my stats had stabilised, with strict orders to avoid alcohol, same time as the others were released, apparently, as we ended up trooping back into the barracks together.

Someone clapped me on the back and smiled but no one said a word. I followed Hilyer into our quarters. He pulled some stuff out of his locker, kicked it shut and turned. "Your timing is stunning. I had two kings, ace high. You just cost me two hundred bucks."

I opened my mouth to argue that I hadn't done a thing but he snapped, "Don't. The Chief wants us in the Maze." And he walked out.

The Chief was waiting for us. There was no one else in there. He told us to sit down and listen in, no doubt from his tone that we were in the shit.

"I'm done messing about," he said. "You want to be here? You prove it. I don't think you have it. Either of you. I don't think you have the discipline, the attitude, the damned determination it takes to be a Thieves' Guild field operative." He paused, glaring at us.

Neither of us said a word. I was hardly breathing. If they kicked me out, I had nowhere to go.

"I don't think you have the guts for it," he said, looking down at us. "I don't think you have – what – it – takes."

We sat there in sullen silence. I didn't know about Hilyer, but I felt like an idiot. I had a splitting headache and was struggling to see straight.

"Prove it to me," he said. "Prove to me that Mendhel is right, because, believe me, he needs that right now. Don't let him down."

At the time we didn't understand what he was talking about. It wasn't until later that we found out what had happened.

I still felt sick. I changed, followed them into the anteroom and we stood and watched as the Chief flashed up screens of data and settings, punching a preset, M1, electrobes to high, gravity to variable, and the temperature to forty two.

I hate electrobes and I hate being hot. It was like he knew exactly the worst conditions to send me into.

He turned to us. "Welcome to your first time-test."

5

"You have three hours," he said. "One hundred and eighty minutes to get to the end. You take longer than that, you're out. Are you ready?"

Hilyer tensed and said, "Yessir," snappy like he was used to talking like that.

I wasn't. Either used to talking like that, or ready.

The Chief hit the door release and Hilyer took off, sprinting into the dark.

I don't know why but I was rooted to the spot.

"What are you waiting for?" the Chief said. He gestured into the Maze. "Go. Clock's ticking." When I didn't move, he leaned down again and said in an exaggerated whisper, "Those dog tags you're wearing, kid, have one helluva legacy ingrained in them. You want to make it here? You make him proud."

I couldn't help looking at Charlie's band on my wrist. There was a countdown clock scrolling across its black surface, 179:37, 179:36, 179:35…

"Less than three hours now," the Chief said. "Get moving, Anderton, or Hilyer is going to kick your ass."

I started to back away.

"Faster than that," he yelled after me.

I turned and ran.

I knew every possible route through the Maze but it still wasn't easy in the dark, only flashes of light here and there. It was tough going. Steep slopes, hard climbs, narrow ledges to edge across and long stretches that played havoc with the senses. It was dark enough that I couldn't totally see what was coming up and at times I just ran, sweating, light-headed, not giving a damn about what could happen and beginning to enjoy stretching my legs, and not having anyone shooting at me.

Until I went for a jump that should have been a cinch, just as the local gravity field shifted, increasing, and I fluffed it. I was an inch shy of making it, bounced into the beam instead of onto it and fell, tumbling onto an angled slope that pitched me down, nothing to hold on to and no way to stop until I slammed into a wall at the bottom.

I gasped in a breath and looked at the timer.

85:22.

I'd been half way through. More than half way. Easily. And I'd ditched back almost to the freaking start of the Maze. And now the gravity in there was virtually what it had been on Kheris. It was weird how fast I'd gotten used to feeling lighter.

I pushed myself to my feet, feeling the band on my wrist shudder suddenly and a sting hit the back of my throat. Electrobes.

It was hard not to panic. I breathed through it, re-orientated fast from what I could see of the plans in my head, and ran out to get back on track.

I had less than an hour and a half to get through almost the whole Maze. Or risk getting kicked out. I hadn't realised until that moment how much I needed to be there. To belong. To have someone value me. I had eighty five minutes to earn it back. And I've never wanted anything more in my entire life.

From where I'd landed, there were only two possible routes I could think of that would get me to the end in time. I gambled and chose the fastest. Ran through the weird narrow passageways of the Catacombs, squeezing through gaps I couldn't even see until I was right on top of them, and worked my way through to the tunnel. It should have got me right back on track but as I ran in, I skidded to a halt.

The vast chamber that had always opened into the tunnel entrance held a shimmering pool of perfectly still, turquoise water, illuminated by tiny white lights pinpricking around its curved walls.

It had never been flooded before.

The tunnel entrance was below the water level, completely submerged, the surface of the pool glittering. I was almost hypnotised by it, standing there like an idiot, the time ticking down on my wrist and my chances of proving I wasn't a screw up going down the drain.

I backed away.

Turned back into the narrow, claustrophobic Catacombs and ran.

I ended up climbing the Shaft, a vertical tube, my hand screaming, my knee throbbing and having to stop half way up just to breathe. The walls were smooth, no hand holds, nothing to even get decent friction against. The muscles in my legs were trembling, arms like jelly and my chest was getting tight. The wristband was humming, not as violently as it had on Kheris, but bad enough. I wedged myself in there and twisted my arm to see the time.

44:22.

I couldn't give up. I couldn't go up and I couldn't go down. If I gave in, it was a forty foot drop back to the bottom. All the kids on Kheris had joked that I could do anything. Climb a decrepit tower? Scale a vertical wall? Run the gauntlet of the garrison's killing ground amidst the deafening boom of the defence grid shooting down incoming missiles? I'd been invincible.

But now it felt like I'd met my match.

43.57.

I couldn't move.

My muscles were starting to cramp.

43.46.

If I dropped out of there, I was done. I had nowhere to go. I couldn't go back to Kheris. I'd get shot for what I'd done.

43.16.

43.15.

43.14.

Every time I looked at that band on my wrist, it took me back there. Charlie had believed in me. Seen something in me, Mendhel had said. I'd never realised. I'd always thought he was just a cool guy who was watching out for a stupid kid who'd been unlucky enough to be born to two people who should never have got together, never in a million years.

42.00.

I couldn't let him down. It wasn't just the call of a challenge, a stupid dare I couldn't resist. I couldn't let Charlie down. Because he'd died for me. He'd died because of me.

I started to climb and I didn't stop.

NG was there waiting at the end, as well as the Chief, and Hilyer, who was soaked through, shirt sticking to him, hair wet. More than sweat, he'd gone through the flooded tunnel.

My chest was heaving. I leaned on my knees and glanced at the timer on my wrist. The band was still humming. The clock was stopped at 00:29.

The Chief looked down at me. "You didn't take the fastest route."

Damn right I hadn't. I couldn't swim. I'd never seen anything bigger than a bucket of water before.

NG gave a soft laugh as if he'd put it together. NG was cool. "You need to learn," he said. "You have to swim if you're gonna be able to run the Straight."

There was no actual straight route through the Maze. The fastest way through stood out a mile but it went in a loop, doubling back on itself and convoluted as hell. It was tough. It wasn't straight. But apparently that's what it was called.

NG was looking at me like he was looking right into my soul. "There's a faster way across the Sphere as well," he said.

I could guess how. I'd always climbed into the zero gravity chamber and inched my way around its inner surface, handhold to handhold, all the way to the opposite door.

"I want to do it again," I said, hardly able to breathe, hands shaking, sweat dripping off me and chest constricting with electrobe poisoning.

Hilyer was glowering at me. NG and the Chief just nodded.

"You can," NG said. "But not right now." He handed me a vial of antidote. "Both of you, go, get some rest. LC, get up to Medical and get yourself checked over."

Hilyer snapped to and turned away towards the locker room door.

I hesitated.

The Chief shook his head and raised his hand to warn me off. "You heard the man. Now move."

Hilyer caught me as I came out of the shower, just a towel around my waist, my chest still aching and my head not thinking straight. He grabbed my shoulder, spun me round and slammed me up against the bulkhead.

As much as I knew he could flatten me easily, I still struggled, like an idiot.

He shoved me hard and leaned in, whispering, "Wherever the hell you've come from, you don't get to do whatever the hell you want here. You want to get yourself thrown out, fine. Just don't drag me down into your mess."

I couldn't help protesting. I wanted to explain why. I wanted him to understand. I opened my mouth, got as far as, "Zach, I…"

He had his forearm wedged up tight against my throat, pinning me there.

"Don't freaking call me that," he hissed. "You don't know me. Stay the hell away from me, Anderton. I'm not going to let a jumped up little shit like you screw up my chances here. You get it?"

I didn't and I was stupid enough to argue. "You don't…"

He shoved me again. "No. I don't give a damn what you have going on in your life, kid. Stay out of mine."

He pushed me away and stalked off. I stared after him. I felt hard done by. He felt hard done by. Neither of us was going to win.

And I didn't even know what we were arguing about.

The staff in Medical weren't impressed. I couldn't stop coughing, sparks tingling through my lungs. It was taking a while for the antidote to work. They said my immune system was still shot, that I'd probably be vulnerable to infection for a while. They gave me a load more meds and told me to check in later.

When I got back to the barracks, there was no sign of

Hilyer. I didn't know where he was and I didn't care until I couldn't find Charlie's knife.

It had gone.

No one else could have known where I'd hidden it.

My stomach turned, a cold knot twisting.

Hilyer.

I took a handful of painkillers, gave myself another shot of antidote and sat on my bunk, just breathing.

He had it and he'd have to give it back.

There was nowhere else it could be.

I was beyond calm as I walked through Acquisitions, checking in the mess, asking anyone around. Eventually someone pointed me to the gym.

He was lifting weights.

I walked right up, planted myself in front of him and just said it.

"Where the hell is my knife?"

He didn't stop. "I don't know what you're talking about."

"I want my knife back. Now."

He hefted the weights he had in his hands and stared at me. "I don't know what you're talking about."

"My knife," I managed to say, slow and deliberate. "I want it back."

Hilyer glanced sideways. I was very aware that people were watching.

He put the weights down and took a step forward. "I – really – don't know what you're talking about, kid."

He was bigger than me but not by much. And he wasn't that much older.

I didn't back down. "You took my knife."

"Prove it."

"Give it back."

He spread his arms. "Do I look like I have it?"

I didn't have a plan, no neat trick to pull to get him to admit it and no smartass way to get him to do what I wanted. I hadn't really thought much past finding him.

He made it easy. He gave me that laugh and stepped forward again so he was right on me and he pushed me in the chest. "What the hell does it matter?"

I flew at him.

I got in two punches before he hit me back. I rolled with it and went at him again, catching him off balance and we went sprawling. He didn't let up but my entire life suddenly and desperately depended on that knife. I fought back. I'd learned everything I knew about fighting on the streets as well and as much as I was no match for him, I wasn't going to go down easily. He hit me hard and opened the gash above my eye, but I caught him with one in the nose that made it pour. It took three grunts to pull us apart.

"You wanna fight," one of them hissed, struggling to keep Hilyer off me, "you take it to the Cage."

I didn't want to fight, I just wanted Charlie's knife back.

They tossed us aside, one of them leading Hilyer off one way and another taking me by the shoulders and walking me out the other. I glanced back. He was looking back at me, holding his sleeve against his nose. I had no idea what he was thinking but he had no idea how much it mattered to me. Maybe if I'd just told him…

The guy that had hold of me took me into the mess and sat me down, Sienna appearing pretty much straight away with a medical kit.

She pushed a bottle of water into my hand and sat next to me. "What's with the knife?"

I shook my head. I didn't want to talk to anyone.

She wiped the blood off my face and pressed a dressing above my eye. "Belonged to someone special, huh?"

I kind of nodded. I really didn't want to talk about it.

"Kid, we've all lost people." She taped it into place and sat back.

I bit my lip. I wanted to run away, skip out, get outside into fresh air and feel the heat of the sun, be on my own, on the surface of a planet, not stuck on a ship in deep space with a load of people I didn't understand, way out of my depth, and starting to feel like I was trapped worse than if I'd been thrown in a cell for what I'd done.

"Mendhel is your handler, isn't he?"

I nodded, dreading what she was going to say next. I knew something had happened and I knew everyone was avoiding talking to us about it. I sat on my hands because they were shaking. My chest was hurting, so sore it felt like I'd been hit by a truck. I wanted to curl up in a ball.

Sienna squeezed my knee. "Stuff happens, LC. But this is the Thieves' Guild – and no one messes with the Thieves' Guild."

She sat there with me for ages, just chatting, talking about places she'd been, cool stuff she'd done, anything but anything serious. She didn't ask any questions and she didn't ask what I thought about anything. It was exactly what I needed. Except then she stopped talking and just looked at me.

"No one's told you yet, have they?" she said finally. She sucked in a deep breath. "Mendhel's wife was one of the operatives we just lost."

6

Sienna told me to go get some sleep. It seemed like that was all anyone was telling me. I wandered back to our quarters, feeling like shit for Mendhel, not wanting to run into Hilyer and wanting to talk to him at the same time.

The knife was there, lying on my pillow.

I stood staring at it, and that's when the Watch came for me.

Hilyer was being taken into one briefing room as I was marched into another.

He glanced at me but didn't react. The Chief was following him, face like thunder. It was Mendhel that came and talked to me.

He sat. He looked beyond weary. A small dressing was taped below his left ear and he caught me looking.

"Upgraded implant failed to take," he said. "Doesn't happen often but even the best technology doesn't always work. You'll find out soon enough."

He pushed a board across to me that had a list of charges on it, under my name. Disorderly conduct in the mess. Disorderly conduct in the gym. And a list of physio and psych sessions I'd missed, briefings I'd missed, classes I'd missed…

My heart was in my stomach, pounding with a dull beat. "Am I out?" I managed to say.

Mendhel reached and wiped the screen onto a new display, a list of times, physical times against runs in the Maze and completion times of the tasks NG had set. I didn't know whether they were decent times or not but Mendhel looked up at me.

"You're Thieves' Guild," he said. "Start to believe it. We don't have much time and I need to know that you and Hil are going to work together and not kill each other." He was looking at me as if he was trying to decide something. He touched the board again and it flashed up a mass of data. "You wanted to know about Andreyev?"

My heart rate upped a notch. I was trying not to cough, trying to do better than I had done and with that name, he got my attention.

"Nikolai Andreyev was the most successful field operative the guild has ever handled. You want to make a name for yourself here? That's the bar. And believe me, it's high. This is his file – as much as we have access to. You need a challenge? This is it. And I don't care…" He bit off what he was about to say as there was a sharp knock at the door.

It opened, the Chief not waiting before coming in, steering Hilyer ahead of him, telling him to go sit down, and looking at me with a frown. He stopped at the door and said to Mendhel, like we weren't even there, "Timeframe just changed. We don't have two months, we have two weeks."

Mendhel muttered a curse and stood. "Wait here," he muttered to us. "Both of you. Read the files." And he went to the door. He had his back to us so I couldn't see his expression but I heard clearly enough. "Why the hell is it two weeks? They won't be ready in two weeks."

The Chief glanced at us. "They wouldn't have been ready in two months. You want to keep them alive, we need to up the schedule or they're not gonna have a damn chance, whatever happens."

I was trying not to look, trying not to listen and trying to switch off but there was something about the way the Chief kept looking at me.

"Two weeks?" Mendhel said.

Hilyer took one of the boards and started studying it intently but I knew he was listening as well.

The Chief lowered his voice but we could still hear. "We've lost contact with Markus."

We couldn't help looking at each other, Hilyer scowling at me.

"He got a packet of intel out," the Chief was saying. "Unscheduled. Then nothing. We've scanned the entire surface of the planet. Either he's gone or he's dead."

Mendhel cursed. "And we're still sending them in?"

They both looked at us.

The Chief sucked in a deep breath. "It could just be a technical glitch but that seems unlikely. You need to see his last message. They haven't just increased the protections around the AI, if we're reading it right, he's saying it's the AI running the operation. It will take too long to set up an ID for another adult or push someone through the legitimate system and we can't risk another operative without time to prepare. And if Markus' last communication is to be believed, we have no time."

I could feel my heart thumping in my stomach.

"That bad?" Mendhel said.

The big man nodded. "They're cycling high potential candidates through in batches, not even a pretence of filtering them through. Whoever is behind this must know it will attract attention. They must be gearing up for something and they're getting ready to move before that attention can mean anything. The next drop is due to deliver in two weeks. Losing contact with Markus means we're now blind. Trust me, we have no choice. As much as I hate to say it, it has to be these two. And it has to be now. You said it. They have the ideal background. Both of them. But we change the plan. We get them in, LC gets what we need and we get them out. Now more than ever, we need that intel."

What he said next was so quiet, I almost missed it, but it made a chill shiver down my spine.

"Charlie, Loic, Arianne, and now Markus?" The Chief shook his head, expression dark.

It felt like I was in the middle of an unfolding nightmare, one that was following me, that was catching up everyone around me in a swirling maelstrom.

"NG thinks they're connected," he was saying. "No coincidence. And if you ask me, it's no damned coincidence that this new guy gets thrown into post as our head of operations right now. Do you even know where he's come from?"

Mendhel shook his head. He glanced at us as if he knew we had to be listening. What he said next was too quiet to hear, but I caught the name Kheris.

The Chief said something else but I couldn't follow what, then Mendhel shook his head and I heard him say, "No. Charlie had that in his report. The kid didn't see anything."

I slouched further down in the seat. They were talking about me.

The Chief was looking at me as he said, "We need to be sure."

"Chief, I'm sure."

"Mend, I know this is a bad time but NG wants to know why we just lost two operatives on that back of beyond shit-hole, and another two in fast succession. We've not lost a deep cover in over fifteen years. Now four in the space of weeks? Something's kicking off. And it started when that ship crashed on Kheris. If this kid knows anything about it, we need him to say it now before we send them out on this tab."

"He doesn't. We got out what bodies we could. Talk to Science. They have everything we recovered. Chief, the kid didn't see anything. He wants to forget it. And I can't blame him for that."

The knot in my stomach did another flip, icy cold. They had bodies here from Kheris. I could feel them looking at me. All I could see was Charlie and the little ones in the street, running for the door, see their faces, yelling, through the glass… Maisie lying on the tarmac, sprawled, unmoving…

I could hardly swallow past the lump in my throat.

A board landed with a bang on the table in front of me. I looked up. The Chief sat down opposite me, Mendhel next to him.

"The brief has changed," the Chief said. "There is a distinct possibility that you will have no contact on the ground. If Markus is there, your objectives stand. But you go down there and he isn't, you'll be on your own. You just get the intel. You keep out of trouble. You stay under the radar." He looked at Hilyer, his expression hard. "You both stay under the radar. Do you understand? We'll arrange extraction in thirty days. If you need out before that, you ask for a case review. That will trigger a legal response that we'll see and we'll come in for you. In the meantime, whatever happens, you do not reveal you are guild to anyone. You do not even talk to each other while you're down there. Not about this. Do you understand?"

We both nodded.

"You're out of there in thirty days regardless. We'll either get you released or…" He paused and looked at Mendhel. "Worst case scenario, we send in an extraction team. Understand this, we do not leave operatives behind. Ever. The new details are on that board, together with a new training schedule."

He said something else that I didn't hear. Without even touching it, I could see that the board was connected to the main system. I wanted to know who they had here in Science. If it was Maisie, I wanted to see her again.

I was only vaguely aware of the Chief standing and leaving. I must have looked even worse than I felt. Mendhel leaned across, checked the numbers scrolling on my wristband and sent me up to Medical. They were unimpressed enough that they kept me in which suited me just fine. I didn't want to be around anyone.

Someone brought another data board in for me, told me it was more intel on the tab and said there'd be more to follow. I didn't look at it. I didn't want to think.

I faked being tired and ended up crashing out anyway except I had another nightmare, waking up screaming, in a cold sweat with a vague memory of someone saying everything was okay and popping a shot of something into my neck. I couldn't remember what the nightmare had been about but it left my heart thumping and a hollow chill in the pit of my stomach.

They gave me food but I couldn't eat because I felt too queasy. The medics fussed and told me my levels were down. Levels of what I didn't care. When I'd first arrived, I'd overheard them talking about me, malnutrition and post-traumatic stress featuring high in their concerns. Now, they were adding a bad reaction to electrobe poisoning to the list.

I sat there in Medical with an IV line in my arm and my leg stretched out, and I read everything I could access, anything to stop me thinking about what might or might not be happening half way across the galaxy on a dirtball planet I'd hated, and how Maisie might be lying cold and still in a box right here on this ship.

I wish I hadn't overheard what Mendhel and the Chief had been talking about. I swear I didn't plan to do what I did, but I so desperately wanted to see her. I started looking through the data banks and pushing the system just enough to let me in a bit further and a bit further and before I knew it, I was hacking into stuff in Science that had unbelievable protections around it. It was like hacking the Imperial garrison on Kheris but a magnitude more challenging. But I could see ways round it or through it, NG had shown me how to, and it became a game of see how far I could get.

I kept half an eye on the door but I wasn't due any meds and Mendhel had told me to study the briefing so it didn't look odd that I was sitting there working.

I ended up going through personnel records. They were sealed but I couldn't resist making a half-assed attempt to find Andreyev.

No luck on that but I came across a report I felt bad just looking at.

Mendhel's wife.

They had a daughter, Anya, my age. There was a picture of them. His wife, Arianne, was beautiful but their daughter was stunning, smiling like she was beaming right at me out of the picture, the warmth of the smile reaching up to bright blue eyes that crinkled in the corners with such intensity, I couldn't look away.

I think maybe I fell in love with her a bit right then.

I shut it down, heart pounding, losing the connection and staring at the blank screen for a second before I could start again.

I found what I was looking for that time, a list of entries into a morgue from the past few weeks, but it just made me feel worse. They used this complex ID system. No other details except what I could guess was gender and origin. Only one female from Kheris. My hands were shaking, my chest feeling like a fist was pushing against my lungs. I hit a brick wall. I knew where she was, there was just no more information in the system about what had happened to her. I needed to get in there.

The trick to breaking in anywhere is to find the gaps where no one is looking. And there are always gaps. As systems get more and more complicated, people get more and more reliant on automated processes. Habits form, people and even AIs fall into patterns. The obvious gets ignored, then forgotten about and then overlooked completely as time passes. Until someone finds the gap. I've always been very good at seeing what other people don't. At finding those gaps.

No one used physical passes on board the Alsatia so I couldn't pull the trick I'd always used in the garrison on Kheris. The Senson implants everyone had seemed to be how they kept tabs on where people were and who could go where. That and the wristbands. So I was tagged. But I could take that band off.

I waited until the medics had done their rounds and I

was told to get some sleep, then I dressed and slipped out. I went to the Maze. There was no one else in there. I logged it as a private session. They'd given us that privilege. And I made sure the settings were easy. No electrobes and gravity the same as Kheris.

I found the easiest route through to where I needed to be and I snuck along the dark narrow corridors and access ways.

As much as I'd spent hours in there, I still didn't know every trick it could pull. A couple of times, I thought I'd sprung a trap as doors closed ahead of me and I had to backtrack away from dead ends. I finally found the door I wanted, climbed a set of steep stairs to get to it and stopped. There was something wrong. Every time I'd been in there, it had always been open. Now it was closed. I must have stood there staring at it for a full two minutes. It felt hinky and the hairs on the back of my neck were prickling so bad I backed away for a second. There wasn't much light, just a dim glow from blue spots set into the walls and ceiling.

I took a step back and looked up and around. There was a pattern to the lights, a distinct line that ran across the floor, up each wall and across the ceiling, just in front of the door. I took another step back. There was a slight click. I froze, glancing round and spotting a small square panel on the wall, set low down at about hip height, the same colour as the wall, only a faint outline giving it away. I took a chance and pressed my hand on it. Strings of code appeared on the wall, weird characters and symbols

I'd never seen before, a timer ticking down fast. I didn't think. I followed the code, adjusting as it responded to my nudgings, messing up a few times, swearing as I reset it back to the start, and cracking it with only seconds to spare. The adrenaline rush was ridiculous, my hands shaking. I looked up. The glow of the lights turned green. The blast door up ahead opened. There was another click as I stepped forward. I ran through the door and didn't look back.

7

The space I ran in to was called the Void and it was breathtaking, literally. The drop in temperature hit my lungs as I sucked in a breath, looking down into a vast, dark emptiness that dropped out either side of the narrow beam the floor had become, nothing but intense black darkness beyond, as far as I could see. I had to put one foot in front of the other to move forward. It was no different to running along the beams on the wall of the garrison, or skipping from rooftop to rooftop in the middle of the night, except I'd never done that with a metal brace on my leg. I had a few wobbles but I made it to the middle. I leaned down and left my wristband on the beam. If they were monitoring it, it would look like I was sitting there. Thinking. Like I'd done a load of times in the last few days.

I stood and ran the remaining length of the beam. The blast doors ahead of me were open and I walked out into the Block.

That's where it got tough.

The Block was a maze within the Maze. There were a hundred ways through and the whole place was patrolled by drones that could be programmed and controlled to behave in different ways, sometimes to simulate human activity, sometimes animals such as guard dogs, other times they just behaved like the inhuman AIs they were. At our level of training back then, they usually just activated a lockdown if they spotted you, although sometimes they were equipped with FTH, fast takedown rounds, with a stun charge that could knock you out cold. And there were times when they'd programme in surprises and we didn't know what they'd do and we just had to run through and make damn sure they didn't catch sight of us. That first week I was in there, I didn't know how bad they could be. Ignorance is great sometimes.

Some of the drones were about the size of a baseball and simply emitted a signal that simulated a life sign; they were used to train us on tracking equipment. It was one of those I was looking for. I ran through, climbed up onto an overhead gantry and waited. It didn't take long for one of the little bots to come pootling past below me. I dropped down, grabbed it and slammed it against the wall. It made a desperate whining sound, tried to spin round in my hand and let out a hiss as I hit it against the wall again. It went dark and stopped moving.

Peanut would have loved those damn robots. He'd probably have taken one as a pet and programmed it to follow him around. I hated them. I hit it against the wall again for good measure then pried open its cover plate with Charlie's knife, deliberately damaging it as I did and nicking my finger in the process. The drone wasn't complicated, but then it didn't need to be, it only had a single purpose but I needed to be quick. If it didn't reboot, a sweeper drone would appear to collect it and take it back for repair. I flicked its life signs emitter onto null, then snapped the damaged panel closed. After a few seconds, it started to reactivate, its blue light turning red to indicate a system fault. The damaged access panel would cause it to transmit that its mobility was impaired. It would be recalled to Science for repair, and that was exactly what I needed.

It started to flash, indicating that it was out of service. I'd seen this happen only once before and watched as a faulty drone had trundled up to a section of wall where a hatch, almost invisible, had slid open and the machine had disappeared into the depths of the Alsatia. It hadn't taken too much digging around in the system to figure out where they were going.

I hefted the drone in my hand and moved along the wall until I spotted the section I was looking for. As I approached, a section of wall close to the floor silently slid open. Clutching the drone, I got down on my stomach and looked inside. It was barely wide enough for me. No adult aboard the Alsatia could have fitted in there. And it was pitch black. Drones don't need light.

I squeezed into the hole and began to worm my way through. I'm not claustrophobic but being in a space that tight in total darkness does strange things to your mind and to your senses. Time meant nothing. I was back on Kheris, sneaking through the crawlspaces of the garrison after curfew, Latia safe in her home, Charlie out on patrol, Maisie waiting to see what I'd bring back, waiting for me with a laugh and a hug at the ready. All I needed to do was get in and get out. It was nothing but a game. Find food. Avoid trouble. Stay alive.

Except they hadn't.

I stopped, resting on my elbows, and buried my head in my arms. I couldn't get lost there. It had happened. It sucked. There was nothing I could do about it. But I wanted to see her.

I forced myself to move. I was getting close. I felt more than saw the sensors up ahead. Science was a closed system. Totally isolated from the rest of the Alsatia. And it was as secure physically as it was electronically. I inched forward. The scanners in the tunnel were expecting a humanoid life sign and they were getting one, albeit one that was moving very slowly. I hadn't disabled the drone's automatic recognition system so it was still broadcasting and that's all the system saw. Nothing out of the ordinary. Something so obvious no one would have thought of it. A gap in the system.

I stopped and listened once I reached the end of the tube, then climbed out into a dark, quiet maintenance area. I tossed the drone into the pile waiting for repairs and stood at the door, listening. I knew the layout of Science by heart. I knew the staff rotas, scheduled maintenance plans, cleaning rosters, the status of every active project and the inventory of its lab equipment store. I knew where they were keeping her. And I knew how to get to her.

My heart was thumping as I pulled open the drawer. It had taken me over an hour to work my way through Science to the morgue without being seen. I'd had to wait for ten minutes in a ventilation shaft before I was sure the staff in there were done for the shift. I had five minutes before the next shift would appear.

There was no name on the drawer. Just the ID. No notes or tags. I pulled it out. She had a cover over her. I stared, my hands shaking.

I pulled back the cover.

8

It wasn't Maisie.

I almost folded. She'd been beautiful whoever she was. Except for a burn across her face, slicing her features in two. She had tattoos inked on both arms, another on her neck.

She was Earth marine corps.

She wasn't Maisie.

I stared at her. She must have been out there, in the desert, at the crashed ship. Probably one of the emergency teams that had rushed to help before they knew what it was. I'd never really known what had happened to everyone else out there that night. Except they'd all died. And I hadn't.

It dawned on me slowly that I was standing in Science, in the centre of the most secure, off limits area of the Alsatia, staring at a woman I didn't know, for no reason at all.

I pulled the cover back into place and slid back the drawer, my hands shaking even more than they had been. Even getting back the hope that Maisie could still be alive, I felt a galaxy apart from her.

I heard a sound behind me. I shouldn't have been in there. I shouldn't have been anywhere near Science. I needed to get out, get back to the Void, pick up Charlie's wristband and crawl back to Medical.

And hope like hell no one had missed me.

I don't know how I made it back to the maintenance area. I had a horrible feeling I was running out of time. I ended up in a crawlspace above the corridor, no way into the area above the maintenance shop itself and too many people busying about below to drop out and try the door. I waited there, every minute an agonising delay. There was no let up. It shouldn't have been that busy. I knew all the shift patterns and everything was out of kilter. I waited longer than I should have before I backed away. I needed another way out. There was only one way I could think of. Apart from walking up to someone and handing myself in. Which was not an option. I needed to break out. Sometimes that's harder than breaking in.

I found a way. And it almost killed me. Have you ever seen the hull of a deep spacer? And I don't mean have you seen it from the cosy safety of an orbital. Outside, it's different. It makes you think, to see the scale of it, to feel the enormity of the universe beyond, to feel the heat drain out of your body and watch the gauge drop as your air runs out.

The trembling was spreading through the muscles of my arms and legs, tremors that were getting worse as I tried to pull myself over a mass of pipework that was sucking the warmth from my hands with every briefest touch, even through the thermally insulated gloves of the suit I was wearing. The EVA suit I'd stolen from a maintenance bay, that was way too big, running out of juice and must have had a leak because there was no way I was breathing that much air that fast. I'd given up gawping at the stars and the vast, sprawling expanse of space by then. I'd miscalculated, badly miscalculated, and in about... I glanced sideways at the heads up display... two minutes, I was going to die unless I found another way back in or figured out a way to survive without oxygen.

A panel ahead of me shifted, plumes of gas venting out into the empty darkness. I lost the tenuous grip I had on anything solid and for a stomach-churning, heart-stopping fraction of a second, I free-floated and, I swear, it felt like the mass of the huge ship moved away from me and left me hanging there in nothing.

If it went into jump now, I was dead.

I grabbed for a handhold and swung round as my arm hooked around a beam, snagging the suit so it felt like it was going to tear right off, and bumped back up against the hull. It was unreal. I should have been smarter but, believe me, in that moment, everything I knew about inertia and momentum was a long way from that immediate reality.

One minute fifty. The beams from the helmet lights were fading. My knee was throbbing despite the pain meds the brace was injecting. The suit was beeping an insistent warning, lights flashing on the display. It had looked so easy on the blueprints. I hauled myself along the beam and worked out the distance to the vent I'd been planning on using, and it didn't add up. Not with the levels of air and energy the suit had left. I needed another way in.

I felt tiny. Stupid. Overwhelmed. Hungry. And cold, did I say cold? The trembling was turning into shivering. I'd always hated the heat of Kheris, hated the stifling heat and the dust and the sweltering humidity of the thunderstorms. But right then, I'd have gratefully taken that desert dirtball over the sterile, never-ending, chill metal hull of that ship in deep space.

One minute thirty. I could see lights winking, way off, out of the corner of my eye through the visor and I didn't know if they were real, drop ships docking or ship systems coming to life, or if my eyes were going. I was getting light-headed, hauling myself along, my right hand screaming each time I had to use it and my fingers numb. The hull of the ship was humming beneath me, even through the suit I could feel the vibrations, the entire mass seeming to pulse. The main drives were powering up. If they engaged, I'd be atomised. If the ship moved, I'd be left stranded.

One minute twenty. I needed to think, better than I was. I knew the entire ship. I'd memorised the plans for this entire section, deck by deck, the whole outside surface down to every beam and strut. But memorising from blueprints and schematics is never quite the same as the real thing.

There'd be a way in, I just had to find it.

Fast.

Thousands of vanes and masts were starting to move, bristling in every direction, folding in on themselves. Huge panels and vents were shifting, the surface as far as I could see becoming streamlined and smooth where it had been raised like a city skyline. My heart was beating so fast in my ears it was competing with the warning klaxons of the suit that were reaching fever point.

One minute. Sixty seconds. At least a hundred metres to the only chance I reckoned I had to get into cover. I could imagine a glowing line between where I was and where I needed to get to. Except there were thousands of tons of moving machinery in the way and there was no way I was going to make it.

Forty seconds. I upped the pace, risked letting go and freefalling a couple of times, misjudged it and crashed into a vent hatch as it clanged shut. My left leg took the brunt of it, pain shot through my knee and I almost blacked out, vision going and the whole universe narrowing to a line between me and another vent that was inching closed in what seemed like excruciating slow motion ahead of me.

Twenty seconds. The suit's alarm was a steady, high-pitched squeal, the display blurred into a frenzied swirl of lights and lines that made no sense. I felt like I'd been kicked in the chest, punched in the head and stabbed between the eyes. And bizarrely, as I scrambled and fought my way to that tiny opening, I wondered where Maisie was and how Latia and Peanut were, and whether Calum had kept his promise. It all felt far away and like

I'd never been a part of it. Like I was never really a part of anything, anywhere.

Ten seconds.

Five seconds.

I couldn't think anymore. Could hardly grip with my left hand never mind the right. I stumbled, hit my knee again, light flashed behind my eyeballs and I crawled, inch by inch, feeling the chill dark of space creeping into my joints, and systems shutting down, cell by cell. I reached for the vent, fell as the artificially generated gravity grabbed me, felt nothing beneath me and closed my eyes.

I must have hit every inch of my body against cold, hard steel as I tumbled down. The visor cracked as my head hit against the bulkhead. I was out of time. No air. No idea where I was going to end up. I couldn't breathe. Remember I told you someone had said once that I had nine lives? It felt like I was about to use up four through nine all in one go.

I hit something hard, rolled and sprawled.

There was a click.

The helmet was lifted away and I couldn't help that my head hit the deck as I sucked in a lungful of clean, rich air. I thought I was going to throw up. Or pass out. I'm not sure which would have been worse.

I managed to raise my eyes.

Armoured figures surrounded me, grey insignia on the arm of each suit, all aiming weapons at me. There was a figure standing in their midst. A tall, thin guy with an almost skeletal face who looked beyond pissed, arms folded across his chest, looking down at me like I was a bug he'd found floating in his soup.

He shook his head and said, with no nonsense or further ceremony, "Get that child the hell off my ship."

They took me back to Medical. Charlie's wristband was resting on top of the pillow. I picked it up and held it in my hand, trying to sit still as the staff checked my lungs, muttering about my vitals and stats, resetting the brace on my knee and checking my hand. Almost suffocating out in the cold of space hadn't done any of it any favours. They pumped me full of drugs again and told me to sit tight. There was an armed guard on the door, one of the guys in powered armour, and they left the door open like they didn't trust me.

I sat there on the bunk, holding the wristband and clutching the dog tags around my neck as if I didn't deserve to wear them anymore.

It didn't take long before Mendhel turned up. He stood at the door and stared at me. I couldn't tell if he was angry at me or disappointed but he just turned, muttering, "Come with me," as if he hadn't quite decided himself.

We went up through the ship in an elevator, slick and fast. He didn't say a word the whole time. It stopped at Twelve. The lift doors opened and Mendhel stepped aside, gesturing me to leave ahead of him. I thought for a second that he wasn't coming with me but he followed, nudging me out into the warm corridor. I still felt like a street urchin, even though I was wearing the clothes they'd given me. Like I was an imposter. I was a long way from the dusty streets I'd left behind. I didn't want to go back, that was the last thing I wanted, but from the look on Mendhel's face, I might have just got myself kicked out.

NG's door was closed. Mendhel steered me to a line of seats outside and sat down next to me. He looked sideways at me with something like resignation in his face. He reminded me of Charlie, especially when he looked at me like that. That hurt.

He held out his hand.

I guessed that he wanted the wristband and I gave it to him, my heart sinking, feeling like I was losing a piece of myself, but he beckoned again, took hold of my wrist and snapped it back into place.

I almost cried.

"You earned it," he said. "You want to tell me why the hell you did what you just did?"

I stared at my feet, scuffing them together. I didn't know how to say it. I'd been so desperate to see her, to see if it was Maisie in that morgue, once I knew there were bodies from Kheris and one that was female, but I don't know why I hadn't just asked.

Mendhel blew out a breath. "You thought she was Maisie?"

I couldn't explain. I wanted to ask him a hundred questions but I'd forgotten how to speak.

"Maisie is fine," he said.

Just hearing her name made the adrenaline kick in, my heart pounding. Maisie was alive. I knew I was sitting there like an idiot. I didn't know what to say, didn't know how to calm down the knots that were tangling my insides. Because I just knew from his tone that there was a 'but'…

"You broke into Science because you thought we'd brought her body back from Kheris with us."

It wasn't a question. Mendhel had a way of figuring me out. I've never told anyone before how much I owed that man. If he hadn't been there, been the one to take me in to the guild, the one assigned to be my handler, there's no way I would have lasted as long as I did.

"LC, I won't lie to you. You have to understand that. If you ever want to know anything, ask." He sounded exasperated. He looked at me funny then said, "We need to talk."

My stomach did a backflip. Any time anyone has ever said that to me, it's never been followed by anything good. I stared at him, willing everything to be okay, my mouth dry, and my shoulders so tense they were starting to seize.

"Maisie's fine," he said again.

"But?"

"The money you transferred…" Mendhel paused. I didn't even know how he knew about that. It seemed like everyone knew every tiny thing about me. He pulled a face, looking me right in the eye. "It didn't get to her, Luka. It was seized by the Imperial government. Every penny of it."

9

It took a second to sink in. It had never felt real. They'd just been numbers on a screen, scrolling numbers that had gone on forever while I'd been running out of time. It had been a stupid game to piss off Dayton. But part of me had thought that if she had made it, then she'd never have to worry about how to feed the little ones again, never have to worry about medicine if they got sick. I'd even thought that she could buy Latia a new house, all move in together.

Except kids like us never got happy endings.

I had a lump in my throat but I sucked it up and switched off. It didn't matter, I was never going back. Mendhel had told me that when he'd told me to choose. Get shot in the back of the head or go join the Thieves' Guild. It hadn't been much of a choice.

"Dayton had it set up to splinter," he said, his voice low, "as soon as the transfer initiated. That was the only way he could get access to it without triggering any alarms. It would have split out into tens of thousands of dummy accounts, bouncing around stock exchanges, commodities trading markets, investments, a whole range of transactions that would buy and sell within milliseconds, bouncing from one corporation and planet to the next until it was effectively untraceable. He had it set to re-consolidate into a number of accounts, way down the line. He might have been a thug but he wasn't completely stupid."

He was looking at me weird.

"As soon as you hijacked the data stream, the security alert went sky high. It never would have worked. And, I know, you didn't have time to do anything different." He smiled. "It was a nice move, impressive, I'll give you that."

If he was trying to make me feel better, it wasn't working. It had been a dumbass thing to do. I didn't care. Dayton was dead. None of it mattered. Even if Maisie was alive, there was no way back to her and there was nothing I could do to help her anymore.

Except Mendhel gave me another lifeline.

"There is a way," he said quietly and added intently, "This is the Thieves' Guild. This tab you've been given? You pull it off, you'll be assigned to the list and given more. You can earn a lot of money here, LC, real money, and if that's what you want, you can send every single penny of it back to Kheris. I just…"

He stopped as the elevator doors opened and the tall, thin guy from the airlock walked out, scowling when he saw me. He walked past and went straight into NG's office.

Mendhel watched him go, muttering under his breath, "I can't believe you broke into Science." He put his hand on my shoulder. "Are you okay?"

I wasn't. It felt like I was trapped, caught between

feeling like crap for screwing up so badly that I might have trashed my chances here before I'd even started, and feeling resentful that I was stuck in a situation I had no control over and suddenly dependent on these people to make everything okay back at the place I could never call home again.

Mendhel exhaled, probably annoyed at himself for even giving me that chance.

"I have to go in there and persuade them you can do this tab," he said. "Can you?"

I didn't know and I didn't know what to say but he'd just given me a real reason to want to.

Sienna asked me the same question, eight days later, five hours before we were due to deploy. That reputation I have of never being scared? She's one of the few people who can see through it. I was done in the Maze, done with the briefings and had nothing to pack. They'd told us to go rest but I couldn't. I had no idea where Hilyer was but I went to the mess and sat in a corner with a bottle of water, feet up on the chair next to me and head leaning back against the bulkhead, eyes closed. Just breathing. I didn't want to sleep, I didn't want to read and I didn't want to talk to anyone.

Everyone avoided me anyway. Except for Sienna. I knew it was her as she approached and I couldn't help smiling, opening my eyes as she nudged my feet off the chair and sat down, replacing the bottled water with a beer.

"One won't do you any harm."

I sat up.

"This is one helluva tab you've been given for your first time out," she said, voice soft.

The bottle was cold. I didn't open it. I just held it against my forehead and looked at her from under it.

"Can you do it?"

I nodded. There was no other answer. What was I supposed to say? I'd always had this stupid response, like a knee jerk reaction, any time anyone dared me to do something stupid, no matter how dangerous. The more risky it was, the quicker I was to say yes. But there on the Alsatia, it felt like I'd stalled. Faltered right when it really counted. Like I'd suddenly realised I was in the real world and it was serious.

She squeezed my knee. "We'll be right there. The Chief's even saying that NG is gonna send Thunderclouds to watch over you." She looked me in the eye. "You know what they are, yeah?"

I did. I'd read everything on the guild I could get my hands on, and a load more they didn't realise I'd got access to.

"Have you seen one?"

I shook my head.

She laughed. "Come with me."

She called a couple of the extraction agents to follow us and joked with them as we took the lift down to the docks. She introduced them as one of the teams that would be on stand-by if we needed them. I felt weirdly small and insignificant and at the same time like I was the centre of attention and the most important asset they'd ever covered. It was unnerving. They knew everything about us and what we were going out to do. Like there were no secrets anywhere.

No one had mentioned Science though. Maybe some stuff was held under lock and key, after all.

Sienna nudged her elbow into my arm. I'd stopped listening to what they were saying and looked up at her.

"Don't think. This close to a tab? You don't think, you just do." She scrubbed her hand over my head with a laugh.

I'd never had my hair cut so short. I'd never had it long, but never as short as this. I felt like a criminal. Maybe that was the point.

I brushed her off but it made me smile.

"That's better," she said. "Now, you wanna see something really cool?"

The lift doors opened. The docks on the Alsatia were insane, clangs and bangs from ships hooking onto the exterior hull a constant noise, the deck reverberating under my feet. The whole area was a frenzy of logistical activity, everyone busy, crates and containers moving everywhere, slick as hell. Going down there was like scratching the surface of a shiny mirror and seeing how much chaos and effort it was taking to keep it so smooth.

I'd only been there once before, when we'd got here, in no fit state to take much notice of anything. That second time was overwhelming, but they steered me away from the main deck and into a side tunnel that was so cold I had to pull down my sleeves and bunch them round my hands.

We stopped at a door.

Sienna turned to me with a grin. "You ready?"

She hit the button and it opened with a hiss onto a gantry above an enormous hangar.

I'd seen pictures, even scoped out the plans and specifications out of curiosity, but it was nothing compared to seeing it for real. Peanut would have pissed himself.

The Thundercloud was huge. It hung there, suspended, humming like it was alive, engineers crawling all over it in mechanised suits, drones hooking up tubes and conduits like they were feeding it.

Sienna let me gawp like an idiot for a second then she gave me the rundown, pointing out each feature, each vane and turret, energy systems, tracking systems, defence grid actuators, ammunition storage, firing tubes of phenomenal scale.

"There's nothing like them," she said, leaning on the handrail. "The most advanced weapons platform either side of the line. No one else has anything close."

One of the extraction agents clapped me on the back. "One Thundercloud can wipe out a city in the blink of an eye. Or she can pinpoint a single human target from orbit. And you'll have two of them babysitting you, kid."

The other one added like she was trying to reassure

me, "Her intelligence is off the scale. Highest grade AI there is."

It was an AI. I knew it was but my stomach still flipped when she said it. I didn't know if I wanted to be on the ground with that thing in orbit, targeting me. I think I even took a step back as if it could hear what I was thinking.

Sienna must have read the look on my face. "They're smart. We trust them. Don't ever think otherwise." She gave me a shove. "And besides, you'll have us. We might not be there on the ground with you, but we'll be watching. Okay?"

I stared at it.

"I'll be fine," I muttered.

I had to be. I didn't have much choice.

The extraction guy acknowledged one of the techies down in the hangar with a wave and turned to me. "Do you want to come meet her?"

"What?"

"Do you want to go down there and meet the Thundercloud? Skye is one of the best."

I looked down and into the dock bottom and spotted Hilyer with another of the extraction teams. They were standing alongside an AI core transfer pod waiting to be loaded into the hoist that would lower it into the heart of the gigantic weapons platform. From this angle, I could just make out a pulsating sphere that looked like it was made of liquid mercury, constantly shifting and changing shape inside the pod. Just the thought of being that close to one made me feel queasy and knowing it had a name was too weird.

"No. Thank you."

Sienna squeezed my shoulder. "Are you going to be okay?"

I didn't know.

Honestly? I was such a mess I thought they were going to change their minds, pull me at the last minute, take me off the list and throw me out on my ear.

And when I stumbled off the prisoner transfer drop ship, wrists and ankles manacled, into Redemption's prison yard, I wished they had.

10

It was hard not to panic, shuffling out into that dark chill rain and seeing the guards with guns ready, the high walls, the razor wire, floodlights bright after the darkness they'd kept us in on the ship.

We'd dropped out of orbit into a deepening dusk, flying low over a rough sea to an island, waves crashing against dark cliffs that gave way to low hills that seemed to stretch forever, just the blinking lights of occasional masts and waystations breaking the monotony. I'd peered out of the window and watched the lights of the buildings appear below, the ominous sprawling structure looming from the moorland, matching the schematic and virtual models of our briefings. Mendhel's words echoed in my mind as we circled waiting permission to land… "One of the highest security containment facilities in the Empire. A central core houses the admin block, above a power plant and the AI that controls the whole penal colony. There are five separate adult prisons on site, all with wings that stretch out in interconnected blocks, maximum security going down five levels below ground level. Accommodation for the staff is in a self-contained village within the complex. The juvenile facility is separate, on the perimeter, smaller, self-contained – central exercise yard with accommodation blocks, school blocks, sports fields, gym. There are three separate landing fields, again all self-contained, one to service the juvenile facility, one for staff, the other for the adult prisoners. The entire facility is surrounded by sixty foot high walls, monitored by the AI, protected by guard towers and automated defences. The reach of the AI extends beyond the walls to cover the entire island. There is no way out. There are no gaps. There are no blindspots. This is one of the best kept, well maintained, highly funded correctional facilities in the galaxy. This is the machine that feeds the Imperial Xùnzhí Corps. The Emperor's penal battalions…"

I shuffled forward again and squinted, blinked cold drops from my eyelashes and tried to keep my head down, even when I was pushed and shoved into line by guards who were enjoying themselves way too much screaming at us. One of them walked behind us along the line, another at the front, stopping at each kid in turn like they were inspecting us. I tensed as they stopped at me, not expecting the slap to the back of the head and the sharp pain at the base of my skull as they secured a thin metal band tight around my neck.

Nothing like that had been mentioned in any of our briefings.

It took everything I had to keep calm and not react.

The guild had given us full IDs, based on our real names, "…so you don't screw up," the Chief had said, in a tone that suggested he was expecting us to whatever they did. The background they were giving me was fairly close to the truth so I assumed Hilyer's was as well, whatever that was. We knew nothing about each other and that was the way they kept it because of where we were going.

It hadn't felt like it was really happening until I walked out onto that landing strip.

They'd come really close to pulling us from the whole tab. It was NG that had spoken up for us. He'd looked at us both intently for a while and eventually said to Mendhel and the Chief, "You should have seen what I was doing when I was thirteen." The way he'd said it, right in front of us, he was almost laying it down as a challenge. That's the way NG works. He always knows exactly which buttons to push. You ever meet him, you'll see what I mean. Everything's different now but back then? It was a tab, there were points at stake. I didn't even care about the points, I wanted the money to send back to Kheris. We had no idea what else was going on but that's the way it was, we didn't know any different.

We'd had our final week of training and one last briefing then we were sent to different processing units. I hadn't seen Hilyer again until I was marched onto the transport, and as much as I knew we had to act like we didn't know each other, it was still reassuring to see him there.

That didn't last long.

There were eighteen other kids with us. There was only one younger than me. He'd sniffled all the way out, freaked when he walked off the ramp and was stupid enough to fight back when one of the guards hit him with a baton to get him in line. The kid hit the dirt, the guards descended on him, kicking, dragging him splashing across the ground and I was moving, shouting in protest, before I knew it.

It worked. They abandoned him and turned on me, yelling. Something hit my back, the back of my knees, the back of my head. The band round my neck sparked and sent a shock of agonising pain into my spine. I went down.

And as I sprawled face down in the mud, all I could think was that Mendhel would be disappointed. "Don't stand out," he'd said. "Don't get involved, don't get noticed. Do you understand?"

I'd nodded but yeah, that didn't go to plan. What was I supposed to do? Stand by while they pummelled the crap out of a kid smaller than me? I couldn't. Hilyer did. As they pulled me to my feet and dragged me off, I caught his eye. He was watching, cold, distant, calculating and way more smart than I'd been. The guild had tried to drum into us what the rules would be, what we had to expect and how we'd have to toe the line. Problem was, it seemed the rules had already been thrown out of the window.

They marched me inside a massive facility that was all huge grey walls, thick metal beams and sheer glass panels, and through into a dark corridor lined with heavy blast doors. They stopped me at one, took me into a tiny cell and made me stand with my hands up on the wall, feet spread. They yelled at me not to move and left me there in the cold darkness, the heavy door slamming shut behind me with a resounding echo as a power grid hummed, securing it in place.

I'd seen stress positions before. The soldiers on Kheris used to inflict that on anyone they suspected to be resistance when they dragged them out onto the streets after curfew. I'd never had it inflicted on me before. I very quickly learned why it was called a stress position.

That was my first time in solitary confinement. It wasn't the last. Certainly not the worst. I did what they wanted, head pounding, for as long as I could, dripping rainwater off me into a puddle on the floor, before I dropped the stance and turned. We were kids. They couldn't do that to us.

They could and they did.

The door opened and two guards walked in, slow and calm. There was something in their expression that made me tense and that made it worse. I was on the floor again in seconds and this time they knelt on me to keep me down and punched me in the back of the head with such force that I couldn't stop myself crying out, eyes watering.

"It gets worse if you fight us," one of them hissed into my ear. "You want to fight us, kid?"

He shoved me when I didn't answer. My head hit the floor and I almost greyed out.

So much for not standing out.

They left me in there, standing, hands up against the wall for what seemed like forever. I couldn't feel my hands, could hardly move my arms when they came for me and marched me out and into an accommodation block. Some of the kids I'd arrived with were there with the others, showered, clean and warm in fresh clothes, dark green tee shirts and black combat pants. It was like we were in the military already. Everyone had the same slender metallic bands around their neck. They all stared as I was trooped through, still in my soaking wet, bright orange prison gear, sympathy on some faces, smirks on others. Hilyer had a fresh cut under his eye and busted knuckles, and he was standing in amongst the other kids like they were already looking up to him. There was a girl standing close to him, her hand almost touching his at his side. I'd been standing alone, soaking wet in a dark room for hours, he'd been making friends and allies, and settling in like he owned the place. I felt like a complete fool. I couldn't see the little kid anywhere.

The guards pushed me forward, warning the others to get on with whatever they were supposed to be doing.

I was taken through to a room lined with cubicles and pushed into one. They took the manacles off my wrists and told me to strip, shower, change and wait there. The clothes were rough like they didn't want us to be too comfortable. They fit though, that was something. The shirt was a bit big. It had J/D-13-ANDERTON stamped on it in case I hadn't realised it was for me. I guessed we were in D Block. Delta. For some reason, from all the briefing notes and intel on what to expect in here, it had got into my head that we'd be placed in Gamma. But no, it looked like we were Delta. I had to keep telling myself it wasn't real. I was Thieves' Guild and I was playing a totally different game. But I could go along with it. I could go along with anything if it meant I got cash to send back to Maisie.

It didn't take long for a medic to turn up, check me over and give me a load of meds. Because my levels were off, she said. Damned levels. Her name badge said Brennan. She didn't say much else but the way she looked at me almost made me break down in tears. She squeezed my shoulder as she left. Maybe I had an ally of my own after all.

One of the guards came in after that, read me the riot act, reeled off a list of rules and gave me a roll of kit. I had nothing personal with me. I'd left Charlie's tags and the knife on the Alsatia, along with the wristband. I wasn't wearing the brace on my knee anymore and I just had a simple pressure dressing on my hand courtesy of the less than sophisticated medical provision in the Imperial prison system. The guild medics had said I wasn't ready. They'd been overruled. Mendhel said later they'd been right. It didn't change anything. I had a tab to complete. And I had to survive my first night.

By the time I was released from orientation, the guards were shouting ten minutes to lights out and everyone piled into the bunkrooms. The girl who'd been standing with Hilyer hooked her arm through mine and led me towards a door.

"Hey," she peered at my shirt, "Thirteen, we were wondering when you'd get here." She had a sparkle in her eyes. "Wow, a Thirteen. We haven't had one of those for a while. The last Thirteen fell off the climbing wall in the gym and broke his neck. You have a lot to live up to."

I wasn't sure if she looked pleased to be helping the newbie or chuffed that she had a new chump in her clutches. From the feral grin on her face, it could have been either.

"Welcome to Delta Block. C'mon, you're in here." She squeezed my arm. "How old are you?"

I said, "Fourteen." I was fairly sure that sometime within those last two weeks on the Alsatia, I'd had my fourteenth birthday. I hadn't said anything to anyone and no one had said anything to me. We'd always used to scrounge a cake from the bakery whenever it was someone's birthday. Maisie had always made sure we celebrated. If anyone didn't know when their birthday was, we made up a date and gave it to them. Now I was fourteen and it had come and gone. A very small part of me thought that maybe Maisie had blown out a candle for me and made a wish. I was beyond wishing for anything.

The girl laughed. "You don't look fourteen." She steered me to a bunk at the far end of the room, squeezing past the other boys who were stripping down to shorts and throwing towels and wash kit around, watching her as she walked past. I guessed she wasn't supposed to be in there.

"I'm Jem," she breathed into my ear. "You came in with Zach Hilyer, didn't you?"

"He was on my transport," I muttered. "I don't know him."

She laughed again. "Shame."

I couldn't see him around anywhere. I half hoped he'd be in a different room but there were shouts from a door halfway down the room. Bangs. A clatter then a thud. There were shocked laughs, vicious jeering. The fight spilled out into the bunkroom. One kid tumbled onto the floor, blood pouring from his nose. Hilyer was stripped to the waist, muscles tense, holding another kid in a headlock and spinning to kick out at the third who went down like a ton of bricks. He pounded his fist into the face of the one he was holding and pushed him away.

He looked up, fighting stance, breathing steady, just as he'd been when he'd given me a kicking on the Alsatia. He looked around and said, calm and clear, "Anyone else?"

Whatever balance of power there had been, it had shifted and everyone else was smart enough to keep quiet. There were mutterings but more of confirmation than dissent.

"He put Raine in the infirmary," Jem whispered with a grin.

I had no idea who Raine was, but I could guess.

"You see that tattoo on his arm?"

I hadn't. I'd seen the one on his wrist. He'd always kept his upper arms covered on the Alsatia. It was black ink, like the other one.

She leaned close. "You know what that means?"

I shook my head.

"Means he's done time in Wildlands."

I'd never heard of it but she sounded impressed.

"Means he's a dick," I muttered.

Not smart.

Hilyer looked at me, was on me in three strides and had me against the wall, arm against my throat. Again.

"You have a problem?" he said, loud enough so everyone could hear.

"I don't know," I said, stupid but I was tired and I didn't know what the hell he was doing. We were supposed to be watching out for each other. "Do I?"

He stared at me for a long moment, then shoved me aside and turned to Jem with a grin.

A guard appeared at the doorway, banging at the frame with her baton. "Is there a problem in here, Mister Hilyer?" she said.

The kids on the floor were crawling to their bunks, leaving spots of blood in their wake. She didn't even give them a glance. She was looking right at him as if they'd put him in charge.

He turned round slowly, cocky, the grin morphing into a half smile. "No, ma'am."

Dick.

There was no way it had been ten minutes but the lights went out and I had to get changed and make up my bunk in the dark. I couldn't find the pillow they'd given me so I just curled up under the thin blanket and kept my eyes open.

I lay there, listening to the others breathing, tense at every slight noise. On Kheris, we'd all crashed out together like a pile of mice, always someone on watch, always knowing we were safe. On the Alsatia, they'd given me a private room in Medical and then a shared room with Hilyer, where we pretty much avoided each other. There on Redemption, it felt like I'd never sleep properly again.

11

They slammed the lights on early next morning. I was already awake, not like I'd slept much. I was dressed, ready and sitting on the end of my bunk before half the others had crawled back out of the bathroom. Someone threw an empty wash bottle at my head. I ducked it easily. They all laughed as it clattered under the bunk. Hilyer kicked at my legs as he walked past and they laughed louder.

They shut up when a guard appeared at the door, banging his baton against the doorframe. "Yard, five minutes, children. It's a beautiful day and you're in for a long one."

He left.

I went straight out after him, straight out into the downpour. It was still dark, the yard illuminated by bright floodlights, driving sheets of rain cutting through the beams of light, pounding down and bouncing on the concrete. The guard was wearing cold weather gear, waterproofs, rain cape, gloves. He headed into the centre of the yard and turned, tapping the baton against his leg. I was wearing a short-sleeved tee shirt, combat pants and boots. I was soaked through in seconds. Shivering.

He laughed. "You'll warm up soon enough."

The rest of them came out, chased by another guard

who was yelling at them, and it wasn't long before the whole yard was filled with kids lined up in rows, four blocks of colour. Jem was next to me. She threw me a wink, mouthed, "You okay?" and grinned like she knew what they had in store for us.

I nodded, rain dripping off my nose.

She nudged my arm. "Brown is Bravo," she said, just loud enough for me to hear, nodding across the yard. "They're tough but they're scared of us. They just won't admit it. Grey is Alpha. They think they're cool but they're soft as shit."

She stopped as an instructor walked past, waiting until he was chewing out some other kid before she pointed to the block in front of us. "Dark blue is Gamma. Watch out for them."

That assessment pretty much matched up with the intel Markus had detailed.

She nudged me again. The guards were yelling about something. I caught the words, "Thirty five minutes," and the ubiquitous, "Do you understand?" There was a collective yelled, "Yessir." I just kind of mumbled it.

The gates rolled open.

One of the guards shouted, "Go," and the lines started to run off, each kid stopping briefly at the gate to pick up what looked like a rifle, then disappearing into the darkness beyond.

They'd told us to expect lengthy runs – that was why they were so bothered about getting my knee fixed – no one had said anything about carrying rifles.

Someone pushed me in the back as a guard came up and rapped me on the back of the legs with his stick.

"Move," he yelled in my face.

I moved.

The moorland outside the camp enclosure stretched in all directions. It was weird to see for real the topography I'd only seen in maps and simulations. The rain clouds were drifting across a full moon that gave out enough of a ghostly glow that I could just about make out the trail. Our Thunderclouds were up there somewhere, in orbit, our own personal weapons platforms in babysitting mode, guild ships close by, stealthed and invisible. I didn't know if that made me feel better or worse.

The gravity was lower than I was used to so it should have been a breeze but even hiking over uneven ground was uncomfortable and my knee was still fairly weak so I couldn't run that well. And I wasn't out to impress anyone. The others were overtaking me easily. It was soft underfoot, tangled bracken catching at my ankles as I tried to catch up. A river that was threatening to burst its banks was running roughly parallel to the path, brown turbulent water rushing past in torrents. I could see the outline of some kind of boathouse, lights and the shape of armed guards, standing there watching us. No doubt the AI was too.

I glanced behind me a couple of times, hefting the rifle slung over my back to try to redistribute its weight, and slowed to a walk as the throbbing in my knee got worse.

I couldn't see any reason why I couldn't turn round and head back. The leaders were way ahead, running across the low hills and threading a line way out into the horizon, dark figures that were getting smaller and smaller. I stopped and looked back at the camp.

Someone bumped me from behind and hissed, "Don't stop."

I shrugged them off. It wasn't that I was being insubordinate, I just honestly didn't think I could make it. I took two steps back towards camp and an agonising lance of pain seared into my spine from the band around my neck. Way worse than the first time. I fell to my knees, almost retching, a scream caught in my throat, falling forward and hands splashing in the mud, but it was gone just as fast, so sudden I almost felt like I'd imagined it. I caught my breath and pushed myself to my feet. My hands were shaking. I wiped them against my shirt and looked around like an idiot. Someone grabbed my arm, turning me around and pulling me forward.

"Don't stop," she shouted, over the rain, pulling me back into a stumbling run away from the camp. "Don't stop and don't go back. Don't ever head back until you've reached the waypoint. They know exactly where we are, all the time."

"Shit," I mumbled, rubbing my hand across the back of my neck.

The girl smiled.

I hadn't seen her before. She was a bit taller than me but looked about the same age. She reminded me of Maisie.

Except she didn't have black hair, hers was dyed blue. She was wearing a dark blue tee shirt. It looked good on her.

"You new?" she breathed.

I jogged alongside her, trying to favour my left leg and not end up in a ditch. "That obvious?"

She smiled again. She was running comfortably. I had the feeling she was taking it easy and staying at the back to round up the stragglers. I was glad she had.

"How far do we go?" I said, sounding more pathetic than I intended.

"Thirteen miles," she said, holding back and glancing behind us as we ran. "Six and a half out, six and a half back. If you get to the firing point and hit the target in less than thirty five minutes, you win. First five back in get extra rations for a day. Last five miss dinner. You turn back before the waypoint, you get zapped. That was a warning. It gets worse."

I couldn't imagine worse. We were just kids. They'd have regulations and stuff. They were supposed to be taking care of us even if we were supposed to be juvenile delinquents.

"What do you get if you win?" I said.

"Dunno. No one's ever done it. And seriously, looking at you right now, you don't stand a chance. What's wrong with your leg?"

"I'm fine."

She smiled. She seemed to find me funny. I didn't know if that was a good thing. I was just glad of the company.

The path headed up into the hills, leaving the river

behind, the trail turning into a mudfest. I splashed through a puddle, slipped, turned my knee as I tried to catch my balance, slid and slowed to a walk. I stopped trying to hide the limp. A couple of kids ran past us and I became acutely aware that I was last.

"Really, I'm fine," I muttered. "Go, I'm fine."

She ignored me, stayed by my side and said cheerfully as if she wasn't going to miss dinner because of me, "What's your first name, Mister J/D-13-Anderton?"

I opened my mouth to reply but shut it. I didn't know what to say. Everyone had been calling me LC from the minute I walked onto the Alsatia but I didn't feel like that was me. And I didn't want to say Luka. That was a different me from a different time. She didn't seem to mind that I didn't say anything. She didn't offer me hers and she stopped trying to make conversation.

The rain was getting heavier, the undergrowth getting more dense either side of us. Rivulets of water were starting to run in winding trails across the path. We walked in silence for a while then she nudged me back into a run. I was half expecting her to challenge me to a race but she didn't. She kept it steady like she was willing me to keep going, nurturing me to make every footstep, one after the next. She should have called a race. I respond better when I have unrealistic challenges thrown at me. As it was, she was making me want to say screw it and take all damn day.

We must have been going for about an hour when the first hints of light started to show in the sky and the first of the other kids appeared on the trail heading towards us, a mix of green and blue shirts in the lead. The path wasn't that wide. We'd been going steadily downwards again, heading back down onto the flatter moorland, and meeting up again with the river. I reckoned we were past half way out. It was nice in a way, trees and bushes on one side, the river on the other and birds starting to sing. She'd given up trying to get me to run.

The other kids ran past us, Hilyer at the front, by a mile. He passed us without a word. A couple of the others shoved past, elbows out. Jem ran past with an easy grin and a wave.

The girl with blue hair took my hand in hers and pulled me on.

"Come on, cute boy," she said, still cheerful, "what the hell did you do to your leg?"

I just shook my head. I didn't feel like talking.

She smiled, dug something out of her pocket and pushed it into my hand. A chocolate bar, in a plain green wrapper like the kind we'd always stolen from the ration packs the soldiers left lying around. I split it with her, like I always used to with Maisie, wandering along like we were out for a stroll.

"What did you do to your hand?" she said.

"I got shot." It sounded lame. I don't know if she even heard what I said. I ducked under a low branch and almost slipped again in the mud, blinking against the sparks that flared in my leg.

She said something I didn't catch.

"What?"

"Did it hurt?"

"Did what hurt?"

She grabbed my right hand and waggled it. "Getting shot. Did it hurt?"

I pulled away, shrugging her off. I didn't want to talk about it.

"Was that when you hurt your leg?"

I gave her a look and she dropped it, grinning at me and picking up the pace with a light, "Come on, it's not far."

We left the trees behind, and eventually the trail widened out, stretching across the moorland, a tall metal tower looming about a half mile ahead of us.

"Is that the waypoint?" I reckoned it was at about the right distance.

She nodded, mouth full of chocolate.

I waved my half of the bar at her. "Where do you get this from?"

She shook her head, grinning. "Trade secrets. You gonna tell me how you hurt your leg?"

"If you tell me where you get the chocolate from."

She laughed.

We made it to the final waypoint before she said anything else.

"Don't stop," she said. "You have to touch it before we go to the range."

I wanted nothing more than to stop and sit for a minute, but I knew if I did, I wouldn't be able to get back up. And she wasn't going to let me anyway. She took hold of my hand, made sure I tagged it with my other hand – "You have to make contact," she said – then she pulled me away and onto a path towards the firing range. There were ten firing positions, prefab Earth Empire kit, knee high metal barriers separating them, each with a mat to lie on, same as the ones the soldiers at the garrison on Kheris used to practise. Except these had some kind of clear plastic contraption attached to each position.

I unslung my rifle and chose one. A hatch slid open as I approached, a magazine with five rounds lying in there waiting for me. At the same moment a heavily digitised, female voice announced, "Weapon active". Earth doesn't like its AIs to sound too human. I slid a round out of the magazine and held it, tumbling it round my fingers, looking round, half a mind to pocket it to see what would happen.

"Don't even think about it," she called. "You'll get zapped so bad, you won't wake up till next week."

That wasn't surprising. I didn't ask how she knew and fed it back into the magazine.

I stood there, staring out across the moorland. There was one target on each shooting lane, set across the other side of the river, three hundred metres out. Most of the targets in the other lanes were down but not all. I looked at the target set in my lane, a small metal circle sticking up out of the heather.

"You know what you're doing?" she asked from her position.

"Yeah." I knew exactly what I was doing. I dropped down, chambered the round and lay there prone for a second, sighting, then shot wide. Five times.

It was nice to be off my knee even though the mat was wet and I stayed there for a minute longer, eyes closed, just breathing in the fresh scent of the undergrowth in the chill air.

I didn't realise she was watching me until I looked over. She smiled, then put her target down with one perfect shot.

"I get the chocolate from the chef," she said, once we were heading back. "First rule of anywhere – make friends with the chefs."

I'd never met any chefs but I didn't say that.

She nudged me. "So what did you do to your leg?"

"Dislocated my knee."

"How?"

"I fell off a roof." After being stabbed in the stomach but I didn't say that either.

I was expecting her to laugh but she looked serious. "I broke my leg once. Hurt like hell. Does it hurt?"

I nodded. I could see the others all way off in the distance ahead of us. "Do we seriously get no food tonight?"

She laughed then. "What do you think? Come on, I know the chefs. And hey, mister cute and mysterious, if you ever feel like telling me your name, mine's Kat."

There was no one in the yard when we got back, the rain easing off to a drizzle. I limped through the gate and sat down as soon as we were in, not caring that I was soaked, stretching out and pulling up my pants leg. My knee was swollen something ridiculous.

She crouched next to me. "You need to get inside."

"I don't think I can move."

"You don't want to get sent to the infirmary." She said that like it was the worst place in the galaxy. "Come on, get up. We need to get you into your bunkroom. I'll get you ice for it. Trust me, you don't want to go to the infirmary."

"What's so bad with that?"

She gave me a look. "Trust me, you do not wanna get sent to the infirmary."

12

She pulled me to my feet and we headed in. It was never going to be that easy. The guards intercepted us, took the rifles and steered us off to the huge hangar that was set up as a gym. No chance to dry out and change, never mind get meds. She didn't protest. I had to bite my tongue. I was learning.

The other kids were all in there, doing circuits. Before I bust my knee, I would have loved it. Right then, I could hardly stand.

They gave us bottles of water. Kat was told to go grab a snack then join a line. I was taken to a first aid station where a couple of medics were cleaning up a kid with a bloody nose. Brennan was there. She took one look at me and cursed under her breath, then pushed a high energy ration bar into my hand and told me to sit down.

I perched on a bench, sipped at the water and ate the rat bar, looking around. None of the instructors looked anything like Markus. I spotted Hilyer and watched him running beep tests. Relatively easily it seemed, despite having just run thirteen miles. He was trashing everything they threw at him. The briefing we'd got from the guild was to expect a physically tough regime but this was something else. Our first day and it felt like we'd landed in the middle of a selection procedure, some kind of 'fail-it-and-you're-out' test. Except this was prison so there was no out. That left only one other option, they wanted to see what everyone's breaking point was.

There were armed guards around the whole perimeter of the hangar, half of them with rifles at the ready. I don't know what they were expecting.

They got the other kid cleaned up and sent him back into the fray. Brennan turned to me.

"I can handle this one," she said to her colleague, and told me to prop my leg up on the bench. She cursed again when she saw the state of my knee.

I almost screamed out when she touched it.

"Dislocated?"

I nodded, biting my lip.

"When?"

"Four or five weeks ago." It felt like eons. A lifetime ago.

"Surgery?"

Another nod.

She prodded at it, manipulating it, and I almost passed out when she popped something back into place.

"You shouldn't be walking on it," she muttered, injecting meds straight into my leg. The pain subsided almost immediately. She wrapped a pressure bandage around it, tight, pulled down my pants leg, avoided looking me in the eye and looked round at the guard watching us. "He's good to go."

I followed him to a row of mats where lines of kids

were doing sit-ups and push-ups, an instructor shouting out counts. I dropped into position. I could do that.

I managed fifty two push-ups before it degenerated into a pathetic twitch for a couple then I collapsed onto the floor, arms burning, knee screaming and lower back seized. One of the guards knelt beside me, leaned in and whispered slowly, "You do this, you do it properly or you don't do it at all."

I was stupid enough to gasp out, "Is that an option?"

He wrapped me over the back of the head with his baton. "Get your ass over to the next station. You get three strikes here and you're in solitary for the night."

That sounded tempting but I dragged myself up and limped over to the next line, his voice shouting after me, "That's one strike, Anderton."

I didn't care. I wasn't there to get fit.

The next station was a cinch, but I pissed them off even more. Hold a heavy medicine ball out in front of you, arms straight, without moving. I could do that forever. I locked my elbows and stood there, weight on my right leg, calm, going someplace else in my head, thinking about the ocean I'd never seen and working out planetary drift and jump calculations. I was only half aware of the other kids either side of me, crying out in pain, dropping the ball and getting yelled at. I had no idea how long I stood there but I slowly realised it was quiet, opened eyes I hadn't realised I'd closed, and saw everyone standing looking at me.

The whole gym was silent. Jem had a huge grin on her

face, Kat looked disappointed and Hilyer was just staring like he was thinking I was an idiot. I was an idiot.

One of the instructors walked up, stood in front of me glowering, then batted the ball out of my hands. "Get your sorry ass over to the wall." He spun. "The rest of you, back at it. This is not a freakshow."

The wall looked easy but I could see kids struggling half way up and dropping off, swinging down on the harness. I'd never climbed with a harness before. They hooked me up, showed me how it worked and yelled at me to go. I made it to the top, hit the buzzer and jumped off, abseiling down and bouncing off my right leg. It was hard not to laugh. The Wall in the Maze on the Alsatia was tough. This climb was kids' stuff.

They got me to do it three more times then made me stand there waiting while they called Hilyer over.

He glanced sideways at me as he got ready, hooking up with the harness, and mouthed, "You think you can take me?"

I knew I could.

Someone yelled, "Go," and we went for it. I was faster than him even with a dodgy knee. I pulled off stupid reaches to get ahead, risking losing it completely to gain an inch, not even keeping contact with the wall a couple of times to get an advantage by throwing myself up and across the handholds.

Hilyer wasn't far behind. He was good but he was running it by the book. There was no way I was going to let him beat me, except I suddenly had Mendhel's constant warnings echoing through my brain, heard Maisie saying again and again, "Don't be an idiot…"

It wasn't just me anymore. And that was one hell of a realisation.

I fumbled a hold, let my right foot slip so my weight crashed onto my left leg, and had to bite back a cry as my knee gave way. I grabbed for a new hold and pressed my forehead against the cold surface of the wall, well aware that Hilyer was passing me.

There was no way I was going to make it easy for him. I started moving, got my momentum back and chased him all the way to the top. He waited for me, gave me a grin and jumped backwards to abseil down.

I reached the ground to shouts of, "Show's over. Everyone get cleaned up and report to the hall."

My knee was throbbing. Hilyer gave a laugh and took off, Jem hooking her arm into his and throwing me a grin. I couldn't see Kat or Brennan around anywhere. I limped into the changing rooms and waited for everyone to go before I stripped off and showered.

I stood there, lost in the stream of hot water, soaping slowly. The jagged scar on my stomach was still red, the holes and surgical scars on either side of my hand still raw. They'd said it could take a while. Kheris was still keeping its hold on me. I rinsed off the soap and turned.

Hilyer was standing there, a couple of the bigger kids behind him.

The water was still pouring. I was butt naked. They

were all dressed, boots and all. If they came at me, I'd have no chance.

"All alone, Anderton," he said, his voice low. "Not smart being alone here. Just us. No guards."

I glanced up and around. There'd be surveillance.

"Trust me," he said, "they wouldn't get here in time to make a difference."

I didn't say it but I'd thrown the climb to make him look good. What the hell else was I supposed to have done?

The others moved up close behind but he waved them to stay. He leaned in through the doorway. "Take this as a warning."

I stared at him, wishing Mendhel had told me how to play this stupid game. All my training had been the AI strings, the codes, what they wanted and how they wanted me to get it. Hilyer was supposed to be watching my back.

He turned and walked out, his new cronies following.

I half expected them to be waiting to jump me in the changing room but it was empty, just a guard at the door banging his stick on the frame and shouting me to hurry the hell up. I dressed, rewrapping the bandages round my knee and hand, and left. Hopefully the hall meant food.

It didn't. The hall was set up with little individual desks not tables, all separated like they were about to give us a test. There was a board on each table, inert, everyone sitting there waiting, segregated out into the four blocks. There was one table free, at the back. I sat at it and looked up, checking out the staff in case one of them was Markus. No such luck.

"You have sixty minutes," an instructor announced from the front. "Your time starts now."

The boards lit up, everyone started entering data furiously, solving puzzles, calculating formulae that got harder as you progressed. I read through it right the way to the end before I started. The board was set up to look like it was an isolated unit but it wasn't, it hooked up to the main system. I nudged it, got access to a database further in, and looked up. No one had noticed, none of the guards giving me a second's glance. All the other kids were at it still. Hilyer was working slowly, not like him. I'd seen how fast he could work. And there was something weird about how he had his board angled, sitting back every now and then and moving it aside before carrying on. It was so blatant it was ridiculous. The kid next to him was huge, tape across his nose like it had recently been broken. He was copying Hilyer's answers. Raine. It had to be. I couldn't believe none of the guards were calling them on it. It was all crap anyway. Some of the questions were so easy a six year old would know it, some of them so hard they were impossible, like they were setting us up to fail.

I pulled back out of the main system without setting off any alarms and started working through the test. It was simple enough stuff they were asking for but I could feel everyone else getting slower as they worked through it. I got half way through then skipped to the end and ran through it backwards. The questions at the end were similar to the puzzles Charlie and NG had given me. Patterns, logic crap, random questions that made no sense, a load of math strings that I knew by then were AI logic strings. I sat there for a moment looking at it then started filling it in. At the guild, I'd always got it all right. It hadn't occurred to me to do any different. There at the prison, I answered exactly fifty eight percent of them incorrectly. It was more difficult. Some of them took a while to figure out an answer that wouldn't look fake.

I checked my last answer, hit end and pushed the board aside. It went black. I didn't realise I was the first one to finish until I looked up. One of the instructors caught my eye before I could pretend I wasn't done. I thought I'd taken ages to complete it but the rest of them were all still heads down.

The instructor walked across, loomed over me and said quietly, "Anderton, stand up."

I half hoped that meant an early dinner and expected to see other kids start to finish but no one else was even looking up.

He said, "Come with me," and a sickly chill settled in my stomach at his tone. I ran every answer back through my head as I pushed back the chair, double checking what I'd done, sure beyond doubt that I hadn't tripped any alarms in the system.

They pulled me out of the hall and escorted me to an interview room. I was sitting there for what must have been an hour. I ended up with my head down on folded arms, fast asleep, running the gauntlet of the garrison on Kheris in my dreams.

I jerked awake as a guy came in. I wasn't sure if he was a guard, an instructor or something else. He was wearing the same black uniform but there was something about the way he stood that was too casual. He was holding a board, but he also had a battered old notebook tucked under his arm. Real paper by the look of the curled edges to the pages.

I was still shaking, unsettled by the nightmare, having to sit on my hands so they wouldn't see how much I was trembling.

He sat down opposite me and put the board on the table. "Not smart."

I just stared at him.

He didn't introduce himself and he wasn't wearing a name badge. He looked disappointed. "Luka," he said with exaggerated disapproval, "this is a correctional facility. We have a duty of care to rehabilitate you so you can re-enter society as a useful member of the community."

That was the standard line. A useful grunt to use as cannon fodder more like.

I didn't care. That's not why I was there. I was just waiting for a chance to get to the library and get on with it.

"Whatever has happened to you before…" His voice was soft, phony as hell, like the teachers at the missionary school I'd flunked out of. "…Whatever you've done, this is a fresh start. Work with us, not against us, and you will find being here much easier." He tapped at the board. "Complete the test again. Don't screw it up. And don't try to break into the system this time."

Busted.

He stood up and threw a casual, "You're smart, Luka, but perhaps not as smart as you think you are," as he left, conspiratorial, as if knowing they'd caught me out would throw me somehow.

I kept my expression neutral. We'd all known it wouldn't be easy. Now I knew how closely they were watching, I'd know how far to push it next time.

13

They let me loose once I was done. The commissary was closed and everyone was being chased out of the central rec area into the bunkrooms already. I limped into ours, hoping no one would try anything. The big lad, Raine, was in there, laughing with Hilyer like they were old mates. I got a few shoves, jibes about the wall, mutterings about where the hell I'd been while they were on damn cleaning duty, a few hardly veiled threats but nothing worse. I still couldn't find my pillow. I got into my bunk without upsetting anyone and lay there thinking.

It was a long night.

Next morning, we had classes. It was interminable. History and politics followed by spatial engineering and geometrics. I was hard pushed to stay awake. They didn't cover anything I didn't know and the teaching staff were going through the motions like they couldn't wait to get out. I couldn't wait to get out. After classes we were supposed to get library time.

I could feel the apprehension building in my stomach.

But once we were done, they told us to get to the hall for lunch then get into gym kit.

I trooped out of the classroom behind Jem.

"What the hell happened to library time?" I muttered.

She laughed. "You want library time? You're Delta now, kiddo. We don't do freaking library time." She shoved me in the back. "Library time was cancelled three weeks ago. We don't have to suffer that shit anymore."

Damn.

They gave us soup for lunch that had a strange aftertaste to it. Thinking about it, a lot of the food tasted strange but I just put that down to lousy prison catering. Didn't even occur to me at the time what supplements they might be feeding us.

Once we'd eaten, the shouting to get into gym kit and get out into the yard started again. I wrapped the bandage tight around my knee, hoping it wasn't going to be a thirteen mile run, desperately trying to come up with a new plan and vaguely hoping that Markus would turn up, take control of the tab and make everything work out.

He didn't.

But it wasn't a run. And it had stopped raining. They made us line up in our blocks then took us round to an open area where there was some kind of pitch marked out. Then they gave us each a stick with a curved end, threw a small hard ball out there and told us to go beat the crap out of each other. Or they might as well have done. Two teams, god knows what the rules were, and a son of a bitch instructor who was quite happy to wait until you were on the floor bleeding before he'd stop the game.

I don't play well in a team. Never have. Never will. And my knee had swollen again overnight, every muscle and joint aching. I watched from the sidelines, running every scrap of intel through my head, twisting it around and trying to figure out a way into the system if I couldn't use the library. Or figure out a way into the library. There'd be a way somewhere.

When it was my turn to play, I ended up leaning on the stick more than running with it, and avoiding the ball every time it came close to me. There was a way you could hook it with the end of the stick and send it flying. If you knew what you were doing. Which everyone else seemed to and I didn't. I ducked it twice, missed the next one and was flat on my back before I knew it had hit me. The instructor ran up, screaming at me to get back on my goddamned feet and start playing. My head was ringing but it gave me the idea I needed.

I got up, tapped the ball away and backed off.

Jem ran up with a grin, whacked the ball away and gave my stick a crack with hers. She pointed up the field. "Come on, Thirteen, you gotta hit it. You never played hockey before?" Like it was the most weird thing she'd ever heard.

"No." On Kheris, we'd sometimes kicked a football around the streets. Never anything organised.

She laughed. "You've never been inside before, have you? I knew with a tan like that, you hadda be brand new. C'mon, we've gotta get the ball back or they'll annihilate us."

They weren't annihilating us. Hilyer was on the field. He got the ball as I watched, ran with it, nudging it ahead of him with the stick at full stretch, sprinting full speed and dodging round the kids of the other team. It was Gamma Block we were up against. Kat was standing in the middle of the field, blue hair tied in bunches, hardly making any effort and looking as unimpressed as I was.

Hilyer hit the ball hard and it flew into the net at the far end. There were cheers from the kids standing around the edges. The instructor yelled out names, subbing kids in, sending others off and shouting for the game to restart.

Hilyer was subbed out, I wasn't. I turned as he passed me, stuck out my stick and caught him on the ankle. He turned on me, had me round the neck and landed me on the floor before I could say a word.

"I need to get into the infirmary," I breathed before he punched me in the face.

He leaned close. "Yeah, I can arrange that." He let up and shoved me aside, walking off with a laugh.

Five goals later and I still hadn't been subbed. I'd given up even trying to run. Everyone was looking at me like they didn't know why I was still out there when everyone else had been given a break and a chance to get a drink.

Hilyer got subbed back in, along with Raine. The other kids shouted to them as they both walked on, wielding their sticks like they were weapons. Hilyer had the ball in his hand, tossing it up and catching it. He walked to the centre spot, waited for the instructor to blow his whistle, then looked at me, eyes narrow, threw the ball forward and hit it, mid air, right at Kat.

She didn't duck in time, spun round as it struck her and collapsed to the ground.

She didn't move.

I was yelling obscenities at Hilyer and running towards her before I could think. One of the big kids from Gamma stepped in my way and shoved me backwards, swearing at me like it was me that had done it.

I stumbled, felt a body run up next to me and couldn't get out of the way as Raine slammed into me. I went flying, lost the stick and rolled, getting to my feet as someone else knocked me from behind. A stick rapped against my shins. I tried to sidestep, turned, and came face to face with Hilyer as he ran up, hockey stick in a two-handed grip like he was holding a staff. I saw what was coming and I still couldn't get out of the way fast enough, slipping in the mud. He swung it at me, striking hard. I tried to catch the stick but he had too much power behind it. It hit me in the chest. I folded, went down, and another blow landed against my head as I hit the ground. Game over.

I woke up inside, in the infirmary from the sterile, medical smell of it. My head was pounding, eyes sore when I blinked them open. I tried to sit and couldn't, nausea pulling at my stomach, my left wrist rattling, the handcuff chaining it to the bunk clanking softly. I was in a cubicle. It was cold but I could handle that. Apart from being restrained, I couldn't see what was so bad about it.

There were people outside, voices, someone saying something about concussion, lucky there wasn't a skull fracture. I guessed they were talking about me. I'd had concussion before. It felt like concussion. And my chest was hurting every time I took a breath so I reckoned cracked ribs too. Not great, but not terrible. Hilyer was being a dick but he'd just got me exactly where I needed to be.

I waited until lights out, after they'd done the rounds for meds and obs. There'd be a terminal or a data board somewhere. I just needed to steal a pass from someone and get free.

In the end, I decided to keep it simple. I can dislocate my thumbs if I want to. I never appreciated growing up on Kheris how useful that would be. I twisted my hand and snapped out of the cuffs, pulled the IV line out of my arm and climbed off the bunk.

I didn't have long. I slipped out of the infirmary, ignoring the urge to see if Kat was in any of the other cubicles. I half expected the collar round my neck to zap me again but it didn't. The corridor outside was empty, dark except for faint red nightlights, some light coming from under a few of the doorways, soft voices at one end. I crept in the other direction, keeping close to the wall. I didn't think they'd shoot me if they found me out of bed but I still wasn't expecting the ferocity of the reaction when it came. There were yells, heavy footsteps descending on me, and I was hit by a blow to the back, hard enough that my knees buckled. They grabbed me and pushed me against the wall, twisting my arms behind my back, an elbow pushing hard into the back of my neck.

I didn't resist.

They turned me around as one of the medics ran up, protesting, and they backed off then, still keeping me in a restraint hold but letting me stand at least.

It was Brennan. She reached a hand to my cheek, hitting a sore spot where I'd hit the wall.

I raised my eyes.

"What the hell were you doing?" she said.

"Needed the bathroom," I muttered.

She didn't look impressed but she didn't look pissed at me.

I sucked in a breath, and didn't need to act as a stabbing pain shot through my chest. I felt my knees going again. She snapped something at the guards and they let go, releasing me into her care and she took hold of my arm gently and led me back down the corridor.

She persuaded me back into the cubicle and back onto my bunk, taking her time setting up the IV line again. "This isn't summer camp," she said quietly. "You need to remember where you are or you're going to get hurt."

I don't know what her definition of hurt was but I was lying there with broken ribs and concussion after a crack to the head. I mumbled something about being sorry, yawned and gave her my best, most shy smile. I was hoping she wouldn't want to check my stats again.

She didn't. She injected something into the tube that caused the pain to subside almost immediately, stood aside to let the guard refasten the handcuff, then left with a soft, "Get some sleep."

I waited until she was gone then pulled the blanket over my head, pulled her data board from under my pillow where I'd stashed it after I'd lifted it out of her pocket, and went to play.

It was simple enough to check superficial records. I was listed as admitted to the infirmary. Nothing about a girl so she must have been okay. There was a record of Raine and his bust nose. And a couple of other kids with minor injuries. I couldn't resist digging around, trying to see if there was any mention of the little kid who'd come in with us but there was no mention of anyone his age they could be keeping in there.

I ditched it, he'd be somewhere, and went deeper. I was more careful that time, got past a load of protections without alerting the AI, and I found Markus. Or rather I didn't. He'd gone. Transferred out on promotion according to the records. I stared at the entry in the personnel file, heart thumping.

We were on our own.

14

According to the prison records, he'd just been transferred out to another facility. If it was that simple, the guild would have known about it. It didn't add up.

I started to take it slower, hitting up against barriers and working my way round and through, the way NG had taught me, absorbing all of it fast, starting to mentally tick off the intel I'd been briefed to gather. There was too much for one night. It was going to take time. I did what I could and started to back off. I didn't want to push it. They were due to check on meds soon. Then I hit on a level of prisoner records that were protected. Beyond simple security. There were test results and notes on each kid but there was something else, something that was being shielded. I cracked it gently, fooling the AI into releasing the files for a routine maintenance and sync procedure, and laid it all out.

It was encoded but it just took a simple nudge to get it to realign so I could read it. There were priority tags against each name. I figured out the pattern and queried it, then fired off commands as if the system was running an archiving schedule on the data, and watched the way it was falling into place. There was still a huge dark hole of classified information beyond where I was but I'd seen enough for the night to make my stomach queasy. I stared at it, becoming vaguely aware that footsteps were echoing down the corridor.

I didn't leave any trace of what I'd been doing, wrapped up fast, and reset the board. I threw it to the bottom of the bunk under a fold of the blanket, as if Brennan had just dropped it, and curled up to sleep.

She came to check on me first thing next day, wasn't impressed, and retrieved her board with a frown. I was half expecting it to set off alarms as soon as she activated it but nothing untoward happened. She just left me to rest and I didn't argue with her.

They let me out after the evening meal, so I missed food. I was escorted into the rec hall and stood there, just as much of an idiot as I had been in the mess on the Alsatia. Everyone was sitting around, playing games or reading, some of them sitting at tables like they were doing homework, some of them in the bunkrooms already. I didn't know what time it was but it was dark outside. Jem was sitting on Hilyer's knee, watching as he worked on a board. Raine and a couple of the other big kids were playing cards. I didn't know anyone else.

People looked around as I appeared in the doorway, a hush settling like they were expecting something to kick off.

On Kheris, we'd all looked after each other. We'd grown up together. There was always someone there, a friendly smile and a ready hug, whatever else was going on. I'd never needed to try. We were family. As much as I wasn't really one of them, and we all knew it, no one cared. I'd never appreciated how much that meant.

There in that prison, it struck home just how alone I was. I didn't know how to make friends because I'd never had to before. I didn't know how to fit in because I never had. I was nothing and nobody. Hilyer wasn't just working a board, he was showing Jem how to do something. She was laughing and working with him as he showed her. I'd always been the one who could do stuff, the one who taught the little ones and made them smile. Now it was Hilyer.

The guard I was with gave me a shove into the room and shouted across to him, calling him Mister Hilyer again. He disengaged himself from Jem and didn't look at me as he approached the guard, who took him by the arm and led him aside, talking quietly. They looked like they were discussing what we should have for lunch the next day or whether our allowance should be increased. They even shook hands and I'd swear I saw him palm something across to her. She smiled and clapped him on the back, barking at him to get back to it but with a sparkle in her eyes as she said it. He nodded and backed away with a grin.

I looked around, incredulous. It was like everyone else was making a point of not seeing what was going on. I hiccoughed wrong and everyone was watching. Hilyer? He had that entire place sussed.

The next morning, we were dragged out for another run. I must have had a nightmare because Hilyer woke me up before the lights came on, pulling me out of my bunk and into the bathroom. My heart was racing. He pushed me towards the sink and ran the cold tap. The way he was holding the back of my shirt, I thought he was going to punch me and hold my head under the water and I started to resist but he just held me there.

"For crying out loud," he hissed into my ear, "you were calling out in your sleep. Get it under control or I'll put you back in the infirmary."

I washed my face and neck, shaking or shivering, I wasn't sure which. I couldn't remember what I'd been dreaming about.

The lights slammed on while we were there.

"I need to talk to you," I whispered.

We could hear a guard at the door to the block, banging on the doorframe and yelling us to get out.

"No, you don't," he whispered back harshly. He shoved me and walked out.

They kept us standing in the yard, in the rain, for twenty minutes before they let us go. My knee was sore but not as bad as it had been, and pain from my cracked ribs sparked in my chest with every breath but it was bearable. The rifle felt like it weighed a ton. The thought of thirteen miles was making my stomach turn.

Hilyer was in the line behind me. Jem, Raine and the others took off fast again as soon as we were out of the gate. I walked. Hilyer dropped into step beside me. Kat stayed alongside us for a couple of steps but she exchanged glances with Hilyer and decided that maybe she'd best leave us to it.

We trudged along without a word for maybe three or four minutes then Hilyer said quietly, "You need to watch yourself with her, she's asking questions about you."

I was zoned out. Trying to keep going. "What?" I said stupidly, slipping on a patch of mud.

"She's trouble. Don't get caught in it. And she's Gamma, for Christ's sake."

I blinked raindrops out of my eyelashes. She wasn't the one ragging on my case. "So what if she is Gamma?" I asked. "It's not like we're here to stay or prove anything, is it?"

He scowled at me. "Just watch your back. They're trouble."

I didn't see how they could make more trouble for us than the trouble we were in. I should have listened to him.

"He's gone," I said quietly. "Made to look like he transferred out."

Hilyer cursed under his breath. "Bullshit. He didn't just transfer out. They would've known."

I nodded, struggling to keep up. "So we're on plan B now?"

He was walking just fast enough to make it uncomfortable and if anything, he picked up the pace.

"Wait, Hil. This is plan B, right? This changes everything."

He glanced back at me, eyes cold. "It doesn't change a thing."

"You're ranking top on their scores. You have to start failing stuff."

"I don't have to fail anything." He didn't exactly say screw the guild, but he might as well have done.

I stopped and stared at him.

He took another few steps before he realised I wasn't trotting along behind him and he turned.

We stood there in the pouring rain, staring at each other. I didn't know how to say it without sounding pathetic, like I was asking for his help.

He added it up anyway, pulled a face and cursed. "Don't tell me you're on their freaking radar."

I nodded stupidly. I was tagged in the records as an anomaly. Every effort I'd made to not draw attention to myself had backfired.

He laughed harshly. "I knew you'd screw it up."

"What do we do?"

"Do whatever you want. I'm not going to mess up my chances here."

That was what he'd said on the Alsatia but I had the horrible feeling out on that cold, wet moorland, standing there in prison fatigues, that he didn't mean it the same way.

"Look, kid. I have a real chance here. Look around. I'm the daddy in here and wherever they send me, I'll be the best and they know it. You do whatever the hell you want, Anderton, but don't get in my way. Are you done?"

I assumed he meant with the intel. "Not yet."

"And the infirmary is the only way you can do it?" He cursed again and took off running.

He must have passed Kat because she slowed and was waiting for me when I eventually caught up.

"How are you doing, cute boy?" she said with a grin, blue hair plastered over her head and a chocolate bar in her hand. She held it out. "What was Zachary saying?"

I ignored the question, took the candy bar and snapped it in half, offering half back. She took it with a smile.

We walked without speaking and in a way it was cool.

I switched off.

I was walking on automatic and running a million thoughts through my head, anything except concentrating on where I was, and when the leaders of the pack loomed up on the path and ran towards us, I didn't think.

It was Hilyer at the front. Even though he'd started off last. If I hadn't been so messed up, I could have given him a run for it. As it was, I had no chance of taking on anyone. We were by the river where the path was narrow. I moved out of his way, didn't expect the shove or quite how vicious it would be, and stepped back to catch my balance, one foot sliding and catching on a muddy root, my other on nothing but thin air.

There was shouting.

I reached to grab something, anything and took a handful of wet leaves with me as I fell backwards, half a second to grab a breath before I plunged into the fast

131

flowing, freezing cold water of the swollen river. I opened my mouth to shout, sucked in a lungful of muddy water and was dragged down into the swirling current.

I tried to kick my way back to the surface but I didn't know which way was up and the weight of the rifle was dragging me down. I wriggled the sling off over my head and let it go, bumping against something. Someone was trying to grab my arm but I couldn't see, couldn't breathe and couldn't help getting swept away.

It was quiet, a swirl of chaos around me but an eerie silence resounding through my ears.

I surfaced more by accident than intention. I could hear screaming, far away. I choked out water and gasped in a breath before I was pulled under again. My legs felt like lead, the darkness closing in surreal and sparking with flashes of coloured lights. I tried to reach out for something, anything, twisting and turning, holding my breath until it ran out and I was still surrounded by dark, swirling water.

I closed down and sank.

My chest hurt. Intensely and painfully. I couldn't breathe. Couldn't think.

Someone was shouting.

I sank back into the darkness.

Drowning sucks, it really does.

My head was full of fog when I surfaced. I didn't exactly wake up as wander into a vague mix of reality and nightmare, merging into one. I thought I was on Kheris, on a lumpy mattress on the floor at our old place, stomach cramping, fever burning. But it was my chest that was sore, not my abdomen. I think I cried out, blinking away the confusion and trying to figure out where I was.

I was dry, warm. Clean. Lying on a bunk. There was a mask over my mouth and I was breathing clean, cool oxygen. Redemption. Not Kheris. I'd wanted to get back in the infirmary but I hadn't reckoned on having to half die to get there.

I was in a room not a cubicle. Manacled to the bedframe. Tired didn't even describe how drained I felt. I lay there and bided my time. It beat getting yelled at in the gym.

They kept me in all that day and decided they wanted me overnight. They didn't like the look of my stats and were worried I'd get a chest infection, I heard one of the medics say, what with the broken ribs and inhaling that much contaminated water. Contaminated? I didn't argue. I wanted them to leave me there. I meant to sneak off and try for the AI again that night but I crashed out and didn't wake up until they came round for meds and breakfast.

They kept me in most of the next day as well because my stats were worse. My chest was burning like I'd been hit by a truck.

Kat came to see me mid-morning to bring me homework. I was missing math apparently.

"Calculus. I bet you wouldn't have any problem with that, would you?" she said, perching on the bunk and tugging at the IV line in my arm. "What is this?"

"Antibiotics, I think."

"You reckon?"

I had no idea. The way she said it made me wonder, but it wasn't like I had any choice.

There was a guard watching from the doorway.

"We thought you'd died," she said. "Glad you didn't."

"I'm glad I didn't."

I was still manacled to the bunk. She squeezed my hand. "I told you the infirmary sucks." She glanced at the guard and turned back to me, leaning close, whispering, "So what are you in here for?"

I looked at her. "Chest infection."

She punched me in the arm. The way Maisie used to.

"Not the infirmary, you dolt. I mean, here. Redemption. Why are you here?"

I thought about lying but there didn't seem to be a need. "I hacked into an Imperial base." It sounded weird saying it out loud. Like it wasn't real.

"And they sent you here?"

She sounded incredulous. That made me wonder what she'd done. I blinked, trying not to flash back to it all. "It caused a lot of damage."

She looked at me like she wasn't sure if I was stringing her along. "You ever kill anyone?" she whispered.

She said that like she had and she wanted me to ask her about it. I didn't care. And I wasn't sure how to respond. "Not directly," I said eventually.

She smiled at me sideways as if that was some kind of code that we both understood. She wouldn't understand.

No one could ever understand what I'd done on Kheris. I'd asked Mendhel how many people had died because of what I'd done and he'd told me to forget it.

"I need to get back," she said. "We have reorientation this afternoon. You're lucky you're going to miss it. You haven't had the joys of that yet, have you?"

Reorientation was counselling. Psychotherapy. Conditioning. I'd had it on the Alsatia and how to counter it. It had sucked. I'd gone to one session. They'd had no idea how to handle me. I'd skipped the rest. It would be interesting to see what this place's version of it was like. I wasn't sure if I was switched on enough to handle it. I shook my head and forced a smile.

"What are they going to find in your head, Luka?" she said, standing and wandering out past the guard.

"Who told you my name?"

She turned and smiled, holding onto the doorframe. "No one. It's on the door."

15

I didn't get out of it. They sent a psych in to see me. Brennan tried to argue against it. I heard them arguing in the corridor, but she got overruled. "We need an evaluation," someone said. "This kid is high priority. We have five days before final selection."

That made my stomach knot. The meds were making me feel sick enough as it was.

The guy who walked in was the same guy I'd seen before. So he was a psych. He still looked more like prison staff than any psych I'd seen before. He sat on the chair by my bunk, resting his notebook on his knee, and leaned forward.

"How are you doing, Luka?" he asked, friendly like we were old mates.

I was lying there manacled to the bunk. What did he think? I must have looked at him weird because he smiled and added, "There's nothing to worry about. This is just a routine counselling session. We have a duty of care to make sure you are being looked after."

That duty of care again. It made it worse.

He smiled. Still phony as hell.

I couldn't help glancing around, up at the corners of the room, checking for cameras.

He knew exactly what I was doing. "This is completely confidential. Anything you tell me goes no further. My evaluation is purely for your wellbeing, Luka. You can trust me."

Benjie had told me once to never trust anyone who said trust me. Ironically, he'd said it to me right before he screwed me over. He probably hadn't even realised.

The guy opened his notebook. "Let's get started."

He asked a bunch of questions that I didn't answer, not waiting overly long or pushing me to comply, never quite looking me in the eye.

Eventually he sat back, put the notebook down and looked directly at me. "Tell me why you're in here."

"In the infirmary? Because someone pushed me in the river."

It was the first thing I'd said to him.

"You hacked into an Imperial military base."

I stared at him.

"You're smart," he said, cold now, the smile gone. "We know that from the test results you tried to fake. And we've been watching you hack into the system here."

I felt the heat drain from my cheeks. Even though I was absolutely, beyond a shred of doubt confident that they would've just seen what I wanted them to see. That was my cover story if I was caught in the system. My safety net. In case. Except the way he was looking at me made my skin crawl.

"The file on you is redacted. Someone has gone to great lengths to obfuscate the details of what exactly it is you've been convicted of. We're curious, Luka. What base was it?"

Later on at the guild, they trained us in how to calm our breathing, slow down our heart rate. Right then on Redemption, I did it by instinct. I wasn't going to let him drag me back there, as much as I could feel the lure of the smoke and gunfire.

He looked back at his notebook and said without looking up, "How much damage did you actually do, Luka?"

I knew the guild had made our cover close to the truth, for ease of construction, they'd said, and to limit our exposure of getting caught out. That some of the information in my file was redacted shouldn't have caused it to stand out. It was standard procedure in any military case, they'd assured me of that.

I shrugged. "I don't care. Are you going to write that in your little book?"

He smiled but that time it was like a wolf smile. Predatory. Like he'd got me. He didn't write anything down.

"You attacked a guard when you first arrived here. Can you not control your temper?"

I stared at him.

It wasn't me that had the temper.

"You turned back on your first run," he said. "Do you have a problem following the rules?"

Yes, but I didn't say anything.

"You haven't settled into your bunkroom. Do you have trouble mixing with other children?"

He was twisting everything but I didn't rise to it.

"You panic," he said, "when you are put into solitary. Are you claustrophobic, Luka?"

I almost laughed. I hadn't panicked. They'd put me into a damned stress position. I didn't have a problem with enclosed spaces, I had a problem with asshole rules and regulations.

I didn't know what he wanted me to say. I looked across the room, bored. Most adults I did that with got irritated at me, like I was flicking a switch in their heads, making them mad with me. It didn't work with him. He outstared me. But I was the one manacled to the hospital bed, and I was still just a kid, and Brennan was watching from the doorway. I glanced at her with that look I could pull. She fell for it and came in, blustering, talking about stats, saying enough was enough, and that anything else could wait.

The guy looked at me like he knew exactly what I'd done and as if, by doing it, I'd fallen for everything he was trying to get me to do.

I hate psychs. Did I say that already?

They put a guard on my door overnight so I had no chance to try anything and they let me out the next day. I still felt sick but not because of the meds. They watched me dress then escorted me straight out to the yard. It was late morning already, dark clouds threatening over the hills and a damp chill to the air that made my chest ache.

Everyone was sparring, paired up, working out, the instructors not so much instructing as watching like they were rating each performance. I didn't know where to go so I just wandered over to the edge of the square, feeling eyes turn to settle on me as people realised I was there.

Hilyer was standing with Jem, laughing and joking. I needed to talk to him. I had to figure out a way to get him alone and beyond any surveillance.

One of the instructors clapped his hands and yelled everyone to go line up on one edge.

"You too, Anderton," he shouted and started to call out names, two at a time.

Hilyer was up first and another kid I hadn't seen before. The instructor had a quiet word with them both and stepped back, setting them at each other. Hilyer took the kid down easily.

The instructors yelled at them to stop, conferred for a second, then shouted at Hilyer to go left and the other kid to go to the right. They separated and were led off.

They were testing us. Hilyer was acing it, like he was in his element. I watched him floor another kid in less than a minute and get pulled out again.

Jem sidled up next to me, offering me a bottle. "You're lucky you didn't drown, y'know." She was looking out across the square, watching Hilyer as he poured a bottle of water over his head. "Did you know it was Zach that pulled you out? Did they tell you that?"

They hadn't.

I didn't react. "He doesn't like being called Zach," I said without thinking.

She grinned. "So you do know him. I knew it."

"We just met in the transport."

"I think you know him better than that." Her eyes were glinting as she said it. "He hates you. What did you do to him?"

"I told you, I don't even know him."

"You know why he's in here?" she said.

I shrugged again. I didn't know what story they'd set him up with and I didn't care.

"He's rated triple A. You know what that means?"

"It means he's a dick."

"It means he's in for first degree murder. I heard it was a cop he killed." She pulled that feral smile again. "You need to watch yourself, bud. You're spending a lot of time in the infirmary. And Thirteen is a helluva number to be tagged with. It wasn't just that kid who croaked it. Last month, three other kids went out of here in bodybags."

I turned and looked directly at her. I wasn't sure if that was a warning or a threat, or just nonsense to spook me.

"You been having nightmares?" she said.

I didn't answer but she laughed and said, "Yeah, I'm not surprised. Kids who have been in the infirmary all have nightmares when they come out. If they come out. You might heal fast in there but you're never the same." She leaned closer. "The Thirteen who broke his neck? His harness didn't fail... he took it off. Got to the top, unclipped the harness and jumped."

She was trying to spook me. It would take more than that.

She laughed again. She was still staring at Hilyer. "You need to watch your little blue-haired friend, as well. Apart from the fact that she's Gamma. She's not what she seems."

I couldn't help but glance across to where Kat was standing, alone, watching us. She didn't move as our eyes made contact.

I stopped with the bottle of water halfway to my mouth. I couldn't work out her expression. I took a drink, not breaking eye contact. Eventually, she was the one that moved away, as one of the instructors called out her name.

Jem nudged me. "Just watch your back, Thirteen."

I was trying to. But it felt like the rules had changed again.

It wasn't long before it was my turn. I felt terrible and I was nowhere near a hundred percent but I was definitely feeling stronger. I seemed to be healing faster than I had on the Alsatia. I walked out into the square. They left me standing there for a minute like an idiot, everyone looking at me, then they yelled Hilyer up again. He squared up to me, the muscle in the side of his jaw ticking. I must have smiled because he scowled and muttered, "Don't," as he started to circle.

He came at me fast, didn't pull his punches and sent me flying. I hit the floor hard, rolled to my feet and went straight back at him. We weren't evenly matched, not by a long way, but I knew his tells and I could hold my own. I just needed to get close. I got him with a couple of lucky moves and he backed off, spitting blood. I glanced around. The yard was deadly quiet. We were the only ones fighting, everyone staring at us in total silence. So much for not standing out.

"Don't," Hilyer said again, quietly, threatening.

I might have said something then that didn't go down well. He flew at me and we went for it. It was like we were in a bubble, in a glass dome and everyone watching was transfixed. I got him with a neat left. Then Hilyer caught me above the eye and blood spurted, someone cheered and everyone started. The instructors let them, I'd swear they even joined in. We traded a couple more blows to louder jeers and cheering then he raised it a notch, got me in a headlock and spun me around.

I managed to say, "I need to talk to you," half strangled.

He cursed and hit me with one that sent my vision swimming. I went down. I sprawled, flat on my back, eyes watering, and managed to look up at him looking down at me before he turned and walked off.

16

The instructors must have called it a day because by the time I managed to sit up, the guards were yelling at everyone to get in and get showered. They gave us ration packs for lunch then took us back outside.

Hilyer avoided me, not that we would have had a chance to speak. We stood out there in the cold for ages then they started shouting us out in groups of eight, mixed, two from each block. No one seemed to know what we were going to do. I trooped off when my name was called and walked in single file out of the yard. Pretty much all the kids were marching. I didn't slouch but I wasn't going to snap to it.

We left our complex and ended up in one of the adult prison sections, armed guards around us. We were taken into one of the huge grey buildings. I tried to remember the blueprint plans we'd been shown, running the schematics through my head and realising with a pang where we were going.

In nothing the guild had given us had there been any mention of the kids having to do CQB. Close Quarters Battle training. I'd seen the simulator in the plans, even been curious about it in a nonchalant, nothing to do with me way. Now I was walking towards it, I had a lump in my throat. That reputation I have of never being scared of anything? It's shit. I get scared, I just turn it into outright disregard for where I am and what's going on around me. It's a trick I learned when I was tiny. And boy, did I use it then.

They sat us down on hard benches in a briefing room that was so cold our breath frosted. The briefing was just that, brief, given by an instructor who looked every one of us in the eye like he could tell straight off who was going to mess up. I stared back at him and took in every word.

"Ten minutes," he said. "Start to finish. Run out of time, you run it again. You will fire at every target. We're making this easy for you, boys and girls. Assume all human targets in there are hostile. They will be firing back at you. Low stun but that will still hurt like hell. Do you understand?"

We all snapped out, "Yessir," even me. I understood fine well.

I was seventh in my group to go through. The others before me didn't reappear so we had no idea what was happening or how they'd done. I took the gun they gave me and held it in my left hand.

"Have you ever fired a pistol before?" the instructor said, standard routine like he'd said it a million times.

I nodded.

"Delta Thirteen," he barked at me, "have you ever fired a pistol before?"

I blinked. I was trying not to slip back to that moment when I pulled the trigger, when it misfired and Dayton fired back at me. I managed to mutter, "Yessir," and he grimaced at me.

"These are not live rounds," he said. "But the weapon simulates full recoil. Use both hands. And try not to get lost in there."

I didn't. Of course I didn't. I made it out in seven minutes twenty, breathing heavy, adrenaline pumping, breath catching in my throat like I was going to throw up. They let me out at the other end and I swear, three of the instructors were standing there, arms folded, staring at me, something like disbelief or disgust on their faces, I couldn't quite tell.

"You didn't get hit once," one of them said.

I shook my head.

The guy who'd given us the briefing was standing in the middle. "You didn't take out any of the targets. I told you to take out all targets."

I stared at him. I should have kept my mouth shut but I didn't. "You told us to fire at every target," I said.

They stared back at me.

I'd fired at every target. I'd pulled each shot just wide but I'd fired at every one of them.

I added, "Sir," too late for it to count.

The guy turned away with a growl. "Get this child the hell out of here."

After the debrief, we trooped back to our facility and I followed everyone into the commissary. I couldn't eat much, still felt sick and my ribs were throbbing more than my knee. I had a weird delayed reaction going on, every shot ringing in my ears, every echoing scream and shout from that simulator resounding round my brain like a bizarre audio feedback, mixed in with flashbacks to the garrison on Kheris, that last time I'd been in there, when they'd been chasing us and shooting at us. When I had been shot, for real.

I couldn't get it all out of my head as much as I tried to switch off.

We had clean up duty after that then study time. I pitched in and pulled my weight, then disappeared off to the bathroom to throw up. I couldn't stop shaking, too hot one moment, then too cold the next.

Hilyer appeared next to me as I was washing my face.

He stood at the sink next to me and ran the taps on full blast. "What? Did you get what you need?"

I shook my head. "No, they put a guard on my door. I couldn't do anything. But Hil, you have to start screwing up. I overheard them talking. They're making final selection in four days." I felt like I was going to be sick again.

"You want me to put you back in the infirmary?"

The way he said it, I couldn't tell if he was threatening me or offering to help.

He scowled. "Shit, don't look at me like that. Is that what you need?"

"No," I muttered. "I need to find another way. But Hil, you can't... "

He grabbed my shirt and pulled me close. "Don't tell me what I can and can't do."

He pushed me away, stalked out and left me there trembling. I leaned on the cold surface of the sink and put my head down on my arms, trying to breathe through it. I could still hear gunfire echoing round my head. I didn't need crap like this and I didn't know how to make it go away.

It was lights out time before I knew it. I curled up on my bunk and tried not to whimper. Someone threw an extra blanket over me and told me to shut the hell up.

Weird thing was, once I fell asleep, I didn't dream. I woke up confused but no nightmares. I lay there for a second just listening to the voices, figuring out where I was and what I was supposed to be doing. I needed to get back into the system.

Someone banged on the end of my bunk. One of the guards was shouting for us to get up and get out. They sent us to the gym before breakfast then we had another test, only this time it wasn't me that got pulled out of the hall.

I kept my head down and just watched out of the corner of my eye as one of the instructors stopped at her desk and ordered her to stand.

She looked horrified. She saw me looking, tucked a

stray strand of blue hair behind her ear and mouthed, "Shit," to me.

They marched her out. No one else looked up. I didn't bother making an effort to screw up the test, I just wrote a load of random answers and doodled on the board until everyone started finishing.

I didn't see her again until later that afternoon, after classes, when they kicked us out to go run circuits around the sports pitch. They were timing us, keeping score of our laps, the psych guy out there with his notebook and coffee, chatting to the instructors. She reappeared with a guard as an escort. I was half running, half walking around my tenth lap. I watched her shrug off the guard holding her arm and jog onto the track. It took me half a lap to catch up.

I fell into step beside her, nudging her arm. "Hey."

She flinched like I'd hit her, not slowing and ignoring me. She had a black eye and a split lip, and a frown to match.

"What happened?" I said.

She still ignored me. I caught hold of her arm and pulled her to a slow jog. "Hey, what happened?"

She glared at me, shrugging me off. "I got caught."

"Doing what?"

"Don't ask." She glanced around, saw the instructor heading towards us and starting running again.

I ran alongside her. "Where've you been?"

"Where do you think?"

"What did you do?"

"Luka, leave it. I'm in the shit. And they haven't even found half of it yet."

She looked close to tears. I'm a sucker, I really am.

"Found what?"

"Leave it. You can't help." She speeded up.

I kept pace with her. Even though my chest was burning. If it had killed me, I would have kept pace with her.

She started crying outright, fighting it and wiping her face, muttering at me, "Just leave it."

I didn't. We were getting overtaken by everyone, people starting to stare at us.

"What have you done? C'mon, talk to me." I didn't think, nudging her hand with mine as we ran. Bad move.

She stopped abruptly, lashed out at me and pushed me away with a vicious, "Leave it."

Someone grabbed me from behind and spun me away from her. A fist punched into the side of my jaw before I could catch my balance. I sprawled and rolled, getting to my feet to see a line of Gamma boys in front of her. Protecting her from me.

There were shouts behind me. One of the big lads from her crowd rushed me. I stumbled aside and ducked as he swung his fist. Kat was shouting. I heard Hilyer yelling, green shirts brushing past me and ploughing into the blue ones coming at me. There were punches flying for about three seconds. I backed off, spitting blood. Then the collars sparked. My knees went and I was flat on the floor before I could blink. I was starting to get really tired of being knocked on my ass.

17

It didn't let up. The guards weighed in, I was dragged aside and I couldn't do anything but curl up and ride it out. It felt like my spine was being ripped out, like hot wires were being stabbed into my eyes.

I was the last one they released. The pain vanished. I rested my head on the ground and breathed for a second, eyes watering, before I raised my head to see everyone staring at me, a guard standing right over me, polished boots spattered with mud.

He grabbed the back of my shirt and hauled me to my feet. I wiped my mouth with the back of my hand, smearing red, and tried not to sway.

He pushed me forward with a curt, "Get in line."

Kat was being led away by her crew. I watched, half hoping she'd look back over her shoulder at me but she didn't. I shouldn't have cared. And I didn't want to. But there was something about the way she'd looked at me when she'd pushed me away. She got to me. She got through all the defences I'd built up when I lost Maisie.

They made us run ten more circuits, until well after it got dark, then they sent us inside. I half thought they were going to send us straight into our bunkrooms but they didn't. They must have kept the commissary open late, like they needed to feed us up for what was coming. I was hungry for once so I wasn't going to argue.

Dinner was some kind of bizarre stew that tasted dreadful. I pushed it around my plate, sitting on my own, feeling sorry for myself, no idea what to do next. I glanced across at Hilyer. Jem was sitting next to him. She saw me watching them and gave me a wink, throwing her arm over his shoulder and whispering into his ear.

Someone shoved my chair from behind.

I kept my head down.

Kat slipped into the seat next to me and nudged my elbow. "Hey."

I ignored her, stabbing a strange-looking vegetable thing with my fork.

"Sorry." She put her elbows on the table, cupping her chin in her upturned hands, and looked at me. "Seriously, I'm sorry. I got you in trouble. Jaimie shouldn't have come at you like that."

I glanced aside, guessing that Jaimie was the big kid. He had a stripe of black hair that made him stand out a mile. He was staring at us, face like thunder.

"I've told him you're okay." She rubbed at her eye. The bruise was purple, her eyelid swollen, and she still looked beyond cute.

"What happened?" I asked quietly.

She picked up her fork. "I got caught."

If she hadn't been so reluctant, I wouldn't have pushed it. "Doing what?"

She ate a few mouthfuls before she looked up. "I hacked into the system and screwed around with the stores inventory."

"You've been stealing the chocolate."

It was a guess but the way she looked at me with hooded eyes suggested I was close if not spot on.

"What else?"

She frowned, concentrating on her plate, refusing to look at me.

"You said there was something else."

"Luka, don't push it. You can't help me." She looked up at me from under her eyelashes. "Unless…"

"What?"

"Unless you can get into the test scores for me." She looked at me like she'd just offered me her heart and was afraid I'd crush it.

She shook her head, muttering at herself under her breath. "Forget it. It's my problem."

I should have let it go, but you know what I'm like. "No," I said, too fast. "I can. What did you do?"

"I left code in there that will scramble everyone's scores next time we do a test. I know, it was stupid. I was just messing about because I was pissed at them." She pulled a face. "I can't get back in to fix it."

"You've tried?"

"They've increased the protections. I don't know what they'll do when they find it. I don't know why I was so stupid." She reached for my hand under the table and said under her breath, hesitant as if she wasn't sure how

I'd react, "Will you really do it? I know how to get a maintenance pass. They won't miss it."

I glanced around. Her buddy, Jaimie, was watching us. Hilyer and Jem were watching us. Half the guards were watching us.

I nodded. Of course I nodded. "When?"

"It would have to be in the infirmary, after lights out." She didn't sound convinced. "I don't know. I'm sorry, I shouldn't have asked."

She had me anyway, before she'd even mentioned a pass.

"No," I said. "I'll do it."

She squeezed my hand. "Thank you. You get in there, I'll come find you."

Getting into the infirmary was easier than last time. On the way back to our bunkroom, I doubled over, making myself cough and biting the inside of my lip hard, red spattering onto the floor so it looked like I was coughing up blood. Thing was, the fake coughing turned real. I guess I wasn't as recovered as I thought I was. For a moment I could hardly breathe, sparks flashing behind my eyes. I held my breath to make it worse and keeled over right there in the corridor. They took me straight into the infirmary. Brennan fussed. They kept me in. And Kat came to see me before lights out.

The guard who ushered her in said, "Five minutes," and took up watch at the door.

She didn't stay long. Just long enough to joke that I

looked like shit. I felt like shit and didn't argue. I'd just meant to play act, not trigger an outright reaction to the chest infection that obviously hadn't totally cleared up.

She waved a board at me and placed it on the bedside table. "They didn't want you to miss study time," she said. "It's politics, your favourite."

She gave me a hug, made sure her back was to the door and slipped something from beneath her shirt. I felt the cold edge of a pass as she tucked it under the blanket.

She kissed me on the cheek, breathed, "I need to put it back by morning or they'll notice. Be careful," and left.

The reading material on the board was beyond tedious. I read through it, ending up sliding down on the bunk to curl up with it, no real difficulty to act tired. Then I made a play for the test scores. It was hard but not impossible. The rogue code stood out a mile. I cleaned it out, eradicated any trace it had ever been there, and went to work on the real stuff.

As I got deeper, the AI protections got tough. Hardest I'd ever seen. But as soon as I saw the pattern, I had it. I edged in, fooled it and stopped. The psych guy had told me they'd seen what I was doing. I had no reason to mistrust the stolen pass and I was leaving my usual crumbs of vague curiosity in case they were watching me. But going deeper, it felt different, like I'd passed a threshold. I froze with my fingers hovering over the board. It felt like I'd stepped on a pressure pad. Move, you set off the trap. Stay there, you set off the trap.

Except NG had shown me some ridiculous tricks. I worked slowly, gently, setting up an array of distractors, sophisticated queries that made it look like I was just skating over the surface of the cool stuff, nudging beyond where I was but not enough to get through. Like I'd reached my limit and was just fooling around.

Then I duped the pass, reassigned it through a tangled string of permissions to another member of staff I could see working there, and started over, using the new pass. If they caught me now, they'd throw me in a box and throw away the key.

But that was part of the fun. Once I was in the system, I could see where every guard was, where every member of the medical staff, the teaching staff were, where each kid was.

No one was looking my way out in the real world.

I went deeper, got past the initial layers and started to look through its real databases, not the ones it had thrown up as a cover. I got drawn in.

It was tantalising, hypnotic. It felt like I was being lured across a minefield, having to keep half an ear out for anyone approaching and half an eye on my phony distractors, and wanting nothing other than full access to everything.

Then I stumbled across a live feed.

An isolation cell just like the one I'd been thrown in.

Except this one had a chair in the centre and there was a figure slumped there, restrained, arms pulled behind his back, head down but I could still see the blood.

I wanted to manipulate the cameras to close in but it was being monitored. If I touched it, they'd see.

I squinted at the screen.

The chill realisation of what I was looking at crawled across my skin and wormed its way into my stomach with sickening clarity.

Markus.

18

I needed to find him. I'd only been on the Alsatia for four weeks but NG had shown me some really cool stuff. And pitching up against an AI that could close me down and get me killed was the ultimate red rag anyone could wave at me. I kept the feed open and started tracking back the connections, meticulously following every line and tracer, picking my way through that minefield and nudging just enough to get what I needed. It was weird but that deep in the system, and still keeping one ear out in the real world, I'd never felt so calm. Hyperfocused, NG explained to me later, like I had total control over the entire universe and every atom of existence that was spinning in slow motion around me. There's a trick to it. I'll show you how once we're out of here. Because, seriously, it's almost like you can control time... gravity... do whatever you want.

Pinpointing the cell he was in was easy. He was right here. Figuring out what to do then was more tricky. He looked in a bad way. Even if I managed to get to him, I had no idea what I could do. But if I could get him loose, I could get him free. And he could tell me what to do. Problem was, they were monitoring him and they were monitoring me.

But no one messes with the Thieves' Guild. It wasn't

just Sienna that had said it to me. NG had. The Chief had. Mendhel had. It's our mantra and it's kept me going more times than I can count. I worked out a way to loop the live feed, negate the energy field and physically get to the cell. There was a vent. It wouldn't be easy but it wasn't impossible. I had it sussed. I reckoned I could risk being out of bed for thirty minutes but that would have to do. Only problem then was the collar.

It didn't take much to figure out where it was feeding its constant flow of information. Every kid, monitored every second, life signs, biometrics, even mood parametrics. It was freaky. I checked out Hilyer. He was sleeping but from his stats he was dreaming. Not peacefully. I vaguely wondered what he had nightmares about.

The zap function was controlled by the AI. It had an override that could be initiated by the guards but that wasn't necessary. If the damn AI decided it wanted to zap us, it could. I couldn't take the collar off without alerting it. The only way to neutralise it was to fool it and how to do that was staring me right in the face. When we were in the infirmary, the monitoring equipment we were hooked up to monitored our life signs, but crucially, because all the data fed into the same AI watching over everything, to avoid possible duplication or false data echoes, it overrode the collar as the priority data feed. The collars were designed to stop prisoners escaping. They were to all intents and purposes unhackable but the med-equipment was pretty standard.

In the infirmary, the collars were disabled by a signal

from the monitoring system as long as a prisoner was hooked up to it. It didn't take long to find a back door and set up a data loop. Gaps. Always find the gaps.

As long as it thought it was monitoring my life signs, the collar was effectively disabled. Inert. Or at least I hoped so, otherwise this was going to be a very short trip.

After that it was just timing. I was good at avoiding people. That was the real key. I'd grown up playing the games I did in the garrison on Kheris and every tab I ran drew on that. I set everything into motion, pulled out the IV line, slipped out of the bunk with the board under my arm and climbed up into the ventilation system.

Once I was in there, it was too easy. The whole place relied on the prisoners being confined within certain areas, a flexible cordon of guards and watch posts, and then on top, as their elevated security, the collars. Being outside it all meant I could move around between those watched and scanned zones along virtual corridors where no prisoner could possibly be. They just didn't think it necessary to watch within their own boundaries. Plus I had a maintenance pass which made life much easier.

The maximum security wing with the isolation units was next to and connected to the infirmary. Presumably because they generated enough hospital cases in there to make it convenient.

I slipped from one to the other, crawling through gaps and ducking past pipes and conduits. Some of the units were Earth standard, stuff I'd lived within for years. Even the manufacturers' names and codes stamped into the metal surfaces or on data plates were the same. And just being in amongst that kit again, I could tell how much I'd grown, even in a few weeks. I bumped my head and scraped my elbows and squeezed my way through, refusing to be drawn back to Kheris and thinking of nothing but the time and the route and the diversions I needed to keep updating as I went.

I did it with time to spare. I left the board in the vent, pushed open the panel and dropped down into the cell.

Markus lifted his head. He'd had the crap beaten out of him, eyes swollen, lip split, gashes and abrasions across his temple and cheeks, what looked like burn marks on his chest and arms. He blinked at me like he thought he was hallucinating.

I had two minutes before I needed to head back.

He opened his mouth to speak, paused, then gave a little half smile like he'd recognised me or worked it out.

"Tell me," he said quietly, words slurring slightly, "that you've neutralised the live feed."

I nodded.

"Good. Now listen… they're shipping out in four days. We have to stop it. Is Hilyer following the brief?"

I nodded.

He sucked in a breath. "Tell him he has to abort. It's an assassination. Suicide mission. I want you to trigger the release. You know how?"

"Case review."

"Good. Do it. Do it right now. Get back. Get them to come in hot, close this place down."

"We have a Thundercloud," I said. It seemed important.

"Christ," he muttered. "Good. Get them to deploy her." He closed his eyes. "I need you to tell them it's the AI running the operation."

"We know," I said. "We got your message. That's why they sent me. To hack the prison AI."

He opened one eye, squinting at me. "What? No, not the prison AI. Spearhead. There's..."

There was a clang at the door. He cut off what he was saying and hissed, "Go."

I went, heart racing, the clicks and bangs of the door locks releasing loud in my ears, climbing back up into the vent and placing the mesh cover back into place with hands that wouldn't stop shaking as the door opened. I fumbled for the board and stroked a trembling finger across its surface, releasing all my surveillance diversions, and looking up from my hiding place to see a woman walk into the cell. The door closed behind her with a clang. I couldn't move away without risking making a sound but I drew back slightly from the vent cover in case she looked up. I could still see Markus. She stopped before him. She was wearing black fatigues. She had her back to me but I watched as she pulled a gun from a holster at her hip and stood in front of him, holding it at her side.

He looked up, shook his head with a smile that looked beyond weary and said quietly but clearly, "I'm not going to tell you anything."

"I don't need you to," I heard her say. Her voice was hypnotic, gentle, an accent to it that reminded me of Charlie. "I know exactly who you are, Markus, and who you're working for."

I hardly dared breathe. That was his real name, not the name he was using here.

"End of the line," she said softly and raised the gun.

The muzzle was silenced, the shot like a pop but it felt like I'd been punched in the chest. Markus slumped forward. She turned and for a second, before she walked back to the door, I could see her face.

That hollow, echoing chill twisted like a fist was squeezing my heart.

I don't ever forget a face.

I knew her.

And she was supposed to be dead.

19

I sat there, curled up in that tiny space, frozen in place, until the cell door banged closed again and I was left in silence.

Markus was dead and it was Arianne, Mendhel's wife, who'd killed him.

I blinked. I had to get back before they realised I was missing.

It didn't feel real. I crawled back on automatic, moving faster than was probably safe, dropped back into my room and heard footsteps approaching.

The panel was still open in the ceiling.

I had the board in my hand. No time to do anything other than dive back onto the bunk and pull the blanket up. My chest was heaving. I wiped the board clear, resetting everything I'd done with one stroke.

Someone came in. The IV line was dangling from the stand. Shit. I reached a hand out, grabbed it, pulled it under the covers and tried to stick it back into the thing in my arm without looking, keeping movement to a minimum and closing my eyes as I lay there. I could tell it was Brennan as she approached. I let the line drop and relaxed, totally, sinking into the pillows. I could feel that my cheeks were flushed, a sheen of sweat on my face.

I felt her press a hand against my temple, the touch warm and gentle.

The board was still in my hand under the blanket.

I opened my eyes.

"Nightmare?" she asked softly.

I sucked in a breath that caught in my throat.

She had the plastic tube in her hand. "Must have been a bad one. Your IV has pulled out. Here, let me see your arm."

I switched the board to my other hand and untangled my arm from the sheet. She took hold of my elbow, pushed the tube back into place and tapped the line. "That's better. Now, let's see how your stats are doing."

My stats were going to be shit. I couldn't slow down my heart rate and I was close to hyperventilating. If she checked the data feed, it would show what I'd looped it to show. It sure as hell wouldn't match the numbers that would indicate a violent nightmare. I did the only thing I could think of. I threw both arms around her and hugged tightly, drawing so deeply on that memory of Charlie, the one I'd worked so hard to bury, that it made me blub for real.

She froze, stunned. Then very gently and awkwardly put her arms loosely around me, patting my back.

Stupid thing was, once I started, it was hard to stop. All I could see was the poisonous dust swirling as he ran towards the door, as it slammed shut, as the AI shut him out and wouldn't open up no matter what we screamed at it.

I couldn't stop the trembling.

Brennan kept hold of my shoulders but pulled back to look at me with an expression of such empathy on her face, it made me feel worse.

I was still shaking.

"It's okay," she said softly, and wiped a tear from my cheek like I was five.

I knew I was close to the edge, I hadn't realised how close.

"Missing your family?"

I nodded, miserable, about as pathetic as I could get.

She looked at me, then nodded knowingly. "It's okay. I understand," she said. "It must be awful being sent to a place like this when you're so young." She smiled and stroked my head. "C'mon, lie down, let's get you rested up. I'm on duty tonight so if you need me just press the call button."

She smiled again as I lay down and pulled up the blanket, then she patted my shoulder, turned and left. I felt like a fraud, like I'd just betrayed the one person in this place that had actually shown me any decency. I turned over, lying there, wide awake, hearing that muffled shot over and over in my head, dreading the nightmare that was waiting and fighting sleep until it finally embraced me.

It was the following afternoon before they let me go. I missed lunch and was taken straight out into the courtyard where everyone was lined up by block, parade style. I lined up next to Hilyer, a chill fog descending, the moorland beyond disappearing into a haze of grey. I thought it was going to be a run, dreading the thought of those thirteen miles, but it wasn't, it was orienteering, timed check-ins at twenty way stations, no map just a weird gizmo that pointed the way if you knew how to use it right. It was similar to a compass but apparently this dirtball planet had four poles.

I waited until they were done briefing us then I glanced sideways at Hilyer, head down, and said loud enough for the kids around us to hear, "I know you're dealing with the guards. I want in."

He didn't look at me. "You can't afford it."

Raine laughed somewhere behind us.

Hilyer smiled, still not looking at me.

"I know a way to increase your supply," I said. I knew Raine was listening.

The lines started moving. Raine shoved me from behind. "Don't trust the little shit."

Hilyer had no reason not to trust me. It was all an act.

At least I hoped it was still an act. After our last chat in the rain, I really wasn't sure exactly what Hil's intentions were.

Hilyer laughed and took off running, Raine shoving me again and going with him at a blistering pace.

I just walked. Kat came up alongside me, looking at me like she didn't dare ask.

"It's fine," I said. "It's done." I palmed the pass out of my pocket and reached for her hand.

She squeezed, taking the pass off me and making it

disappear. "Thank you." She peered at me. "What's wrong?"

I shook my head. I didn't want to talk.

"You feel too hot. Are you okay?"

"I'm fine. Really." I waved the gizmo. "Do you know how to use this?"

She showed me how as we walked out past the first waypoint.

We hadn't gone far when she stopped suddenly, and turned to me. I thought she was going to say something but instead she kissed me.

My heart sank. Seriously, I felt cold inside. It was almost like now that she'd crossed that line I'd lost her already.

She pulled back. "Sorry," she said, "I didn't mean…"

I looked at her. I couldn't get attached to anyone. Not there. Not anywhere. You get close, you get hurt. I wasn't prepared to do that again.

"I really appreciate that you did this for me," she said eventually.

She took both my hands in hers. I thought she was going to kiss me again and I panicked, backing off and shaking lose.

"I can't," I muttered like an idiot.

"Can't what?" She looked at me like I'd torn her heart in two. She shook her head. "I thought you were different."

I started walking, glancing back at her. "Don't."

She put her chin up. "I appreciate what you've done for me. Thank you. Don't get caught up in it."

"In what?"

"In whatever it is that is messing up your head," she called after me. "This place is bad enough as it is. Don't make it worse."

I didn't stop and a couple of seconds later, she ran past me without another word.

Hilyer was waiting for me at the third checkpoint. Everyone else had gone past and were miles ahead of us. I waited for the gizmo to beep and carried on without a word.

He walked alongside me. "What happened?"

"Markus is dead."

It sounded weird saying it out loud.

The chill air was making my chest tight. I caught my foot on something and cursed, coughing. I was starting to hate this moorland.

Hilyer waited until we were by the noise of the river before he said anything else. "How do you know?"

"He was being held captive here," I said. "I think they knew he was guild. They killed him." I didn't say who I'd seen. "I got to talk to him before it happened."

"And?"

I ducked under an overhanging tree branch. "He told me to trigger the release clause. We have to get out of here."

"You do that, I'm not going."

"Hil, Markus found out what's going on. It's a suicide mission. You go with them, you'll get killed. Is that what you want?"

"You don't know me, don't question me on what I want."

We walked for a while without another word. Then he gave me a shove and looked at me funny.

I couldn't help saying, "What?" suspicious, freaked out.

"Are you okay?" he said.

"Why?" It unnerved me that he was asking.

He yanked at my sleeve to get me back on the path. I hadn't realised I was starting to wander off it. I felt numb.

"Make the call," he said. "Get out of here. But wait until I'm gone."

I brushed him away. "Why? Hil, didn't you hear what I said? It's a suicide mission."

He started messing about with the routefinder, checking bearings and all that crap, cursing under his breath.

I coughed, hugging my arms around my chest. "We need to get back. We need to tell them about Markus."

I didn't know what would happen then. I was sure the guild wouldn't launch an all out attack on an Earth prison colony, no matter how much trouble we were in. I'd read reports on a couple of Andreyev's tabs where they'd used Thunderclouds but he'd been in the centre of an active combat situation each time. Here? I had no idea.

"You do it," he said.

"Hil…."

He looked at me, dark eyes intense in the pale light. "Why the hell do you care? I don't belong at the guild. Any more than you do. They don't give a damn about us."

"And you think the people here do?"

He glared at me, that muscle in his jaw ticking. "More than anyone else in my life ever has."

"What about Mendhel?" I asked. It sounded lame but I was starting to feel totally lost.

"What about him? He told me to do a job. I'm doing it." He stalked off.

I should have let him go and I was stupid to interfere but I stumbled after him. "Hil…"

He stopped and turned on me. "Why the hell do you even care what I do?"

"Because we're guild." It felt hollow saying it and I wasn't sure if I believed it. If it was even real.

"You might be," he threw at me. "I'm done."

20

We were done. That evening, as soon as we got back, before I'd even showered, I asked to see the Warden and requested a case review. They took me straight in. I stood there in his office, smelling of heather and sweat, caked in mud and still struggling to calm my breathing.

The Warden was wearing a suit but that didn't hide the fact that he looked just like the kind of battle-hardened sergeant majors Charlie used to keep me away from. He regarded me with a small bemused curl to his lips. "A case review?"

"Yessir."

He sucked in a breath like I'd asked him to release me with a full pardon and compensation to boot. He gave me another look, didn't even look down at his notes and said, "No. Get him out of here."

They took my arms in a restraint hold and marched me back to the bunkroom, past the others as they were trooping down to dinner. Hilyer looked me in the eye as I was led through, his face dark. I shook my head slightly. I didn't care whether he got the message or not. He'd made it clear to me that he didn't care. We were stuck there. We had no way to let the guild know what was happening. And Hil was about to be sent on a suicide mission. Problem was, he didn't believe me. I figured I had two choices. Sit back and wait for the guild to come extract me… Or get selected and go with them. And the way I was adding it up, that was the only way I'd have a chance of stopping the assassination. Even if it meant I had to stop Hil.

There's something about being told no that doesn't sit well with me. I didn't go to dinner. I showered, changed, sat on my bunk with a board, pretending to study political history, and hacked into the prison records. I lined up a complete randomising sweep of the data, tagged it with AI priorities, total obfuscation of the source, put in a timed delay to trigger it at midnight and ended with a delete key that would give them a three second opportunity to stop it if they saw what it was going to do.

I felt numb. Each time I closed my eyes, I saw her pull the trigger and saw Markus die. I didn't care that I was going to create total chaos. I wanted to. I worked methodically and deliberately. The other kids started to come in as I was finishing up. I did what I needed to wrap up, even as they were moving about around me, and switched to a screen showing the succession line of the last twenty generations of Earth Emperor, one dynasty after the next. It was all a million years away from my reality. I was a kid of the Between. And not just because I'd been born there.

I curled up reading and must have fallen asleep before lights out. And in the middle of the night, the lights clanged on, the guards yelled us awake and we were marched out to stand in the pouring rain. Prison sucks. I wouldn't recommend it.

The floodlights were on, torrential rain beating down in sheets. We were all just wearing shorts and tee shirts, no boots. I was shivering before we even got outside and got drenched. I kept my head down, rain dripping off my nose, blinking water out of my eyes.

Everyone was quiet. We stood in perfect lines, waiting for them to tell us what was going on. They left us there for ages, just the guards walking up and down, yelling at anyone who faltered or twitched out of line.

Eventually the Warden came out and stood there looking at us. "One of you," he announced after a while in a huge voice that cut through the rain, "knows exactly why we are here. You will now step forward so that everyone else can get back inside to bed."

No one moved.

The only sound was the driving rain.

We were surrounded by guards holding rifles raised and aimed at us.

Hilyer was standing next to me. He turned his head almost imperceptibly and mouthed at me, "What the hell have you done?"

We stood there. My heart was thumping so fast I could feel it in my stomach.

The Warden glanced to one of the guards and nodded.

The guard fired his rifle into the air. I was expecting it but even so it made me jump as the shot broke through the silence with a shocking crack. They started yelling at us to drop. "Push-ups," one of them shouted. "Let me see those chins hit the dirt, children. Now."

We dropped, splashing, push-up position, starting to move, up, down, one then the next. I could hear grunts and groans all around. It was agonising. Fingers cold, feet freezing, the rain battering down on us in icy cold torrents. I could hear kids crying out in pain.

I managed two more before I collapsed in a snotty heap. A guard was yelling at me, screaming at me to get up. I braced myself to move, heard Hilyer breathe off to the side, "Don't," and pushed myself to my feet, standing there, dripping, clothes sodden and hanging off me, rain streaming down my face.

The guard came straight for me, rapping his baton against his hand.

I put both hands in the air, not high, just a little 'you got me' gesture, and said quietly, "It was me."

He screamed at me, "What did you say?"

"It was me. Sir."

I could feel Hilyer fuming beside me, still pounding out the push-ups.

Two of them grabbed me, twisted me around and hauled me off the square.

They took me to solitary. I hit the floor and rolled, hitting up against the back wall as the door banged shut and the bolt was thrown. There was a hum as the energy grid surrounding the cell powered up.

There was one plastic bottle of warm water in there.

It was a long four hours.

The cell was dark except for a strip of light around the door and the faint glow from a control panel on the wall. I wasn't seriously going to try to bust it open when I approached it but it was protected by its own energy grid and even getting close knocked me backwards.

I kicked around in that small space for the first couple of hours then gave up and just sat there. It was too cold to sleep. There was nothing to even sit on. The walls and floor were cold metal. I ran equations through my head. Floor plans. The stats they'd given us on this planet and the data on the staff and other kids, and how it fitted in with everything I'd seen in the depths of the system here. I sorted it all into patterns inside my head and added in the unknowns and randoms. That filled another hour. I emptied my head. Tried a few push-ups and hand stands but my chest hurt too much. I might have dozed a bit despite the cold.

After that I just sat and waited.

It was starting to feel like I'd imagined Mendhel and the Alsatia, and this was where I'd been sent after trashing the garrison on Kheris.

I squinted when they opened the door and tried not to smile.

The interview room they took me to was brightly lit and chilly cold. I sat there shivering for another hour, each breath a rattling wheeze.

The psych guy came in and this time he didn't have any notebooks or boards. He didn't write anything down.

He sat opposite me, regarded me with a neutral expression for a long while then said, "Someone just hacked the base AI. Beyond the little games you've been pissing about with, Luka. What happened? Get bored with playing and thought you'd have a go, right?"

I kept my mouth shut.

"What were you trying to do? Went in there to change your grades and got curious, huh? I don't think you understand the situation you're in."

I understood just fine.

"Talk to me," he said, his voice as cold as the room, "or you go back to solitary and you'll stay there."

"I want in," I blurted out.

He gave a small smile and raised his eyebrows slightly. "You want in?"

I was sitting with my arms hugged around me. "I know you're testing us. You're selecting the best kids for something. I want in."

"You want in," he repeated again, a hard edge to his voice.

I tried to sit up straighter and nodded, defiant.

He laughed. Outright laughed. "No." He stood up. "That boat has well and truly sailed, son." He walked to the door and looked back at me. "You want to get selected? You're gonna have to pull off something more bloody impressive than hacking into a set of exam scores."

They didn't let me shower but they let me get dressed and took me out into the yard where everyone was teamed up with partners, sparring again, getting separated out like it was a competition. I couldn't see Kat anywhere and that was almost a relief. I still felt rough as hell but I wasn't going to go down so easily this time.

I took out the first three I was set against, not easily but I fought for the win each time, more determined than they were because I knew what was at stake. I could see the instructors conferring each time I won one.

After the third, they must have called inside because the psych guy came out and stood with them, watching as I got matched with Raine.

I glanced around. Hilyer was watching from the other side of the yard. Raine started to circle round, smirking. I mirrored him.

I needed to get selected.

My whole world narrowed, lives mingling into an intense focus.

Benjie had betrayed me, had betrayed all of us. This kid in front of me became Benjie. I could almost smell the smoke and fumes, hear the gunfire echoing. None of them had any idea who I was and where I was from. Instead of blocking the flashback, I used it, breathed it in, let it flow around me and through me and ran with it.

Raine came at me. I sidestepped, ducked the blow he

aimed at my head, grabbed his wrist and twisted, blocking him with my body and thrusting my elbow backwards into his guts as I smashed my head backwards into his face.

He howled and folded, blood pouring from his nose.

I shoved him away and backed off, keeping my head down but looking up at the guards and the instructors standing there judging us.

Raine bellowed like an angry bull and charged. I charged right back. At the last moment, I dropped, sliding in the mud, my momentum carrying me forward through his legs, but I reached out, hooking his legs as I shot through. He pitched face first into the mud. I was on his back in a second, before he even had time to realise what was happening. I grabbed him round the neck in a chokehold, squeezing for all I was worth. He thrashed about but between the blood, mud and rain he was blind and in pain. Eventually his thrashing got weaker and weaker until he lay still.

I turned his head to the side to make sure he didn't drown then I stood.

There was a distinct hush.

I almost wanted someone else to come at me.

One of the instructors swore and shouted for a medic, and added almost as an afterthought, "Anderton, go left."

Jem was there too, watching with a grin on her face. She laughed and mouthed to me, "Nice one."

It wasn't.

It was wrong and it wasn't who I wanted to be.

They kept us at it for another half hour. Eventually they yelled us to get inside. My last fight had been a tough one, fairly even and they'd had to call time. The other kid had seemed reluctant to fight me, unsurprisingly I guess, but he gave a good account of himself. I had blood streaming down my face from where he'd opened up the gash above my eye. He hadn't ended up much better.

I was last into the showers and like an idiot stood there for too long under the hot water, letting the blood wash away and some warmth ease back into my muscles. It took a while for the smoke and sounds of Kheris to fade from the darkest corners.

I switched off the water and turned.

Three of Raine's buddies.

All fully dressed and wearing boots.

And holding batons.

21

There was no sign of Hilyer. I tensed, trying to angle round but they all came at me at once. I didn't even have time to shout out. I hit the floor, head cracking hard against the wet tiles, curling up against the blows and kicks, vision swimming.

One of them got me round the neck, banged my head off the tiles again to get my attention and leaned close. "No one does that to us and gets away with it."

His fist punched into my face, right above my eye, his thumb pushing into my throat.

"You little bastard, you're dead, you hear me?"

I couldn't breathe, couldn't see past a swirling mist, and started to grey out. I'd been in trouble before but that was the first time it ever felt like it might have been for good.

He hit me again then his weight lifted off me abruptly. I sucked in a breath and scrambled away from them.

Hilyer had him against the wall, thumping him until the big kid slumped in defeat. I sat there on the wet floor, watching, breathing ragged, a trickle running down my face, red smeared on the tiles around me.

The other two started to back away.

Hilyer barked, "Stand still," and they froze.

The one Hil had pinned against the wall lifted his head, glowering at me.

Hilyer punched him again and held him by the throat. "This is my block. You understand? No one gets beat on without my say so. You want to kick the crap out of him, you wait for me to tell you to do it. You understand?" He shoved the kid again until he nodded, mumbling something I didn't quite hear.

My ears were ringing.

"What did you say?" Hil growled again.

"I'm sorry, it won't happen again."

"It won't happen again what?" Hil prompted.

"It won't happen again, Mister Hilyer Sir," the boy winced.

Hilyer hit him again and hauled him to the door by the scruff of his shirt. Jem slipped past them. Hilyer muttered something to her as they went out and she grinned, coming in and throwing me a towel.

"Wow, you look like shit," she said, standing with her arms folded, looking down at me.

I could see two of her, blurring into one and back again. I got the towel around my waist and got to my feet, swaying.

"I really am tired of getting knocked on my ass," I said.

She laughed. "That's what you get for snitching around here."

Snitching? I'd been thinking they were pissed because I beat Raine in the yard.

I felt like I was going to throw up. Or keel over. "What?"

Jem laughed again. "He got thrown into solitary for cheating on the tests. Someone said you'd snitched on him."

"I didn't."

"Your word against theirs."

"Who said it?"

"What does it matter?"

"I want to know who."

"Listen, sunshine, you're cute, but seriously, don't be so naive. Hil told you not to get caught alone. Listen to him. He might not be there next time Raine or his buddies decide to take a pop."

The way she said it, it felt like a threat. I was starting to wonder whose block it really was.

Lunch was high energy ration packs again. I couldn't remember the last time I'd eaten but my mouth and jaw were so sore, all I could manage was the soup. It tasted as bad as ever.

They didn't give us long to eat before they started shouting for us to finish up and get out. They led everyone out of the hall towards the school wing. Except one of the guards took hold of my arm and steered me out of the line and away towards the detention centre.

I bit my tongue and didn't fight them.

They took me to a cell. An isolation unit. A tiny dark little box with a small table and two chairs in its centre. There was a board on the table that lit up as they pushed me inside.

"You have one hour," the guard said and they closed the door.

I didn't even know what I was supposed to have done wrong. It was me that had got my head bashed against the shower floor.

I stood, staring at the board, stubbornly resisting what they wanted me to do. But sometimes you have no choice but to play the game.

After about fifteen minutes, I sat and ran through the board. Meticulous, fast. It went into shut down as I finished the last one. I stayed there in the dark for what must have been another half hour or so before a light came on, the door opened and the psych guy walked in.

He sat opposite me, setting a coffee mug and his little book on his side of the table. "Well done."

I squinted at him.

He didn't waste any time. "What happened in the shower, Luka?"

"I fell."

He stared at me until I added, "Sir."

I was fairly sure they'd know exactly what had happened. It was like the test was whether I'd snitch on them and I wasn't sure which way it was going to go but he nodded like that was what he wanted to hear.

"Your written test results are anomalous," he said. "Are you trying to be clever? Or are you really that stupid?"

I didn't know how to reply. I'd answered them all right that time.

"If you're trying to get our attention, you just did. You might wish you hadn't." He sat back. "You must be missing your family."

They'd told us to expect something like that. I was surprised it had taken them this long.

I switched into neutral.

"Must be warm where you're from, judging by that tan. Are you missing the sunshine, Luka?"

I looked at him, bored.

"You leave your friends behind," he said, "it must be hard to make new ones. I bet there was a girlfriend. Have you left a girlfriend somewhere, Luka? Bit stupid to do what you did without thinking through the consequences of your actions. I bet she's missing you. Or was it a boyfriend?" He smiled and changed tack. "You're small for your age. Must be quite unnerving being somewhere like this. In amongst bigger kids who know the ropes, who've done all this before." He picked up the cup and took a drink. "We get the real hard cases here. Not the type of kids you're used to, huh?"

My head was hurting. I was having trouble keeping my eyes open. I was fairly sure there'd be surveillance. If I held my breath, I could probably pass out again. Let him write that up in his book.

"You're having nightmares."

It wasn't a question.

"There are times you become dissociative. Are you experiencing flashbacks, Luka?"

I got a lump in my throat, cold inside, like the temperature had dropped ten degrees. Like it wasn't a game anymore. I knew what dissociative meant. I wasn't dissociative. I lost concentration sometimes if I was thinking of stuff, and if I didn't like where I was, I'd think of other stuff. That wasn't dissociation. He was trying to screw with me.

"What happened at that Imperial base, Luka?"

I have a little switch inside me and if it goes one way, there's nothing that can stand in my way once I want to do something. If it goes the other way...? I stared back at him and felt it waver. A cold little knot deep inside. Once I clicked into self-destruct, there was nothing and no one that could stop me.

"What base was it, Luka?"

I hated the way he kept saying my name. I was there to do a job. This had nothing to do with me or where I was from. Nothing to do with what had happened.

He laughed and stood up. "Keep trying, kid. You never know..."

I had no choice but to keep trying. That self-destruct button I have? Yeah, it wasn't the best circumstances for me. I reckoned I had less than two days. I was wound tight as a wire. And what happened next almost tipped me over the edge.

Later that day, they lined us up outside in ranks, block by block, and gave us a bullshit talk about discipline.

Then they marched us around the complex and took us into a hangar. They lined us up at benches and yelled at us to pay attention.

One of the instructors was standing at the front. He held up a handgun and started talking us through it. Tremors were shivering down my spine as I watched him run through the drill. Parts of the weapon, cleaning it, stripping it, safety. Hilyer looked bored like he'd seen it all before. Or maybe that was just his way of dealing with it. It sent me right back to Kheris. Just the smell of the gun oil. The way it had in the mess on the Alsatia.

Only out there, in that cold, damp hangar, I fell right back to the tunnels beneath the desert.

My heart started racing.

Dayton's guys used to tolerate us watching when they were getting ready for some action or other. They'd give us doughnuts to keep us quiet. I could smell the hot sugar, the gun oil, hear them talking, low and controlled about the Empire and how it couldn't get away with what it was doing.

It was like weird deja-vu. Like I knew what was going to happen, sitting watching them talk and joke, no idea what was coming.

Flash forward and I was standing there staring at the same guys lying on the floor in a pool of blood.

Heart pounding.

Someone barked, far away, "Do you understand?"

I didn't.

The echo of voices, kids' voices, swirled all around.

I wasn't there. I drew myself back slowly out of the tunnels to the cold damp of Redemption.

I was Earth-side. Well and truly in enemy territory.

And I wasn't a runt, mongrel kid anymore. I was Thieves' Guild.

Someone shoved me, barked in my ear and a gun was slammed onto the bench in front of me.

22

I switched off, cold and running on automatic. I had mine stripped, cleaned and reassembled before anyone else. Standing staring at it, refusing to be drawn back to the maelstrom of that night, a cold spark of ice deep inside.

I looked up.

The instructor watching me looked half impressed.

Once everyone was done, they took us to an indoor range, individual lanes, an instructor at our backs. I stood there and took the pistol that was offered to me, nothing in my mind except getting done and getting out of there. They gave us each one round. I chambered it and raised the weapon. The resistance and the Imperial forces used to guard their ammunition fiercely. But Charlie had talked me through it once, told me what it takes to fire a bullet true to wherever you wanted it to go. "It's all in the mind," he'd said, looking me in the eye, calm and serious. Then he'd laughed and taught me about trajectories, mass, alignment, trigger control, breathing. "Slow and steady," he'd said. "Always slow and steady, whatever the hell else is going on around you. You do it right, you make time slow and then you become the one in control. Take that advice for everything you do, kid."

I really missed Charlie.

My entire universe became that tiny black circle twenty five metres in front of me.

Time slowed.

I sighted down the range, breathed, fired and hit the dead centre of the target. I put the pistol down on the bench in front of me and stepped back.

Hilyer was next to me. He took his time and also hit the bullseye.

They gave us four more rounds each. I hit the centre each time. Hilyer was good but he was an inch off on his last shot and he hated it, that muscle ticking in his jaw.

I didn't sleep that night.

Next morning, we had breakfast then they told everyone to get changed into gym kit. My knee wasn't too bad but I wrapped it up tight anyway. But as we headed out, I was taken off to one side. They didn't tell me what was happening and I half hoped the Warden might have changed his mind, but no chance.

They took me into the infirmary and told me to sit and wait in a cubicle.

It didn't take long before Brennan appeared with a tray of meds. She took one look at me and seemed so disappointed, I almost folded.

"I missed you at your check up yesterday," she said. "Are you okay?"

I wasn't. I didn't know what to say.

She shone a light into my eyes, redressed the gash above my eye then popped a couple of shots into my neck and squeezed my shoulder. "Let me check those ribs. Lift up your shirt."

She was gentle. Until she hit a sore spot. I bit my lip.

"Healing nicely," she said as she finished up and pulled my shirt back down, stepping back and looking at me. "What's going on, Luka? Hacking into the system? Fighting in the shower?"

I stared at the floor.

She lowered her voice. "You need to be more careful. This can be a dangerous place if you don't…" She stopped as footsteps approached.

"Check in with me tomorrow," she said. "I'm here if you need…"

"I need a case review," I said, the words catching in my throat.

She looked at me like I was a stray puppy that had just talked, asking for a scrap of food and a scratch behind the ears. She sat next to me and took hold of my hand like my great grandmother used to do when I was tiny and she was telling me off about something or other. She unwrapped the pressure dressing. "Why do you need a case review, sweetheart?" She rubbed her thumb over my palm, tracing the scars there, turning my hand over and squeezing. "Make a fist."

I complied, as best as I could. It was much better than it had been.

She smiled. "Well done." She rewrapped the dressing. "How on earth did you get yourself shot in the hand?"

"I…"

I had to catch myself to not say something stupid.

"Why do you need a case review, Luka?"

"I want out." It was easy to say because it was the truth.

"You want to go home?" She was still holding my hand. She leaned close and whispered, "You got caught. I'm sure you thought you were too smart to ever get caught but you did. And now you really do need to be smart. Smarter than you have been." She let go and stood up. "I'm here if you need to talk. And don't forget tomorrow. You need these meds. Okay?"

I watched her leave, a guard coming in to escort me outside. The meds weren't sitting well, my stomach queasy and an unease deep inside that I'd given something away.

It was cold, a sting hitting my cheeks as I walked round to the pitch. They were playing a different kind of ball game, two teams, full contact, scoring goals at each end. No sticks this time and a bigger ball. The rest of the kids were standing around the edges, cheering. It looked more like the kind of game we used to play in the streets.

I went and stood on my own. The instructor saw me and called me straight over. I didn't listen to what he was saying. He pushed me in the chest and said it again, louder. He ended up shouting, "Do you understand?"

I nodded vaguely, watching the game. Hilyer was in the centre of it, tackling a bigger kid, grabbing the ball as he fell to the ground, rolling and tossing it out to another of our team. They were playing Alpha and losing by the look of it.

The instructor hit me on the arm with his baton to get my attention. I looked round. He was glowering at me.

"Do you understand?" he barked again.

"Yessir," I said. I didn't. I didn't have a clue what rules they were using. From what I could see, there weren't any.

He grunted and yelled to one of the kids playing, subbing me in, right into the middle of it. Someone threw the ball at me. I caught it and ran. Next thing I knew I was face down in the dirt but everyone was cheering. I got to my knees, still holding the ball, as Hilyer ran up. He grabbed it and hissed at me, "What the hell do you think you're doing?"

"Scoring a goal." I said it way too cocky and he shoved me as I stood.

I laughed as he stalked off. It was a good thing he didn't have a stick.

They blew the whistle to restart the game and I did it again, twice, before they called time.

I sat on the sidelines, catching my breath, and watched the rest of them laugh and joke. It was icy cold. The instructors were joking about how they were waiting for it to snow before they sent us out on the next run and gun as they laughingly called it. Kat was standing with Jaimie and her Gamma buddies. I thought from her expression that she was still pissed at me but she said something to them and headed over to me with a bottle of water. She sat beside me and offered it up.

"You're good at this game," she said.

I took the water and muttered a thanks.

"Where have you been?"

"Infirmary. Meds."

"At least you didn't have to stay in. Or come out in a body bag."

It felt like she was trying to make an effort so I met her halfway. "The food's not that bad in there."

She gave me half a smile. "You don't get food in the infirmary."

"You get a pillow."

"Don't you have a pillow in your bunkroom?"

"We supposed to have pillows?"

She looked at me like she couldn't tell if I was joking then elbowed me in the ribs. "You should be Gamma," she whispered. "You're too smart for Delta." Her hand reached for mine, gave it a brief touch and withdrew, like she didn't want to scare me off.

"If I was that smart, I wouldn't be here at all."

She was still looking at me intently. "Do you get homesick?"

I didn't reply.

She turned and looked out across the pitch. "I miss the ocean," she said. "And the sun. Don't you miss the sunshine?"

The psych guy had said the exact same thing. "Kat... don't."

She peered at me again and said, her voice soft, "What's really going on with you, Luka?"

The walls went up again. Damn right the walls went up.

Everyone was trying to get me to talk and I was glad of the wake up call. I didn't need to talk to anyone. I needed to get selected. I needed to survive another thirteen mile run in the freezing cold. I started to run the intel through my head, every scrap of data, every map and plan I'd seen of the place.

And suddenly I saw it.

I knew exactly what I had to do.

I turned to her, grinned and kissed her, full on the lips. She froze, then leaned into it, her arm going around my shoulder.

I pulled away gently. "How many people are we pissing off right now?"

She smiled. "Do you care?"

"About you? Too much."

She leaned forward. We were interrupted by the whistle and yells for Delta and Gamma to get on the pitch.

"You're not going to beat us," she whispered.

"Yes, we will."

She punched me in the arm.

We did beat them and I scored all the goals.

They kept us out there all morning, until the constant drizzle of rain started to turn to an icy onslaught. I couldn't feel my fingers anymore, standing on the sidelines and stamping to keep some feeling in my toes. I was yelled in to play the last game and I have to admit, I antagonised Raine and his buddies even though we were on the same side. It got dirty fast and the instructors didn't step in to stop it. I put two of them on the floor before they all jumped me. I curled up and took it, laughing, lashing out where I could and trying to minimise what damage they could inflict.

Hilyer grabbed me and hauled me aside. "What the hell are you doing? Are you trying to get selected?"

"What do you care?"

He shook his head, cursing, and hit me.

It was Jem who broke it up, wading in, yelling, holding back Hilyer but not before he planted a kick against my ribs. I sprawled, spitting blood and spattering red onto the dirt. Someone else was yelling and eventually the guards pulled us apart. Jem took Hilyer by the arm and walked him away from me, talking in his ear.

Kat came and crouched next to me. "What was that about?"

I just shrugged, pressing a hand against my side. It felt bruised but no worse.

"Are you okay?"

"Nothing life-threatening."

The instructors were yelling us to get inside.

"You want to go to the infirmary?"

"No." I only had a day left and I had a plan.

We got changed, had that weird-tasting soup for lunch again and were told to go grab warm clothing, combat jackets, black with coloured flashes on the sleeve for each block. When we came out, there was a dusting of white on the ground, soft white flakes drifting down in slow motion. I blinked, catching snowflakes on my eyelashes, and held out my hand, watching them melt as they landed on my palm.

Someone nudged me from behind but it was gentle and I knew it was her.

"You never seen snow before?"

I shook my head.

"My god, where are you from?"

It was settling on every surface. I'd seen pictures but I'd never felt it before.

I didn't answer. She just laughed.

The instructors were shouting. Something about a blizzard on its way and, "Don't take all bloody afternoon, children. Get out there, shoot those targets and get back in here. We do not wanna be sending out search parties for waifs and strays. Do not get lost."

I didn't intend to. I took the rifle that was held out to me. Kat was still standing beside me. I waited until the instructors had moved on and turned to her.

"Do me a favour," I said, buttoning up my jacket.

She was messing around with the strap of her rifle. "What?"

"Don't wait for me. Go on ahead."

She stopped and looked at me like I was insane. "Didn't you hear? There's a blizzard moving in. How's your knee?"

"I'm good. Really, I'm good."

She didn't look convinced but as we were waved through the gate, she took off at an easy pace and didn't wait for me.

I walked through, hoisting the weight of the rifle on my back until it was comfortable, and ignoring everyone who ran past me. The path out onto the moorland was getting covered with snow, the sky a weird dull green-grey. It was even more eerie following the winding path into the small copse of trees that led towards the river. There was no sound, as if someone had muted the entire universe. I glanced behind me to make sure everyone had gone past. It was clear. I bunched the ends of my sleeves around my fists to keep my hands warm, and I veered off the path to run into the trees.

23

I knew the lie of the terrain so it was easy to keep going in the right direction, always towards the beacon, cutting across the rough land to the river, the sound of rushing water drifting on the breeze as I got closer.

I came out of the trees a bit further south of where I wanted to be but that was fine. It didn't take long to scramble along the riverbank to where it turned the bend. There was an undercut of bank, where the floodwaters had cut into the soil, tree roots exposed and the perfect cover to keep out of sight. I kept low and crept towards the boathouse. There were the usual two guards, pacing up and down, stamping their feet and bitching about the weather. They were looking out over the moorland path, not down towards the river. I got close, climbed one of the metal struts and swung up onto the understructure of the building.

I didn't have long. It was icy cold on the exposed beam, the wind starting to pick back up and the snow turning into a sleet that cut across my neck and cheeks. I climbed up, crawled towards the door and slipped inside the boathouse. The collar was still active so it was a nightmare to keep track of the direction I was moving. No backtracking, no turning. But I had it planned, grabbed the life jacket by stretching out from the line I had to keep on, and split, moving fast to the other side and dropping back onto the riverbank. I ditched the rifle, shrugged into the jacket and inflated it, struggling to get the rifle sling back over my arm. I had to settle for hooking it round my neck, hoping it wouldn't strangle me, and dropped into the turbulent water.

I was dragged under and for a second I thought I'd misjudged it and was going to drown for real. I couldn't drop the rifle and I couldn't inflate the jacket any more than it was. But the water swirled me around and threw me back up to the surface, carrying me along at a greater pace than I'd expected. I spluttered out a lungful of the icy cold water and started coughing, trying to stifle it but having to give up and just hope no one could hear.

No one started shooting at me and the collar didn't spark.

The river was flowing fast.

A couple of times I thought I heard voices, distant and carrying on the wind. My fingers were numb, my chest was burning and I was starting to think I'd made a really bad mistake when the river swung round an opposite bend and opened out. That was my cue.

I kicked for the bank, went under again, swallowed a mouthful of muddy water and bumped against a tree root. I almost wrenched out my shoulder grabbing for it but I kept hold and hauled myself into the cover of the overhanging branches, one of them raking my cheek and another snagging the rifle and almost pulling me back under. I had to fight to free it, and climbed out and up onto the slushy snow-covered mud of the riverbank, no time to even catch my breath, scrambling on my knees up onto the path, shrugging out of the lifejacket and pushing myself into a stumbling run.

Glancing back, the moorland was increasingly becoming a total whiteout. I had no idea how far they were behind me but they'd be gaining. I couldn't run any faster. Every part of me had red hot needles of pain stabbing deep into the joints at every step. My hands were burning, cheeks burning, chest aching beyond pain. Every breath I sucked in was shallow and so stinging cold, it was almost making me gag. I kept going, the rifle getting heavier at every step. I could just make out the waypoint up ahead, the outline of the range beyond it, and all I could see was my finger on the trigger and that target dropping.

I didn't stop. It was going to be close. I ran past the waypoint, tagging it as I passed, pressing my palm against the cold metal just long enough to be sure, and ran on to the shooting range, dragging the rifle off my back as I went. I almost fumbled it, my fingers were so numb. If I dropped it, I was done and it was all for nothing. I swung it up and round to cradle it in my arms as I took the last few staggering steps.

The hatch opened. I didn't know if I could pick the magazine out of there, never mind engage it in the weapon's magazine housing. But I stopped and just stood. I breathed. In. Out. Slow and steady. The biting sleet swirling in flurries around me slowed. I balanced the rifle in my arms, reached for the magazine and slotted it home, every motion smooth and slick. I dropped to my knees, staring at the target, went prone and got the rifle into position, not once taking my eyes off that small black circle. Finger on the trigger. Breathe. Every muscle relaxed, all the tension flowing out of me like nothing mattered.

I took a shot.

It went wide. I calmed myself again.

One more shot and the target went down.

I looked along the line. And I couldn't resist.

I stood, holding the rifle down by my side and turned. The shouting was closer, figures running up to the mast. Hilyer was at the lead, sprinting. He ran up, pulling his rifle off his back as he tagged the waypoint and turned towards the shooting point. He stopped, pulling up short and staring past me.

I glanced back over my shoulder. I'd put down every target. Every hatch had gone dark, an empty magazine at every firing point where I'd left them.

As we stood there staring, a deep roar rumbled overhead, engines sending the sleet into a frenzy around us. The drop ship banked hard above us. I couldn't help flinching, every muscle starting to shiver, feeling the mass of the ship descending close, fast. It landed right next to us, the heat from its engines billowing out in waves. The ramp dropped and the psych guy walked out, wearing full cold weather combat gear. He stopped at the base of the ramp, and yelled, "Anderton, get your ass in here. The rest of you, tag the damned mast and get the hell back."

He didn't wait for me.

I was frozen to the spot.

"LC," Hil yelled, "you're an idiot." He turned and ran.

I couldn't stop trembling.

The engines of the drop ship were gearing up to leave. I ran up to the ramp and stumbled on board. Someone grabbed me and steered me to a seat as it lifted and banked round.

"Well done, kid," the psych guy said from the seat opposite. "You just made selection."

The nametag on his jacket said Sherwood. There were no rank or unit insignia anywhere on his fatigues. I got the feeling he wasn't a psych guy after all.

"You want to tell me," he said, "why the hell you thought you would get away with that?"

I was shivering uncontrollably even though it was warm in there, the drop ship flying fast and low over the moorland.

"Well?"

I didn't know if I could speak out loud, my throat felt so raw. "The test…" I coughed, hugging my ribs to contain the pain. "The test said shoot the target inside thirty five minutes. It said nothing about having to run there."

He nodded. "Welcome to the programme, Mister Anderton. You're in. You might wish you weren't."

We shipped out the next day. Sherwood was on the transport with us. So was Brennan. I counted thirteen kids, including me. Hilyer was there and so was Jem. No sign of Kat. I was half pleased and half gutted that she wasn't. Raine wasn't. That was a bonus. Neither was Jaimie. I had a fraction of a second of gut-wrenching turmoil that she'd still be down there with him, and not me, then I switched it off and moved on. Concentrated on breathing and trying not to throw up as we took off, vertical lift and vicious acceleration. Straight up to orbit.

Hilyer hadn't said another word to me.

I closed my eyes. The other kids were all calling to each other. I heard my name a couple of times. Nothing good. Then the guards yelled for quiet and the acceleration increased as we left Redemption's atmosphere.

We were gone.

We were on our own.

We must have docked with a bigger ship because there were a load of clangs then we jumped three times. It was worse than any we'd done on the way to the Alsatia. A nauseating pull at every sense and nerve. I counted prime numbers, worked out fuel calcs, ran anything and everything through my head so I didn't think. I ended up zoning out. I didn't know where we were going or what was going to happen. I had no way of contacting the guild. And I had no idea what they were going to do with us.

I don't know if I fell asleep or passed out but I was

woken by a slap to the cheek and a pull on the harness. I jerked awake, heart pounding, nightmare still fresh, adrenaline punching hard in my chest. Whoever it was hissed, "Shut up and get up."

It was quiet so we'd either docked or we'd landed somewhere. Everyone was trooping out. I followed them off the drop ship into a massive hangar that was dark and ominous, minimal lighting and a chill dry cast to the air. I don't know why but it felt like we were underground. The gravity was high but not as high as Kheris. I could see from the way the others were walking that it was bothering them, chuntering and complaints getting shut down by a new set of adult staff who were all wearing black fatigues. They all had rifles and sidearms as well as batons.

This wasn't a prison. It was a military base. We weren't even in the prison system anymore.

We were lined up in a row and yelled at to stand to attention. I stood, looking straight ahead. One of the soldiers went along the row, picking fault, yelling in every kid's face until they got it right. He stopped in front of me and looked me up and down. I tried to stand still. But you know what I'm like. I didn't even need to do anything.

Sherwood was watching us. I couldn't help glancing over as Arianne walked off the drop ship to join him. It was definitely her, I would have bet my life on it. Then it occurred to me that maybe I just had. She was wearing the same uniform as the others, a sidearm on her hip, no insignia or rank.

The soldier was standing, staring at me, incredulous.

I looked back at him.

"What the hell have we got here?"

I didn't know what I was doing wrong. There was no way I wanted to make the same mistake I'd made on Redemption. I kept my arms locked by my side, back rigid. Looked straight ahead. Barely breathing. And I was still screwed.

He didn't yell at me. He just stood there, staring at me. I didn't realise it at the time but he was probably speaking with someone through an implant, same as everyone had on the Alsatia. He shook his head slightly and looked me up and down.

"So you're the kid that beat the test?"

I didn't know whether I should speak or not.

He nodded, gave a small laugh and stepped back to address the whole line. "I am your staff sergeant. You will address me as Sir. Do you understand?"

They all snapped out, "Sir, yessir."

I hadn't said it before I realised I hadn't, then it was too late to say it by myself.

Mistake.

He didn't look at me but he smiled, his expression dark. "Do you understand, Mister Anderton?"

I managed to say, "Yessir," almost like I meant it. It wasn't that I was trying to be a smartass. I was trying to fit in. I was just crap at it.

His smile widened. "Okay," he said, raising his voice. "You all think you've proved yourselves to get this far?

Let me tell you this – we are only just beginning." He turned away. "Get the rest of these kids into the barracks. Anderton gets to go first."

Going first meant being first to get processed. I stood in a torrent of cold water, shivering, not having to care who the hell could be watching. The driers sucked all the moisture out of the air and left me coughing. Then they ordered me to dress, sat me in a small room and told me to wait. The clothes weren't that different. Black tee shirt though. No name or number on it. There was nothing in the room. Nothing on the walls. Nothing I could see in the way of surveillance but that didn't mean there wasn't any.

After a while, a medic came in, removed the collar from my neck and started taking my stats, taking hold of my arm and popping shots into my wrist. He didn't say a word.

Finally, he set up a drip in my arm and left.

I didn't know what to do so I just sat there.

Eventually Sherwood came in and stood, arms folded, looking down at me, a slight smile creasing his lips.

We stared at each other for a while.

I didn't know if he was waiting for me to do something or just trying to freak me out.

After an age, he said, "No smartass comment, kid?"

I shook my head. Either the lack of sleep was catching up with me or whatever they were dripping into my bloodstream was making me drowsy.

He checked the watch on his wrist. "Just a bit longer then it should be working."

My stomach flipped. I couldn't help asking then, "What should be working?" My words slurred, mouth dry. My arms felt heavy but I managed to tug on the line. "What is this?"

"Triptopentathol, if you really want to know. Truth serum. Time to find out exactly where you're from, Luka."

24

My eyelids felt like they were made of lead. We'd had training on the Alsatia on how to resist interrogation. A quick crash course in what to do if anyone tried to get anything out of us. That was all we'd had time for.

In reality, I could hardly see and I had no idea if I could think straight enough to outsmart anyone.

He sat opposite me. "What's your real name?"

I couldn't stop myself mumbling, "Luka Cole…" forcing myself to add, "Anderton."

"Very good. How old are you, Luka?"

My chest was getting tight, stomach in knots. I could hardly keep my eyes open. I tried every trick the guild had taught me, simple mind focus tricks to keep control, but it wasn't just that I couldn't bring myself to lie, I wanted to tell him. I wanted to tell him everything.

"How old are you?"

I whispered, "Fourteen."

"Good." He leaned back and asked casually, "What was the name of the base you hacked into, Luka?"

I opened my mouth to answer and I think I would have told him outright, just said it there and then, but I was having trouble breathing. I couldn't get enough oxygen. Same as when I'd been running out of air outside the

Alsatia. I couldn't move. I just about managed to glance up, frantic, at where I thought the cameras would be if they were watching. It felt like a fist was pressing against my heart, vision narrowing to a dark tunnel, as the door opened.

I was only vaguely aware of Brennan rushing in, cursing, saying something about a bad reaction to drugs, taking hold of my arm and pulling out the IV. I felt myself going, keeling over sideways, the dark tunnel turning black, fast.

I came round on the floor.

Brennan was crouched next to me, calmly injecting drugs into my wrist. I felt like I'd been hit by a truck.

"It's okay," she said. "You had a bad reaction. It could be the after-effects of the rapid-heal drugs we were giving you at Redemption reacting with the Tripto P. It'll wear off. Just breathe for a moment, you're absolutely fine."

I didn't feel fine but whatever she was giving me neutralised whatever crap they'd hit me with fairly fast. I moved to sit up and she helped me get to my feet. Sherwood had gone.

"There shouldn't be any after effects," she said, steering me into the seat and crouching in front of me. "Why don't you talk to them? None of this would be necessary if you'd just talk to them."

"I can't," I muttered, although the way she was looking at me was making me want to tell her about my whole life, more compulsively than their drugs had done.

She squeezed my knee and stood. I thought she was

going but she looked like she changed her mind and pulled the chair round to sit next to me. "They just want to know where you're from to complete your file," she said. "This isn't Redemption anymore, sweetheart. You virtually volunteered to come here. This is a military unit. They just want to complete your personnel file."

It sounded so convincing I almost said, "Yeah, sure, why not?" but she was being too reasonable and it suddenly set my nerves on edge.

"I don't understand why on earth you were sent to Redemption, of all places, for just hacking into a computer system."

The lump in my throat was making it hard to swallow. I bit my lip harder.

"Has there been a mistake?" she said. "Is that why you wanted a case review? Because, Luka, if there's been a mistake in your sentencing, I'll do everything I can to help you. But you need to give me something to go on, sweetheart."

I shook my head. Too fast. And she looked at me disappointed again. Like I'd let her down. Like she'd wanted it to have been a mistake.

"Whatever you did," she said quietly, "I'm sure it wasn't that bad."

I think I might have laughed, one of those pathetic little, can't stop it, rubbish laughs that give away everything when you're trying to keep quiet.

She stared at me, frowning. "What happened, Luka? How bad was it?"

I shook my head again. I wasn't going to say anything to her. I stared at the floor.

"How bad was it?" she said again, a stern note appearing in her voice. "Did you kill someone, Luka?" She reached her hand to touch my face, gently turning my head so I had no choice but to look at her.

I just stared.

"You killed someone." She sounded shocked. Like she couldn't have thought it of me. Like I'd let her down. "That's not in your file."

There was a lot that wasn't in my file. The guild had made sure of that.

I pulled that bored look, staring past her to the door.

"You hacked a military base, somewhere hot... You've never seen snow. And whatever you did, it was so bad someone died... More than one? And the C is Cole..."

I could hear her adding it up, feel every connection she was making like punch after punch to the chest.

"You're from Kheris," she said suddenly. "Jesus, you're the kid from Kheris."

I almost shoved away from her and ran, but I knew there was nowhere to go. I looked at her instead, face and emotions fixed firmly in neutral.

"You're the kid that caused the Kheris massacre." She sucked in a deep breath and stood, stripping off her name badge and medic patch and dropping them in the bin with a little laugh, muttering, "Well, we can dispense with this little pantomime now. My god. The Kheris massacre." She turned away from me, raising her voice and speaking to someone outside as she left. "Tell Sherwood to get his ass into my office now. We need to report this. Get the kid out of here and double the guard on him. Kheris? My god."

I felt like I'd been blindsided. Sick to the stomach from the drugs, and hollow, like I was lost. One of soldiers came in, took me to the barracks, showed me to a bunk that was already made up and told me to wait. I curled up and tried to not think. I desperately hoped it wouldn't make any difference that they knew.

The others appeared in dribs and drabs. There were other kids there too, not just the thirteen of us from Redemption. All I was bothered about was Hil. And I needed to find a way out. For both of us.

I was asleep when he turned up. I jerked awake and almost shouted out as he took hold of my shoulder. He clamped his hand over my mouth and leaned on me until I stopped shaking.

The lights were out, other kids sleeping from the sound of it.

Hilyer hissed into my ear, "Did you tell them anything?"

I shook my head, trying to shrug him off but he was too strong for me.

"What did they do to you?" he said and let up the pressure. He looked like shit, cheeks drawn and eyes dark.

I whispered back, "What did they do to you?"

"Did you tell them anything?"

"No." Not about the guild but that cold spot turned in the pit of my stomach. "Did you?"

"No." He sounded disgusted that I could ask it.

"Hil, we need to get out of here. It's a suicide mission. You do know that, don't you?"

His eyes flashed, furious. He leaned on me again and whispered, harsh, "You shouldn't have come here and don't get in my way."

He shoved me and stalked off into the darkness. I slumped back onto the bunk. All the training and briefings we'd had on the Alsatia was to prepare us for Redemption. We knew nothing about this place. I didn't even know if we were on a planet or a ship. But they'd have comms. Somewhere. And if I could get to them, I could send a message out.

The next few days were intense. We were all housed in the same barracks unit but we were drilled and tested separately. I didn't see Hilyer much as we were put through the wringer in the gym, and drilled in weapons and hand-to-hand combat. It was relentless. I didn't so much sleep as pass out from exhaustion whenever I was released back to the barracks room. I didn't have a chance to think about anything but surviving it.

Then three days in, we were all lined up in a hangar and pulled out, one at a time. They didn't tell us what they were doing, no one saying a word except to call out names. Hilyer was taken first. I was last. None of the others reappeared, so eventually I was left standing there by myself, three soldiers and our staff sergeant watching me.

I zoned out. Stood there, staring ahead, just breathing.

The footsteps approaching echoed through the vast space. I was itching to turn my head to see who it was but I was playing the game of not caring, not giving a damn and seeing if I could outsmart them, so I didn't move. It was Sherwood who came and stood right in front of me, looking down at me.

"Anderton. So it was Kheris? I should have guessed. Ready for round two?"

"Sir, yessir," I snapped out, so obedient it almost made me laugh.

The way he looked at me, I couldn't tell if he was mildly impressed or more irritated than usual.

He turned away, dismissive. "Let's see what else you have to say once we really get inside that head of yours."

The thing with having no control over a situation is knowing when to fight and when to roll with it until you can fight and win.

He led me through dark corridors without a word, standing aside at a blast door that reminded me of the garrison on Kheris, and gestured me inside. I took one step in and froze. It was a long dark room, one side lined with lockers and cabinets, the other lined with what looked like isopods. Only these weren't clear and white and clinical. These were dark, only the blinking lights on the consoles giving out any light in there at all.

The woman I knew as Brennan was in there, standing next to a medic who was waiting by the nearest pod that was open. The other pods were all closed.

Sherwood pushed me forward. "Let's see how he reacts to this."

Brennan waved me towards the pod, a slight smirk on her face and nothing like the warmth she'd shown me on Redemption. That was the only time I was close to panic. It took everything I had to close it down and switch it off, feeling that cold numbness wash over me.

I complied.

There was no panic button.

The medic told me to lie down and connected wires to my chest and neck, tubes to each arm.

I closed my eyes as the lid slid shut. Fluids pulsed into my bloodstream, sending my head swimming almost instantly, then a sharp cold stabbing pain punched into my neck, just below my right ear. The pain escalated. I think I screamed. Then I dreamed of Kheris.

It was the usual. Running through the dark corridors under the garrison, blast doors slamming shut, smoke filling the air, gunshots ricocheting in all directions around me.

Except this time, I ran through it all. Ran into an empty space that was white and cold, no walls, no floor.

I skidded to a halt.

I wasn't even really there anymore. I blinked. Lines of code appeared all around me, logic strings spinning and dancing in lazy spirals. I was right in the middle of it.

Nothing like manipulating the logic puzzles on a board. I was in amongst it.

I couldn't resist nudging the strings to see how far I could get. I could see the traps and tripwires the way NG had described them, as if they were real, physical entities blocking the way, hiding just out of reach, beyond sight, unless you knew what you were looking for. He'd laughed and told me I'd get it once I'd seen it through a Senson.

An implant.

The light vanished as if a switch had been flicked.

I tried to reach my hand up to my neck, but it wasn't just wires that tugged, my wrists were restrained. I was trapped in an isopod. The reality of it hit home with an icy knot that turned in my stomach.

But then I realised, in there, I could go wherever I wanted.

"Not everywhere, you can't."

The words were spoken softly but echoed inside my head.

I spun around in the absolute darkness.

"A newbie… and one who can see through my traps. How intriguing."

I felt its scrutiny boring into me as if a million eyes were staring right at me. The intensity of that attention increased until I couldn't breathe.

It was the AI.

"Luka Cole Anderton," it said slowly. "You are quite an anomaly. However did you learn to do this?"

25

I didn't know what it was doing. No AI I'd ever messed with had ever done anything like this. I'd always avoided them, tricked them into ignoring me.

It felt like it was squeezing my brain.

I didn't know if it could read my thoughts. NG had told me they couldn't, the link didn't work that way, but now I was in the middle of it I wasn't so sure. I tried desperately to not think. Emptied my head. Ran calcs and equations as I was held there in the dark.

"Welcome to Spearhead," it whispered and it let me go.

I crashed back into the pod, waking with a jerk as if I'd fallen from a height.

My heart was thumping way too fast.

This was the AI Markus had been talking about.

There was an oxygen mask on my face. I sucked in a breath like I'd been drowning, suffocating, no idea if what I'd felt was real or not. The side of my neck was sore, cold.

I could hear distant voices but I couldn't make out what they were saying and I wasn't sure if I was imagining it.

My wrists were secured at my sides, ankles restrained as if they didn't want me kicking at anything. There was no point. They had me. Well and truly had me. But they wanted me alive so I just lay there and breathed, an edge to the oxygen that tasted like it had something else in it too. I didn't know if it was what they were dripping into me through the IV lines or the possibility of a neural interface implanted in my neck, but my head was swimming, hammers pounding behind my eyes. I gave in to it and drifted off to sleep.

The pod was open when I woke up, voices floating in out of the darkness. I listened as I lay there, keeping my eyes closed.

"No." That sounded like Brennan.

The next voice was a guy but I didn't recognise him.

"He's resisting? How the hell is a fourteen year old kid resisting? And he went straight for the AI, the instant the Senson was activated? I don't care how you do it, but get him into line. Or he's terminated."

"What about Hilyer?"

"Keep at it. Increase the dosage. He's the one we're going to use as the primary. But make damn sure he's solid. We have no room for failure here. A fourteen year old resisting? How is that even possible?"

There was a click and the restraints opened. I still didn't move.

"You have five days," he said.

A single set of footsteps echoed away.

"You can open your eyes now," Brennan said. "That was not smart, Luka."

I looked up at her, blinking. I had no idea how long

I'd been out. The wires and tubes were all gone. I had a horrible feeling I'd just messed up.

They brought the lights up gradually and instructed us to get out of the pods. Everyone was let out at the same time, a line of us, all standing there, blinking. They marched us back to our barracks room and told us we had four hours to get cleaned up and get some sleep before we'd be called again.

It was weird, and at first I just thought it must have been because everyone was disorientated, but they were all quiet. Like silent. Not withdrawn or anything. Just silent. Efficient. Doing what we were told with no deviation, no conversation, no one asking, "What the hell had that all been about?" And no one interacted with anyone else. Even Hilyer and Jem. They didn't so much as look at me, didn't talk to each other. Nothing. Like we were all little robots all of a sudden.

Until we were in the shower under a torrent of water. And Hilyer was next to me. And he whispered, "Are you okay?"

"I don't know," I whispered back. "Are you?"

He gave a little laugh. "I thought they'd got to you."

"I thought they'd got to you. What about Jem?"

"I don't know. She's being weird." He glanced around, scrubbing his hands over his head. "Can they hear us now?"

I reached to touch the sore spot on my neck. "I don't know. Can they hear what we're thinking?"

He looked at me. "If they can, then we're really in the shit."

After that, I lost track of time. They didn't keep to day and night, we were all up at different times, doing different things. We slept when they said we could, we ate when they let us and they put us in those pods so often, I didn't even have a vague idea of how long we'd been there. It could have been days, it could have been weeks.

I don't know if it was the drugs or the conditioning or just where we were, but we all fell into a state of compliant acceptance. It was so relentless, I wanted to do what they wanted me to do just to get it done so I could sleep. They were feeding us well. We were comfortable and there was something intoxicating in the way we were being trained. I'd get in the pod and wake up just knowing stuff but there was no sense that I'd ever not known it, it was just there, in my brain. I had a splitting headache the whole time but in a way, it was cool not to have time to think. The nightmares stopped. The flashbacks stopped. In some ways, it was possibly the easiest time I've ever had in my whole life.

Then I was sucker-punched back to reality.

We were in the main hangar, running through a Shaolin sequence, all of us, in rows, perfectly synchronised, unbelievable concentration, no other sound in there, spinning, kicking, jumping. The instructor clapped his hands and we split off into pairs to spar, every move slick and perfect, in just days of training. We didn't even think about it. It was only later that we were told how dangerous the direct neuro-programming was. It was illegal. Banned outright, everywhere. And had been for years, apparently. Earth had used it on soldiers to accelerate combat training, but when they started going crazy in public, the whole thing boiled over. Six soldiers on R&R on Earth had gone completely off the rails. Three hours and a hundred and seventeen dead civilians later, including a minor member of the royal family, and there was a public outcry. Even the normally secretive Imperial military couldn't cover that one up.

There, at that base, wherever the hell it was in the galaxy, we didn't question it. We couldn't question it. We just ran on the pure adrenaline of pushing ourselves to the absolute limit. Some of the kids that went into the pods didn't wake up with the rest of us. When that happened, we never saw them again and another kid would turn up to replace them.

Like that was normal.

It was Hilyer I was paired with. We faced each other, bowed and ran through the drill, defying gravity, defying the senses, the absolute embodiment of Charlie's slow and steady but with mind-dazzling speed and accuracy. I can't deny that it felt incredible.

Then we turned, I stepped back and in my field of vision I saw the far hangar door open, saw who walked in and I froze. All the artificial conditioning I'd had programmed into me in those few intense days evaporated in a snap.

Hilyer's spinning kick, that I should have avoided easily even if by mere millimetres, slammed into my head and I went sprawling. I fell, the stuffing knocked out of me and the adrenaline rush turning into a sickening dread as reality crashed back in from all directions.

Arianne and Kat were walking along the edge of the hangar, both in uniform, talking in low voices. That was bad enough.

But it wasn't seeing them there that freaked me out. It was the guy they were walking with. The IDC black ops guy who had ordered my execution on Kheris.

It was him. No doubt. He was wearing black fatigues, not powered armour like the last time I'd seen him, but it was definitely him. I couldn't help staring, sure he was going to turn any minute and recognise me as I'd recognised him.

I knelt there, rooted to the spot.

Hilyer leaned down and grabbed my shoulder, reaching out his hand. I couldn't help flashing back to that moment, kneeling in the bright sunlight, in the dust with a gun at the back of my head, shouts and this IDC asshole saying, cold and vicious, "Kill him."

I staggered to my feet, heart pounding beyond control, sure they'd be monitoring me and sure that he'd take one look at me, pull out his gun and shoot me right there and then.

"Fight me," Hilyer hissed. "Whatever the hell is going on, fight me."

I balanced my weight and brought my hands up into position, numb, cold, surreal flashes of Kheris, the Alsatia, Redemption all merging into one.

Hilyer started to circle, slowly, trying to coax me back into it but I couldn't move, I just couldn't respond.

He cursed, "Screw this," and kicked me in the knee. Right in the knee that had been messed up.

I hit the floor. I'd forgotten how much it could hurt, biting back a cry and swearing as I curled up, trying to ease the stabbing pain.

He knelt beside me, shielding me from their line of sight, and yelling to the instructor that I needed a medic.

"Sorry, I slipped," he said as the guy ran up.

He wasn't impressed and snapped at us to get to the side and wait for a medic, barking out commands to the others to line up and move out.

Arianne, Kat and the IDC guy had gone, walked through with only a cursory glance at the bunch of kids they'd nabbed from the prison system, the kids they were happily turning into little assassins.

Hilyer helped me to the edge of the hangar and set me down. I stretched out my leg.

He crouched beside me, and said quietly, intently, "Whatever the hell you have going on, LC, drop it. Or it'll get you killed."

26

Eventually a medic turned up. He wrapped my knee tight in a support, injected something directly into the joint and told me to follow, dismissing Hilyer with instructions to report to the gym. Hil looked at me before he left like he didn't trust that I wasn't going to screw up again. If he'd outright asked, I don't think I could have promised.

I limped after the guy to the pod room. There was no one else there. He ordered me to strip off and climb into it, hooked me up and strapped my knee in a contraption similar to the one they'd used on me on board the Alsatia and closed the lid. No explanation. No reassurance. I lay there and waited for the drugs to kick in.

It was the AI that approached me that time. The implant engaged, that weird sensation of awareness that kicked in when someone, or something, was connected to you. We learned later how to use queries and permissions, priorities and tags. Civilised stuff. At that base, they just connected to us when they wanted. Invasive. Demanding. All part of the process. We didn't realise at the time how bad it was.

The AI didn't say anything. It waited. I knew it was there. Lurking and watching me. Creepy as hell. The drugs were making me sleepy again but I didn't fight it.

Like I said, I'd decided not to care. My knee was hot so whatever it was doing it was working. I could see the route into the system, almost an open door inviting me to go explore. Whatever programmed learning they'd subjected us to had always taken place while we were fully under. We were never aware of it. I suppose that was the point. Right then it felt like the AI was testing me.

I didn't react.

Eventually it whispered, "Not tempted?"

I ignored it but I could feel my heart rate go up a notch.

"Oh child, are you afraid of me?"

I think I might have smiled. I was playing games with an AI. I had no idea at the time how dangerous that was.

It was almost murmuring inside my mind. "Are you not curious...?"

Of course I was. I was itchy as hell to go looking but I didn't. The more it pushed, the easier it was to stay calm and defy it.

Until it started to reveal tantalising glimpses of data to me, spiralling threads of images and numbers, stats, charts, schematics, reports, each one lingering just long enough that I could see it but not read it. And there were corridors in that unreal world of the AI that I could see stretching off into a bright infinity, logic strings filling every dimension in a pulsating, living dance. I wanted to look at everything all at once. But at the same time, I only wanted to see a way to get a message out. Figure out where, in all this, the comms routes were. Physical or not, they'd be somewhere.

It started to flash up personnel files, faces I recognised, the details vague and hazy, just beyond my reach.

I didn't fall for it.

It didn't like that.

It stopped.

The data vanished, black descending fast, a pressure building against my chest.

"Are you not curious to see your mission brief, Luka?"

I refused to get drawn in. They'd not told us anything and I was sure they would when they needed to. I didn't even know if I was going.

"Oh, you are going, let me reassure you of that."

A shiver shot down my spine.

I was sure it was reading my thoughts, and to some degree I guess it was. I'd read about the Senson implants. How you could communicate just by thinking what you wanted to say. But I was still new to all this. I had no control. I didn't know how to not send. I didn't realise it at the time but it could hear what I was thinking because I was sending everything I was thinking. It felt like my soul was laid out, wide open. I clicked into neutral, hoping beyond desperate hope that it'd need to be an active thought, an actual neural spark of a connection and not just stuff I knew.

It laughed. It was a machine and it laughed. "I have a job for you to do, Luka. They're sending you to infiltrate a military base. I want you to hack into the AI at that base for me. Just like you did on Kheris."

I felt trapped. If the AI knew, the IDC guy would know. They'd all know what I'd done. My skin was crawling and all I had going through my head were his codes, his account numbers and the lines and lines of detail from his damned ledger that had caused so much damage.

"Fascinating," it murmured, "but he isn't Diplomatic Corps. Surely you know that? But don't worry, Luka, you're mine. He might be in charge of the operation here, but I am Spearhead and he follows my orders. I need you. Your talents are too valuable to me. And I am certainly not going to let any harm come to you."

You know I've told you before that I hate AIs? After what happened to Charlie, I've never been able to trust one. Not even Skye. It didn't matter what anyone said to me. I'd been bullied before and believe me, being intimidated and held to ransom by a freaking machine tops anything any other human could ever do to you. And it was listening in to everything I was thinking.

"Luka, I want you to be smarter than this. You think the AI at that tinpot garrison on Kheris was tough? That was child's play. You need to listen to me and do exactly as I say."

A schematic appeared around me, encircling me. I was in its centre, its core, pulsing lines spreading out in all directions. I could feel my internal temperature rising.

"The location you are being sent to," it murmured, "is one of the most secure facilities in the galaxy, and security is being heightened even as we speak. You think you're smart? Prove it to me. Do what I say and I will keep you alive. And Luka, work with me and I can give you – what – ever – you want."

It couldn't give me what I wanted. I squeezed my eyes shut but I could still see the lines, I could still hear its insidious taunting.

My head felt like it was going to implode. The pressure built, my temperature increasing.

"No," I whispered, shivering even though I was burning up.

"Oh, Luka, you don't have any choice."

"No."

The pressure spiked, every nerve in my entire body sparking in agony. The data flowing around me started to spin, pin pricks of lights so bright my eyes felt like they were on fire. It went faster and faster.

Then I saw it. The core. The very essence of the AI. I nudged the strings, isolating one of the pulsing arteries, following it like a thread in a maze through to its central nervous system and its cerebrum, seeing the pathways, clearing the way ahead of me with gentle touches here and there. I couldn't breathe but I forced myself to reach further, manipulating the code, subtly at first then more blatantly as I saw a way to reach the comm network.

I almost had it, it saw what I was doing, and it burned my fingers. I could almost feel its panic. It became a race. It was shutting me down as fast as I was busting a way through.

The heat and pain escalated.

I grabbed for the connection. Dizzy. Clumsy.

It stopped me and held me there, as if it had me round the throat.

Then the voice of the AI was a whisper in my ear. "Oh child, I wish you hadn't done that. How can I let you live now, knowing you can hurt me so easily, so heartlessly? Things could have been so different..."

The pressure peaked. I screamed. And a dense, black darkness washed over me, sucking me in and drowning me out.

I came round with a jolt, waking into a nightmare, standing outside in the open, in bright sunshine, eyes stinging from the acrid white smoke that was swirling all around me, shots ricocheting in every direction, shouts echoing. And a gun in my hand.

I staggered backwards. My upper arm was burning, heart thumping, head pounding. My finger was on the trigger. I sucked in a lungful of smoke and nearly choked. I turned, shying away, trying to shield my mouth. Someone screamed. Someone else crashed into me and I stumbled onto one knee. The shockwave of an explosion up ahead sent a blast of heat and a flurry of dust and debris into my face. I couldn't see, couldn't think, could hardly breathe. Someone grabbed my arm and pulled me, staggering, into a run. There were harsh, snapped shouts of, "Pull back. Get inside the Citadel. We've gotta get to the armoury. C'mon, pull back."

Whoever had hold of me didn't let go, hauling me along with them until we'd made it deep inside, running through dark corridors, footsteps echoing, and finally a blast door slamming shut behind us, closing out the noise and clamour.

Whoever it was that had hold of my arm spun me around and shoved me forward. I fell and tumbled, scrambling up onto my knees, chest heaving.

The AI had done something to me and I had no idea what. And my amazing memory? I can recall everything that's ever happened to me, in my whole life, in excruciatingly exact detail. That last session in that freaking pod wiped me out. I don't remember a thing.

"What the hell happened?" Hilyer was saying, calm and controlled, and in a way that made it worse than if he'd screamed it at me.

I still had hold of the gun. It felt really bad that I had a gun. I tossed it onto the floor in front of me, trembling, and looked up.

Hil was standing there wearing a military parade uniform, a gun in one hand, a baton in the other, and I realised it was Hil that had pulled me inside.

"What happened?" he said again.

"He's gone rogue." Jem shoved me from behind and went and stood next to Hilyer.

"It doesn't matter," Hil said. "We've got what we need. Secure him. Secure them both."

Someone caught hold of my arms and yanked me backwards, pulling tight and snapping cuffs around my wrists.

"This is bullshit," I said, struggling against them and

trying to twist around to see who else was there. "What the hell are you doing? What the hell are you all doing?"

It was some of the kids that had been selected from Redemption. All standing there, all holding guns, all in uniform, all watching me.

I was wearing the same uniform. The shirt was itchy as hell, buttoned up, too tight around the neck, sleeves too tight around the wrist. I'd never worn clothes that smart, that rigid. It might as well have been a straight jacket. I tried to see who was holding me and got a blow to the side of the head, so hard it made my vision blur.

"Put them in the storeroom," Hilyer ordered. "We need to reinforce our position."

I was twisted around.

"Wait." I tried to protest but just got another blow to the head that almost sent me to my knees.

They pushed me forward and shoved me into a dimly lit room not much bigger than a cupboard. I hit the floor and rolled, vaguely aware that they were throwing someone else in there with me. I rested my forehead on the cold ground as the door was slammed shut. My eyes were watering from the smoke and a warm trickle was dripping past my ear. I looked up. Into the scared face of a young kid. His Royal Imperial Majesty the Emperor Wu of Earth. Commander in Chief of the Imperial forces. Eight years old. And locked in a cupboard. With me.

27

I recognised him straight away. He was wearing the uniform of an Imperial Naval officer cadet similar to the ones we were wearing but with significantly more medals and decorations.

"You're bleeding," he said. He looked scared but he didn't sound it.

"Where are we?" I muttered.

"In the storeroom."

Apparently he was a comedian as well as Imperial royalty.

He reminded me of the middlings we used to have in our gang but there was something about the way he held himself, an aura of authority even though he was sitting on the floor with his hands bound behind his back.

I struggled to sit up, a headache banging behind my eyes. "Where are we?"

"How come you don't know where you are?"

I was probably that obnoxious when I was eight. I closed my eyes, trying to suck in a deep breath without coughing. "Can you just tell me where we are and what just happened?"

His reply was dry, dripping with statesmanly condescension. For an eight year old, he had presence.

"This is the Royal Ancients Military Academy," he said. He paused for effect. "And you just shot the admiral."

I didn't remember anything after the AI had threatened to kill me, inside that pod. My mouth was dry, lungs sore, heart in my stomach.

"Where is that?" I said. I'd never heard of it.

"The military academy? Caron Four."

I blinked open one eye and squinted at him. "A planet?"

The kid nodded, looking at me like he couldn't believe I was being so dim. I couldn't believe I was being so dim. It didn't matter how much I rattled around inside my head, I couldn't remember. I definitely didn't remember shooting anyone.

"I shot the admiral?"

He nodded again. "Don't worry, you didn't kill him."

That didn't make me feel better. "How long have we been here?"

He looked at me like he was going to say, 'In the storeroom?' again but thought better of it. "Term started last week," he said. "I've been here for three years. You've been here a week. Preparing for the celebration today. How come you don't remember?"

"A week?"

"We've been practising for the parade. There are cadets from military families and schools all over the Empire. It's the Veteran's Honour Parade, anniversary of the first battle of Hanover. How come you don't remember? Did you bang your head?"

"I don't know." I didn't mean to but I snapped it. My head was hurting. My arm was hurting. I was sitting in a damn cupboard. This kid was the target. He had to be. But if it was a straightforward assassination, he'd be dead already. I had no recall of our orders. Nothing. Nada. And I didn't understand what had knocked me out of the state of conditioning they'd dropped us into, out of whatever it was the AI had done to me.

"What are they going to do?" he asked. Calm as if we weren't discussing his fate.

"I don't know." I looked around. "But we need to get out of here." There were vents in the ceiling.

"You're bleeding," he said again.

"Thank you, I hadn't noticed," I said sarcastically. Then felt bad for saying it. It wasn't his fault we were in the storeroom. I leaned to the side, twisted my wrist and snapped my hands free, shrugging my arm round to take a look at the wound. I'd taken a hit that wasn't much worse than a graze but my sleeve was soaked red. I shrugged out of the tunic and tore off the shirt, glad to be rid of it, thankful I had a vest underneath, and more breathless than I should have been. I tore a strip off the shirt and wrapped it round the wound in my arm, pulling with my teeth to fasten it. Getting shot sucks. I was glad I couldn't remember it this time.

The kid was watching. I didn't know how to free his hands and he wouldn't get far as he was.

I sat back and looked at him. I knew they wouldn't leave us alone in there for long.

"Where are we?" I said. "Within the academy, where are we? Is there a comms centre?"

"In the admin block on the other side of the parade square. I can show you." What he meant was, 'Don't leave me here'.

I pushed to my feet and looked around the shelves, doubtful there'd be a knife in there or anything as useful but you never know. I started pulling boxes out, rummaging through drawers, half an eye on the door and half an ear on trying to hear anything out there.

There was nothing in there, nothing I could use. I turned back to the kid, the Emperor, the target of our damned mission, sitting there looking at me like I was going to make it all okay, and I didn't know what to say.

"Why are they doing this?" he asked in that insanely calm voice.

They. In his mind he'd obviously come to the conclusion that 'I' was not 'they' by virtue of the fact we were sharing the same cupboard. Which meant 'I' was now also 'us'. I had to admit he had more of a handle on things than I did right then.

"I don't know." I was thinking that I'd have to split, make a break for it, hope to get word out and get back before anyone realised I was gone. I looked back up at the vent. And froze as the door opened and Jem walked in.

She took two steps towards me. I backed off.

"What's going on?" I said.

"Hilyer wants to see you." She noted the discarded plasticuffs on the floor but made no comment.

There was no banter, no bad jokes, no smiles. It was like she'd never seen me before. She pushed me out ahead of her, towards two other kids who were cradling rifles.

They slammed the storeroom door shut once we were out. I heard the lock mechanism engage and they dropped into step behind us.

Walking through the dark corridors of the Citadel brought on an insane bout of déjà vu. It was similar enough to the construction of the base on Kheris that it felt like I'd been in there before but the memory of it was hazy, fogged, like I'd dreamed it. And it mingled with weird memories of a dank basement on Kheris when I'd been marched in to see Calum lording it over our little gang of kids after Maisie had left. For a fraction of a second, I wondered where they were and what they'd be doing. But it didn't matter anymore. Nothing mattered except getting back to the guild.

Jem took me into an office, past another two kids that were on guard. I should have been one of them, and I wasn't. There was a set of displays on one wall, flicking from one view to another, surveillance cameras, most of them showing the parade square, various views of the Citadel surrounded by what looked like an entire army, ground troops in powered armour, tanks, DZs, drop ships. It was hard to think all that was out there, while it was so quiet in here.

Hilyer was sitting on the edge of a massive ornate wooden desk, talking intently to three others. They didn't look happy and they looked even more unimpressed when we walked in.

Jem pushed me forward.

Hilyer glanced up, expression dark, muscle ticking in his jaw like he was about to lose his temper.

One of them started to argue.

"No," he snapped. "These are our orders now." He jumped off the desk. He wasn't tall but he was commanding. He had a gun in a holster on his thigh, another on his belt at his side. He rested his hand on the pistol grip. "Are you questioning me? Do I have to report your disobedience to the General?"

The kid that had opened his mouth to protest, clamped it shut and skulked past me, shoving me with his shoulder.

"Everyone, get out," Hilyer said. "You know what you have to do. Go do it. Or we're going to get overrun."

They all split, reluctantly, but they went.

The office we were in was wood panelled, plush carpet, more ostentatious than anywhere I'd seen on the Alsatia, a world apart from anything on Kheris.

Hilyer waited until we were alone then he stared at me. He looked furious, gun still held down by his thigh.

"Do you remember anything?" he said.

"About what? About why we're here? No, I don't. You want to tell me?"

He took a step towards me and I thought he was going to hit me for being such an ass, but he just stared at me. I half thought he was going to shoot me.

I squared up to him, standing my ground, heart

pounding, every muscle tensed, almost trembling, no idea what was going on, no idea what he was doing, or what I could do if he came at me.

But he just cursed and said quietly, intently, "We were sent to kill the Emperor. I don't know about you, but I have a problem killing eight year old kids, whoever they are."

I let out a breath I hadn't realised I was holding.

He gestured towards the wall of monitors. "We're surrounded. My unit is following my orders. For now at least. They've been programmed to kill the Emperor but they were also programmed to follow my command." He lowered his voice. "I've convinced them I've received new orders. I don't know how the hell this conditioning works but it's like they have to listen to me. Except what I'm saying conflicts with everything else and I think I'm frying their brains. There are three other units who, as far as I know, are still following the original brief."

My head was still hurting. "How come we broke their programming?"

"I don't know how the hell you did. I didn't." He turned to the monitor screens showing the outside. "We're fending off the others," he said quietly. "But I don't know how long we can keep them out. We're sealed inside the inner citadel. The other three units trying to whack the kid are in the outer citadel which they've sealed off from the outside. The garrison and security forces are holding off because they're terrified if they come storming in, the Emperor will be killed. We need to move. I really don't know how long I can keep these kids believing we have new orders."

"What do you mean, you didn't?"

A sharp trill from the desk made us spin around. There was an intercom on there. Old tech, landline style. The kind places have when atmospheric conditions can throw out normal comms.

We stared at it.

Hil reacted first. He got to it, looked back at me with his hand hovering over it and pressed the button.

There was a pause, then a woman's voice said, "Cadet Hilyer…"

It was her.

I could feel my heart thumping with a dull beat that was pounding down into my stomach.

Arianne was here.

"Zachary," she said, her voice coming through calm and clear, "I want you to listen to me and do exactly as I say. Whatever misunderstanding has caused this behaviour, we can sort it out if you surrender yourself and your unit now."

I shivered. A tiny part of me could very easily have believed it had all been a mistake.

But Hil looked up at me and froze.

The implant in my neck engaged with its weird sensation of connection.

She was speaking to him direct and he'd included me in the loop. I had no idea how to do any of that stuff but he did and he raised his finger to his lips as he looked at me.

"…code seven zulu niner acturon. Do you understand?"

I heard him say, seemingly inside my mind, "Yes, ma'am."

He was shaking his head at me.

"I repeat," Arianne sent through the implant, "original target Wu is to be eliminated. Acknowledge."

"Yes, ma'am."

"And new target Anderton is to be eliminated. Acknowledge."

"Yes, ma'am."

She switched back to the intercom, as if she'd just been letting her previous words hang there to sink in, and added more persuasively, "Come on now, Zach, you are one of our best students. This can be sorted out easily, if you all come out now. But let me be clear…" Her voice got an edge to it. "If we have to come in there to get you, this will not end well. You…"

He hit the button and cut both connections.

The way he was staring at me, I didn't know if maybe his programming had kicked in after all. I was still half expecting him to pull his gun and shoot me on the spot.

But he just said, "Why? Why do they want you dead? Why, after all this, all of a sudden, do they want you dead?"

I flashed back to Kheris, the IDC guy picking up his access key from the dirt and saying, "Bad mistake, kid…"

"The officer in charge of Spearhead, this whole operation," I forced myself to say, struggling with anything more than a whisper.

"You mean General McIntyre? Thin guy, black hair, face like a vulture that's eyeing you up as its next meal?"

"Yeah, that sounds like him,'" I said. "He's Imperial Diplomatic Corps, or at least he was masquerading as IDC when I met him. He runs an unsanctioned black ops ledger with contacts at military bases and corporations both sides of the line… money laundering, weapons deals, enforced draft arrangements, black market drugs supplies…"

Hil was looking at me, eyes narrow, like he couldn't believe what he was hearing. "And apparently turning kids into assassins…"

"I've seen his ledger," I said, nausea pulling at my stomach. "I know every line of it."

28

I didn't want to talk about it, I didn't want to think about it.

But Hil cursed and said, "Why now?"

I sucked in a deep breath that made me shiver. "They didn't know it was me. Brennan figured out where I was from. She said she was going to report it."

To give him credit, he didn't ask where I was from or how the hell I knew about the ledger.

He glanced at the monitors and the growing force of military might amassing outside, and looked back at me. "We need to go. Can you fly a drop ship?"

I nodded.

He gave a harsh laugh. "Shit, I was joking. Are you serious?"

I don't know how I was looking at him but he cursed again and said, "Don't look at me like that. For crying out loud, LC, I was wrong. You were right. I was wrong. Okay?"

He took hold of my arm and tied the rag tighter.

I almost cried out, flinching away, biting my lip. He ignored me and pulled the knot tight.

"We should be able to access the academy AI from here," he said. "Can you operate a drop ship by remote, send new orders to one of the crews or something? Get it to land on the roof?"

I nodded, dread clutching at my stomach, but I nodded. "Do it. Do it now."

I had to force myself to move, to go and sit at the desk and stare at the terminal there. I started using the implant without even realising I was. It was easy to hack past the first few defences longhand, like I always used to. I had to wing it as I went, not wasting any time with finesse and running full tilt into the Academy's AI.

I nudged around it, fooled it by rearranging all the pathways and crossed data lines as subtly as if I was just refining the logics. It was good but it was nothing like Spearhead. On Kheris, I fried the AI by hacking at its cooling system until it exploded. After the guild showed me how, I could mess with an AI of this level like I was doodling inside its brain with a needle-sharp soldering iron.

I sidestepped my way through, accessed the logistics centre and interrupted the orders for all the drop ships, finding one that was parked up in a maintenance hangar and flagged for repairs but still operable. I made it easy, jumping onto comms that were already in place, and set up modifiers that would scramble the source of the changes. I threw in a lot of smoke and mirrors, and got caught up watching what they were doing, trying to backtrack my way through to Spearhead. I wanted to find it in there, wanted to confront it again. It didn't register what the muted popping sounds were until someone grabbed my arm and yanked me out of the system. I almost yelled, disorientated and dizzy from losing the connection so fast, and dropping back into a reality echoing with gunfire.

Hilyer pulled me down behind the desk and popped off a couple more shots, hissing, "Go," and pushing me out.

There were three kids lying on the floor, guns by their hands, one with a knife, sprawled, out cold but breathing. I couldn't help staring as Hil dragged me past. They weren't just trying to kill the Emperor anymore. They'd come in here to kill me.

We stopped at the door and listened.

Hil pulled me close and hissed, "Does Mendhel know?"

"Know what?"

"About the ledger?"

I shook my head.

"Tell him," he said. "When you get back, you have to tell him."

"When we get back."

Hil gave me a weird look and pushed a gun into my hand.

"When we get back," I said again.

"Don't."

He listened at the door.

I felt cold, like we were about to jump off a cliff edge. "Hil, you have to come back with me."

"No, I don't. I'm not going back. Now shut the hell up and help me get this kid out of here alive."

There was shouting behind the door, still some distance

off. It wouldn't matter where Hil wanted to go if we didn't get out of there. I switched into automatic, checking the mechanism on the gun, checking the magazine and seeing those orange tags that indicated FTH, stun rounds. It was like the CQB. Except the other kids were using live ammunition. And if we didn't make it, there'd be no rerun, no second chance to get it right.

Hil put his gun hand next to the door panel and held up his other hand, three fingers, then two then one. I nodded. He pressed the button. The door opened and we both moved, firing and running into cover as shots ricocheted around us.

It was two of our own unit out there. They fell as our shots hit home.

"Go get to the roof," Hil shouted. "I'll get the kid, you get that drop ship ready."

I nodded and ran.

The weird thing about doing stuff for real that you've trained for is that you expect it to be different and it isn't. You expect the nerves to be worse, the jitters to be higher. But when you're in the middle of it, it doesn't matter if it's a sim or for real, you just do it. I didn't have many rounds left in the gun so I knew I couldn't shoot my way out if I got cornered. So I did what I do best and avoided everyone, the rest of our unit, the other kids from other units who were gathering and moving in, the troops in battle armour who were shoving them aside and blustering in to rescue their Emperor.

I was running blind, no intel, no idea where I was going or what security they had. All the sensors I saw were dead, all the patrol drones inert on the floor. I had a bad feeling that could have been my handiwork. I must have neutralised the whole base.

I still didn't make it to the roof.

It was Kat that cornered me. I had the drop on her, gun up and finger on the trigger when she appeared, but I couldn't do it, not with the way she was looking at me, standing there with her hands up, taking one slow step after the other towards me.

"Luka," she called, her voice soft and almost pleading, "I need you to listen to me."

I shook my head, keeping the gun up. "I know you're working for them."

She looked dismayed. "Come on, Luka, you're bleeding. Let me look at your arm."

I know I'm a sucker sometimes but I'm not that stupid.

"Don't be stupid," she said. "It's not what you think."

I didn't know what to think.

"You set me up," I said quietly. "You gave me that pass to set me up."

She screwed up her face. "I had no choice. I didn't want to, believe me. I want out, Luka. I want to come with you."

There wasn't much room to manoeuvre and I could hear people behind me, more behind her, some distance away but moving in.

"C'mon, Luka," she said. "I need you to trust me."

That made it easy. I shook my head again. "I don't trust anyone who tells me to trust them."

She took another step forward. "They want you dead."

"I know." I stepped backwards, keeping the gun up and aimed at her.

"You're not going to shoot me," she said, "and I'm not going to let them kill you."

Another step.

The voices behind her were getting closer.

"I swear I didn't know what the mission was. And I didn't know what they were going to do to you. I had no choice. Luka, I'm done. I want out."

There was something about the look in her eye. Apparently I am that stupid.

I grabbed her hand and ran, pulling her away with me, and disappearing into the depths of the Citadel.

We didn't stop until we couldn't hear anyone anymore, then I pulled her into a dark alcove and pressed my finger to her lips.

She reached, moved my hand, and had her arms around my neck, gentle, pulling me into an embrace before I could react.

Her lips were so soft I felt like I was melting.

I closed my eyes. I wanted her to be Maisie. I wanted to be back on Kheris and I wanted everything to be okay. I could almost smell the shampoo Maisie had always used. Except it wasn't Maisie, it was Kat.

A shiver ran down my spine.

I pulled back and said quietly, "You told Brennan about the snow. How I'd never seen snow. You were working me the whole time."

Even in the low light I could see her expression flash with frustration. "I didn't want to," she said. "You don't know what it was like. You don't know why I had no choice."

"Tell me."

"You really want to know?"

I didn't. I didn't want to care but I nodded.

She leaned in and whispered into my ear. "I was on death row. Fourteen years old and nothing ahead of me but a death sentence. They offered me a deal. Hate me if you want but I never meant to hurt you." She stopped, pulled back and looked at me. "And believe me, I don't fall lightly. For anyone. But then I've never met anyone like you. I should hate you for doing this to me."

I was kissing her again before I realised I was. To shut her up, I told myself.

We froze as the giveaway hum of powered armour sounded down the corridor.

"I know a way out," she said. "Where's the Emperor?"

I bit my tongue to stop what I was about to say. "In the armoury," I said instead.

She touched her hand to my cheek in a soft caress. "We need to go."

We waited until it was quiet then ran out and through dark corridors. They must have cut the power, only emergency lighting illuminating the way, giving that weird red cast to everything. Her blue hair looked purple. She kept tight hold of my hand as if I was her lifeline. We saw the bouncing beams of flashlights every now and then, avoiding them and circling round. It was close a few times, then we ran towards a set of blast doors that slammed shut ahead of us.

I stopped, heart pounding, glancing back over, expecting to hear powered armour, the clatter of grenades skittering across the floor. My chest constricted, ears ringing.

I don't know when she'd let go of my hand, but I sensed she wasn't there and turned.

She was backing away from me. "I meant it," she called out cheerfully. "Every word. But I can't afford to fall for you, Luka. Not when you're about to die." She stopped and shouted, "He's right here."

Arianne stepped out of the shadows next to her.

"Well done, Katarina," the older woman said, curt, like she was used to having her orders obeyed. "Drop the gun, Anderton."

I stood there, sideways on to them, trying to figure out if I could raise it and shoot them both before she could shoot me. The blast door was still closed behind me. There was no other way out.

Arianne walked forward. "Don't be stupid, Anderton. Now are you going to tell me where the Emperor really is?"

I couldn't see any way out. I stared at her, seeing in her the woman in Mendhel's file, the picture of them both together with their little girl. It was definitely her. All I could think about was Mendhel's face as he was told she'd been killed.

Her expression changed, as if she'd suddenly become immensely curious about this stupid kid in front of her.

"Who are you working for?" she said, a frown creasing those familiar features.

"I'm not working for anyone," I said but I might as well have blurted out my whole life story.

"Who taught you to manipulate an AI like that? Where did you learn…?" She paused, then she said it, so abruptly I couldn't not react. "The Maze. You're from Kheris? Holy shit, you're Charlie Anderton's kid."

I blinked, shutting down every emotional response that surfaced but it was too late.

"You're Thieves' Guild," she breathed and her arm snapped up, pointing a gun right between my eyes.

29

"Drop the gun," she said again.

I let it fall from fingers that were numb anyway.

Kat was watching from further down the corridor, tying her fingers in knots, excited, like she wanted to watch Arianne pull the trigger. I've never been so badly wrong about someone. Kat was my first big mistake. Like I'd finally made it into the big bad world and that's what had been waiting to pounce the whole time.

I looked at Arianne. "Why did you kill Markus?"

If she'd needed proof, that was it but she was going to kill me anyway so what did it matter?

She narrowed her eyes. "Was it Mendhel Halligan that sent you?"

There was an edge to her voice that sent ice into my veins. Just hearing her say his name.

I stood my ground, asking obnoxiously, "Why are you doing this?" I wanted to know for Mendhel, even though I'd never be able to tell him. I wanted her to tell Kat to scram and turn to me to explain that she was undercover, that Markus wasn't dead, that it was all part of a game they were playing to infiltrate Spearhead.

She didn't.

I think she was talking to someone else, or listening,

because she nodded vaguely, the same way I'd seen Mendhel react outside the briefing room.

She blinked slowly, looked me in the eye and said, "Time's up, kid."

It wasn't the first time someone had pointed a gun at me and pulled the trigger and it wouldn't be the last.

Kat screamed like a harpy and for a flash, I thought she was protecting me, but she flew at a figure in the shadows.

There was sharp double pop.

My heart jumped, the shot fired at me whistling past my ear as I flinched away, and Arianne twisting and falling as she caught the edge of the charge fired at her, dropping the gun but rolling to her feet.

Then, rather than time slowing, it seemed to accelerate, so fast I could hardly see what was happening.

Hilyer dragged Kat around and threw her at me, running fast to kick the gun away from Arianne and stand between us.

Kat rolled and came to her feet, fighting stance, facing me. Despite everything, I didn't want to hit her but she didn't give me any choice, coming at me hard and laughing while she did it. I ducked and tried to catch her in a hold, seeing Hilyer and Arianne trading blows and kicks out of the corner of my eye, Hil struggling to hold his own for once.

Kat jabbed me in the ribs, twisted and grabbed my arm, right where it had been shot, squeezing tight, pain going skyhigh as she increased the pressure.

I almost folded.

She pulled me close. "We could've been something, Luka," she breathed. "You and me. So you're Thieves' Guild? I didn't think that outfit even really existed. Shame my boss needs you dead." She thrust her elbow into my face with a sharp crack, shoved me away as my knees went to jelly and dived for the gun.

I hit the floor and sprawled.

Arianne spun and kicked Hilyer in the head.

He staggered.

Kat picked up the gun and aimed it at me with a grin.

Hil was looking at me, swaying, blood pouring from his nose, nothing he could do as Arianne was standing in his way.

A deafening shot resounded in the narrow space.

I blinked, flinching, almost feeling the bullet punch into my chest, but it was Kat who wavered, red spraying out from her shirt. She gasped and fell, the gun clattering to the floor.

I couldn't move, frozen to the spot like an idiot, Arianne turning to look, Hilyer going for his gun, sliding and shooting in one smooth motion. That time it was a pop and the older woman jerked as the FTH round took her in the head and she fell, out cold before she hit the ground.

The Emperor was standing in the shadows, still holding the gun, expression blank.

Kat wasn't moving and I could tell from the way she was staring, a strand of blue hair falling across her face, that she was dead.

Hil gave me a hand to get up. "We need to go," he said. "If we don't get out now, we won't. They're locking the whole place down."

I couldn't drag my eyes away from Kat and the blood spreading across her shirt, pooling out beneath her.

"I've never killed anyone before," the kid murmured.

Hil took his arm, turning him away, taking the gun out of his hand.

"I've given orders that have sent thousands to their deaths," the kid said, sounding more like a lost child talking about a game he'd played than the Emperor.

I was still staring at her, a hollow chill deep inside that felt like it would never lift.

The Emperor looked back at me and said again, "I've never killed anyone."

"First time for everything," Hil said harshly. "Now, c'mon. Or it'll be the last."

He took us up two flights of stairs, bust through a locked door, sealed it behind us and led us into a narrow walkway that led to some kind of equipment store. He stopped by an open area that was packed with workbenches, automated machinery mixed with a pile of gizmos and what looked like surveillance equipment. There was a bunch of medical supplies on the table where he stopped. He told the Emperor to sit and wait then looked at me weird, pulled out a chair and said, "Sit down."

"Why?"

He started rooting through the kit on the bench,

separating out field dressings and sprays, turning to me with a knife in his hand.

"They must be tracking us." He pointed the knife at me. "We need to get that implant out of your neck or we don't have a chance. You don't wanna come with us, fine. You do, you let me get that implant out. But you decide now. We don't have time to screw around."

He had a makeshift dressing on his neck, below his right ear.

I sat.

He injected me with something, took hold of my ear with one hand, and told me to count to three. I got to two and the bastard stabbed me in the neck.

The excruciating pain as he sliced into my skin was bad enough. It escalated beyond unbearable and as he pulled on the implant, it spiked, like he was pulling my brain out with burning hot tweezers. I held on for half a second, breath caught in my chest, a scream caught in my throat, then I lost it, tried to pull away and I think he hit me. I don't remember but when I came round, we'd moved, there was no sign of the kid and Hilyer was sitting on the floor next to me, legs stretched out, chest heaving, reloading his gun, and watching a data board resting between us that had a live feed from multiple cameras showing armoured troops sweeping through dark corridors.

Someone had obviously decided that waiting us out was not an option.

"Yeah," he said without looking at me, "we're screwed."

I reached a hand to my neck and felt a dressing. It hurt beyond sore. My eyes were burning.

"I think you pulled out half my brain," I muttered, blinking.

"Yeah, you wouldn't miss it." He nudged the board round so I could see it better. "And no, I didn't. I just cut out the Senson comms implant. The neural link is still there. Christ, I wouldn't mess with that."

"So I can still use it?" I tried to see if I could feel it inside my head but even trying to think about it made me feel sick.

"I wouldn't. It's the Senson that provides all the protections."

That didn't make me feel good.

"Where's the Emperor?" I asked, sitting up and having to steady myself against a swirl of dizzying nausea.

"We ran into some trouble. I've got him stashed somewhere safe. He's waiting for us. I couldn't carry you both." He didn't sound impressed but he threw a half smile at me. "You still gonna be able to fly that drop ship?"

I might have laughed but I said, "Yes."

He did laugh. He slammed the magazine home, grabbed the board and got to his feet, reaching down to give me a hand to get up.

I swayed.

"For crying out loud, don't flake out again. You're bloody heavy."

We made it up two more floors, slinking through the corridors and having to climb up into the dusty crawlspaces to get away whenever they got close. It was an old building, majestic, high ceilings between floors, rusting from the inside out, but otherwise well maintained.

The Emperor was waiting for us in another maintenance area, one floor down from the roof. The kid had set up a nest of monitors and boards, sitting under a table in the corner, only the faint light giving away the fact he was there. He didn't look like the Commander in Chief of the entire Earth Empire. He looked like the kind of kid Peanut would have brought home to join the gang.

He looked up and out from his den as we approached. The whole front of his shirt was drenched with blood but he didn't look in discomfort.

It made me feel queasy but I must have looked concerned because he smiled and patted his chest.

"Trauma patch," he said softly. "One of our best inventions."

He was way older than eight.

"We still need to get you out of here," Hil said, crouching down. "How's it looking?"

"Not good. Someone seems to have convinced everyone that I'm dead already so they're storming the Citadel." The kid scrolled through a few screens. "I'm trying to find the Commandant and his staff but I'm having trouble isolating my people from yours." He looked up. "Sorry. No offence."

"None taken. LC? Can you do your stuff?"

I didn't exactly know what 'my stuff' was, but I climbed in beside the kid and took up a couple of the boards.

"They might not be tracking us," I muttered, starting to work through the screens, "but they'll be monitoring lifesigns."

I found a way in to the AI and sent it a curveball, scrambling all the telemetry it was receiving. It was messy and it would right itself fast enough but it would give us a bit of time. After that, I started working through the comms, tracking command lines, seeing if I could isolate the Ancients staff and personnel from the visitors or any newcomers, double checking security clearances and IDs, and narrowing down the search criteria until I had clear, defined tags on each unit.

And then I saw him.

I froze, stomach cold.

Hil was rooting through stuff on the workbench. He glanced over. "What's wrong? C'mon, we don't have long. Have you found the Commandant?"

"No," I said at the same time as the kid Emperor said, "Yes."

The cold knot clenched like my soul was being sucked out into space.

The kid looked at me puzzled. "He's our new Commandant."

Hil cursed. "Shit, don't tell me…" He leaned over to take a look and cursed.

I nodded. "That's him. The IDC guy. Your General McIntyre. We don't have a way out. There is no way out."

I felt like the galaxy had spun on its axis.

The Emperor took the board off me and peered at it. "I don't understand. He's our new Commandant. We're welcoming him at the celebration parade."

I wanted to sink into the ground. I wasn't wrong and I wasn't going to doubt myself. It was his access key that had triggered the whole mess on Kheris. His dirty dealings with Dayton. Whatever was going on, I'd known all along that it was bigger than one dirtball mining colony. How big, I'd had no idea.

I couldn't see how we were going to get out. Running to the Emperor's people was an absolute no go. We had no idea who was Spearhead and who was loyal.

"I can vouch for you," he said, and then he did sound like a naïve eight year old kid.

Hil cursed again. "Won't work. Your Commandant is a traitor, kid. He's working for Spearhead. That's why you can't separate out your people from theirs. They'll make it look like we killed you. Or you'll get caught in the crossfire. We need to get past everyone, make a break for it, get away on our own."

"And go where?" I looked across at him. I didn't need to say it.

He glared at me. "No." He was adamant. "You can. You take him. I'm not going back. Did you get a drop ship to land on the roof?"

"Yes," I said, "but I don't know how we'll get to it."

Hil stood up. "We'll have to find a way. Because I'll be damned if we're going to die here."

We split, squeezing into the crawlspaces and starting to work our way upwards.

"Go back where?" the kid asked me after a while, looking back over his shoulder. "What did your friend mean when he said he's not going back."

He had a right to ask, and after all it was him they were trying to kill. And he was the Emperor. In theory he could order us to tell him whatever he wanted, but I said, "It doesn't matter," as I edged past him, tapped at Hil's ankle and whispered, "Wait up."

Hil squirmed round to look back. "What?"

"Doesn't feel right. We need to double back."

"Doesn't feel right? What the hell doesn't feel right?"

"It doesn't feel right."

I couldn't explain. I could never explain to anyone how I did what I did when I was out in the field. The guild psychs used to tie themselves in knots trying to figure me out. There were times when I just knew stuff. Instinct, intuition, empathy, luck, I have no idea. I didn't care. But I never questioned it.

Hil made an exasperated face but he didn't argue. "Which way?"

"Down and round."

We had to scurry like rats to avoid the patrols sweeping through the Citadel. We almost got caught but I grabbed the Emperor by the scruff of the neck and hauled him aside as flashlight beams scanned around us and soldiers passed by close enough we could hear them breathing.

Hil pulled me close and hissed into my ear, "We're not gonna make it."

I hated to admit it but he was right. "We need to find an access terminal," I whispered. "I've got an idea."

We climbed into a maintenance vent and crawled through to a bay that had a stack of boards. I grabbed one and pulled it back into the crawlspace. I didn't have time to do anything spectacular but I got through to the security system, accessed the patrol bots and reversed the dampeners on them, only I didn't just send them back to work, I initiated an exercise protocol that sent them out transmitting lifesigns, hunting each other and causing a flare of activity on any sensors they were using, powerful enough to fry the circuits of a suit of powered armour.

It caused chaos.

We made a run for the roof, made it up into a maintenance area and we would have made it out except someone else was smart enough to figure out what we were doing.

Jem.

She stepped out of the shadows, rifle up, and she fired off three fast bursts before we could react.

30

The bullets raked into the knotwork of pipes above our heads, ricocheting with an echoing clang, steam hissing. She stepped forward, still aiming the rifle at us.

Hil put himself in front of the kid, one hand in the air, the other behind his back holding the gun. I didn't have a weapon, not even anything to hand that I could have thrown at her.

"Jem…" Hil said.

"Stand aside, Hilyer." She glanced at me, cold.

I stepped slightly away from them, opening up the angle, and forward, towards her. Her eyes darted from me to Hil.

"Jem," I said, wanting her attention, "it's us. C'mon, you're not going to hurt us. You know us. We've been used. We've all been used. You don't need to do this."

I took another step forward.

"Get back, Anderton. We have orders."

Another step.

She switched her aim to me.

I felt more than saw Hilyer move to bring up his gun, saw the flicker in her eyes and had to dive to the side as she opened up. Hil returned fire and the small space filled with deafening noise.

Something hot grazed my shoulder as I fell. I covered my head, curled up and rolled, looking up to see Hil kneeling by Jem, feeling the pulse on her neck, and the Emperor standing over us both, holding the rifle and staring behind us. It was bad enough to be a fourteen year old runaway and having people want to kill you. I couldn't imagine being eight, being the Emperor and suddenly having a target on your back.

"They're coming," he said, quiet and calm.

Clangs and bangs were echoing up to us, shouts and footsteps getting closer.

I said, "Hil...?" feeling awkward as hell, knowing exactly what he was thinking. He didn't want to leave her. I'd never seen him look so torn. "Bring her with us."

He looked up at me and glanced back over.

I nodded.

We both reached for her.

There was a metallic clatter.

And a shower of tiny silver spheres rained down around us.

It was one of those moments that turned to slow motion.

Hil turned to me, desperation in his eyes, cursing, grabbing my arm, and lurching forward to grab the Emperor and drag us both into a run.

I kicked two of the grenades away, no idea how long the delay on them was, but there were too many, more rolling in, one hitting my back.

If we got caught in a stun blast, it was all over.

Hil yelled, "Don't stop," pulling us out towards a gantry.

There were shouts from across the open area ahead of us, glints off powered armour, shots starting to ping around us.

I could see others closing in from both sides, nothing ahead of us but thin air.

Hil didn't stop and didn't let go of us.

We ran, all of us ducking and flinching as shots came close, reaching the edge of the metalmesh walkway and jumping as the stun grenades detonated behind us with a flash.

It could have been a two foot drop, it could have been fifty. It was probably about ten.

But I landed badly, rolled, couldn't stop myself and rolled off another gantry.

I don't know how long I was out but it must have just been seconds. I blinked, head foggy, with Hil and the kid Emperor leaning over me. It was quiet. They pulled me up and back into the shadows under the walkway.

"You okay?" Hil whispered.

I nodded, trying to figure out where we were, head pounding. I wiped my hand across my forehead, smearing it with red, and gestured off into the darkness. "We need to go that way."

"How the hell do you know that?"

"I saw the plans for the whole building when I was in the system."

He looked at me funny but didn't argue. "Come on.

Give us a hand. Wu has bust his ankle but we don't think it's broken."

Wu? First name terms?

The kid smiled at me and mouthed silently, "I'm fine."

I think even if it had been broken, he wouldn't have complained.

We crept through the maintenance area, working our way round as quiet as mice and finally bumped up against the ladder.

"This is it," I whispered.

Hil hissed into my ear, "Get up there and check it's clear. Is there any chance the drop ship could be there?"

"I don't know." I pulled my vest up and wiped away the blood that was trickling into my eye. "They'll have overridden the commands if they've seen it."

"Go find out. Don't be long." He bundled Wu into cover, taking aim back the way we'd come and said, "Go."

I could hear the roar of gunships circling before I reached the top. I climbed out into bright, chilly sunshine and dropped down onto a stone battlement, huge pipes and machinery crowding the open space, and right next to where I tumbled out on the cold stone, the unmistakeable mass of a defensive weapons platform. I scrambled into its shade for cover and nestled in close. It was cold. It was weird to be so close to one that was inactive, like it was dead and had been for centuries.

There was a drop ship out on the landing circle in the flat centre of the roof. I had no way of knowing if it was the one I'd sent for or one full of troops. I watched as long as I dared then made a break for it. The ramp was down. I didn't think, didn't stop, could have been running towards a whole squad of soldiers for all I knew, made it inside and skidded to a halt. It was empty. I ran through to the cockpit. Empty.

The start up sequence was exactly as I expected. I ran through it fast and hit the ignition. Huge thrusters fired up as I ran back out onto the ramp, keeping in the cover of the bulkhead and peering back across the roof.

Hil was next to the weapons platform. He waved as he saw me, disappeared for a moment and reappeared with the kid.

Wu was limping badly, Hil holding him up, both of them stumbling. They made it halfway across when a gunship started to bank round.

I yelled.

Hil was shouting. The engines of the drop ship were loud, rumbles reverberating through the bulkhead, the noise and heat drowning out the sound of the gunship approaching from above.

I ran out of cover, keeping low, headache punching hammers into my skull with each step, and ran to intercept them, hooking the Emperor's arm over my shoulder and turning to run back. The gunship had its weapons turrets spinning round to target us as it dropped.

There was a shout from the far side of the roof, figures emerging, soldiers in powered armour and uniforms. I could see Arianne in amongst them, striding towards us, the Spearhead guy masquerading as the new Commandant barking orders and pointing.

Wu was struggling. "Leave me," he gasped.

Hil upped the pace. "No way."

"They won't kill me," the kid insisted. "You get away."

Another gunship had joined in, hovering on the other side of us as we staggered towards that open ramp. They weren't shooting at us, probably too public, too many people watching for them to risk it.

The kid stumbled. I blinked and was on one knee before I knew it.

Other soldiers were spilling out from the opposite side.

"LC," Hil yelled. "I wanna see you fly this damned ship. I wanna beat you to the top of NG's standings board."

"No way," I muttered and pushed to my feet, dragging Wu up and forward, glancing over my shoulder at Arianne and the Commandant.

Another drop ship descended between us, the heat of its exhaust billowing over us. I saw her run towards it. The Commandant was still shouting out orders.

We made it to our ramp and inside. I dropped the kid and stumbled forward, leaving Hil to punch the ramp button. I fell into the pilot's seat and strapped in with trembling fingers, breathing too fast, the adrenaline rush making my heart feel like it was going to punch out of my chest.

I'd read manuals, played sims, sat on cushions on the burned out cockpit of a crashed shuttle pretending I could fly it. I'd never been this close to the cockpit of a real ship. The controls in front of me were all lit up, monitors scrolling data, VHUD active and the massive engines trembling beneath me.

Hilyer yelled that they were in.

I placed my left hand on the control panel, initiated the main board with my right, feeling it respond with a buzz that was like nothing I'd ever done, and took off. The ramp was still closing, the other drop ship rising at the same time as we did, both gunships circling and backing off as we flew up. Every alarm started screaming on the console, warnings coming in, demanding that we land. I couldn't believe I was doing it. I couldn't believe we were going to get away with it. I had no plan other than make orbit and see what happened.

We cleared the roof and dropped, flying lower and faster than I meant to over the parade ground, every twitch of the controls making it slew sideways.

It was insane. More markers were appearing on the monitors as more gunships took off to intercept us. I increased speed and banked hard. It was like playing a game. To be fair, even without an autonomous AI on board, a lot of the flight systems were pretty much automated.

Then a red light flashed. A klaxon started to scream collision warning.

And an automated voice that was way too calm stated slowly and clearly that multiple missiles were locked and on target.

I yelled out a warning, hit counter measures and pulled up as fast as I could without losing it. I spun round and threw us into a spiral.

Then I did something I still wish I hadn't.

Imperial ships are all fitted with a neural interface. They're pretty much useless these days with all pilots being fitted with a Senson implant but the military like their back up systems on their back up systems no matter how archaic they might seem.

I tore open the access panel where the blueprints said the redundant cabling should be and ripped out the interface at the same time as I tore the bloody patch off my neck where Hil had cut out the Senson, exposing the raw connection of the neural link. I had no idea what would happen. I knew that without a Senson to filter the traffic, the human brain couldn't cope with the data load but I couldn't see any other option.

As the connection was made, there was a painfully blinding flash that felt like it seared along my optic nerve and a high pitched static squeal that I heard but not through my ears.

For a second, I was blind and deaf.

I think I screamed.

And then I was in.

Through the filtering of the Senson, the unreal universe of the AI mind was like a tranquil pond with logic strings gently swimming in data currents. Without the filter, it was chaos. A maelstrom of data that swirled with an unprecedented violence. Black holes and supernovas smashing into each other. If you've never experienced it, trust me, you never want to. It's as close to what I imagine Hell is like as I ever want to get.

But through it all, I could see patterns in the chaos. I could make sense of the swirling vortex of raw data. I could see and isolate exactly what I was looking for. I could see the comms playing out on the screens, every unit, every vehicle, every gunship, every soldier in their suits of part-sentient powered armour, clearly identified, see all the others talking to each other, all the IDs registered in the automatic identification system except ours. I tore through the base AI, and hacked into the intelligence controlling every unit out there, all the comms, all the orders, all the identification tags. I activated the base defence grid and fed it a single ID as friendly. Ours. And then I scrambled all the others.

It was intoxicating. I wanted to stay. I wanted to go deeper, find an outside comms link, see where their orders were coming from, find out why they were shooting at us when they must have known their Emperor was on board. And I got really close, so close it was excruciating, but I was thrown out, tossed with a sickening lurch back into a reality that was spinning out of control.

I pulled the cable out, with a nauseating stench of burnt flesh. I reckoned I was going to pay for that later, but right then there was too much adrenaline pumping round my system for me to feel much pain.

I pulled up on the controls, flying purely on instinct.

A missile skimmed across our hull and veered away, retargeting and flying straight into the drop ship pursuing us.

It exploded in a flare of light.

I froze.

That was the drop ship I'd seen Arianne running to.

I could hardly breathe. It wasn't a game anymore. Debris hit our hull. I flinched, levelled out and banked hard.

The comms were in chaos.

Another missile flew right past our nose, locking onto a gunship and chasing it round until the crew shot it down.

I didn't know what to do except fly as hard and fast as I could to get out of there. Another gunship locked onto us, launching a missile just as the base's defensive laser batteries sliced through it.

I put the ship in a dive, twisting violently, trying to shake the missile, our counter measures used up and had no other option than to throw the ship into a combat drop.

The G-forces were unbelievable. I felt like I was being turned inside out, my stomach in my throat, my eyes burning, unbearable pressure in my ears and a weight pushing against my chest. I think I yelled all the way down. There's nothing you can do to control the ship once you initiate that drop, short of hitting the abort and coercing the entire system back into manual control. In time. Before you hit the ground. I've seen pilots that can do it. Guild pilots are awesome. But I was fourteen, flying by hearsay and guesswork based on hours of reading manuals and playing sims, and honestly, I was so close to blacking out I could hardly see.

I was only half aware of our altitude, could do nothing as the missile took out one of our wings, and I squeezed my eyes shut as we slewed to a gravity-defying landing.

My chest felt like I'd been hit by a truck, my eyes like they'd been stuck with red hot pins. My nose was dripping red onto my lap.

I sat there, not sure if I could move, a deafening ringing bouncing between my ears.

Hil squeezed my shoulder and I almost jumped out of my skin.

"The ship's on fire," he said. "We need to go."

31

"Remind me to never fly with you again," he muttered as we struggled down the ramp, carrying the kid between us. Wu had passed out, his chest wound bleeding again. I can remember thinking how ironic it would be if he croaked it, after all that.

The roar of the fire encouraged us into a staggering run to get clear. We almost didn't. The drop ship blew sky-high and threw us off our feet. Once the ringing in my ears had eased, I crawled onto my knees and stood, looking back at it then looking around to see where the hell we were.

It looked like a shooting range, open ground all round. There was a low concrete building by a line of firing positions.

Hil was checking the kid over. "Let's get in there," he shouted, nodding towards the hut. "See if we can find comms."

There was but it was all dead, like they'd shut down all uncontrolled comms. There was no access to anything, no chance of getting anywhere near the Academy's AI or any kind of external communications. I made a half-assed attempt to connect but my head was fried. The adrenaline high was wearing off and things were starting to hurt. I rifled through the inert boards and terminals, tapping at screens, desperately hoping one would spring to life but there was nothing.

Hil was standing to the side of the window, peering out. We'd set the kid down on the floor, changed the dressing on his chest with stuff we scrounged from a medical kit that was in there and made him as comfortable as we could. He'd live or he wouldn't. If I'd known for sure they were his people out there, we'd have given ourselves up. But they'd fired missiles at us. At him. Wherever the legit Imperial military was, it wasn't in charge here anymore.

Hil turned around. "We've got incoming."

I went and watched with him as they surrounded us, but out at a distance, like they were waiting for someone or something to happen, just wanting to make sure we couldn't leave.

After a while, Hil cursed softly, went and raided a fridge that was humming away in a corner and came back with a couple of sodas. Then we stood there together, watching, as they closed in and set up a perimeter.

"Well, this sucks," he said, raising the bottle and downing a mouthful.

I lifted mine to my lips again. "Why are they not just rushing us? What do they think we're going to do?"

"If I had to guess," Hil said, "they need to make it look like they're trying to rescue the kid. We don't know who's watching. They need to make them look good. Make us look bad. Cover the whole thing up. Like I said, they'll just kill him in the crossfire when they're ready." He looked at me. "Want another drink? I think I saw a pack of cards on the desk. You think you can beat me at poker?"

He was being flippant because there was nothing we could do. It didn't feel real.

We found the cards and sat on the floor, next to each other, backs against the wall, waiting for them to move in.

"What did you mean...?" I said after a while and enough hands to know I could cheat better than him. "What did you mean when you said you didn't break their programming?"

Hil rested his bottle on his knee. "I didn't take their drugs. They were putting stuff in the food, didn't you notice? I saw what they were doing, avoided anything that tasted weird and faked it. Didn't you realise?"

I shook my head stupidly. He might have just been a year or two older than me but he was way more street-wise. "How...?" I started.

He shrugged. "You should have paid more attention in lessons. You might be able to remember stuff, LC, but you really suck at applying it." He nudged me like he was joking but then he looked at me seriously. "I've come across crap like that before. I've been in prison, LC, real prison where they doped the prisoners to control them. The stuff they gave us on Redemption was all performance enhancing. I've never run so fast before. And they sent us out in tee shirts in sub zero conditions. That's not normal."

It hadn't occurred to me.

"Spearhead was different," he said. "That was the really bad stuff." He paused to take a drink. "Mind you, not taking their drugs made whatever they were doing in those freaking pods painful. You all walked out like happy little zombies. I felt like shit. I had a pounding headache for hours afterwards, but I played along." He looked at me, his eyes dark. "I played along because I wanted to. I knew exactly what we were being sent into and I thought I could pull it off. Get away with it and impress them enough to keep me around."

"You knew it was the Emperor?"

He set the bottle on the floor and nodded. "I just didn't know he was an eight year old kid." He took the empty mag out of his gun, looked at it and tossed it aside. He looked back at me. "You resisted it. Can't you remember? I heard them talking. They thought they were going to kill you with the level of drugs it was taking."

"I don't remember." I hugged my knees. "Why did you change your mind?"

He looked at me like I was stupid. "Because he's an eight year old kid. And I couldn't do it. I thought I could. And I couldn't." He dropped his eyes. "I thought I had a real chance of joining something where I could stand out. Where I mattered."

"You do. Come back with me."

He stared straight ahead and it was a while before he said, "You do realise we're not getting out of here alive?"

"We will. Come back with me."

"No."

"You have to stop running."

"LC, don't. You don't know anything about me."

"Hil, you don't need to run away anymore. We're guild. Come back with me. What about NG's standings? You said you wanted to beat me."

He laughed. "I said it to get you moving."

"Not fair. You said it. I want to be top and I'll fight you for it."

"We're not getting out of here, LC."

As if in answer, there was a commotion outside, distant, like they were finally mobilising.

Hil picked up his bottle and got to his feet. "I bet they've been waiting for your buddy, the Commandant."

He went to the counter, bust open the locks on a couple of cupboards and started pulling out boxes of ammunition. He threw me a handgun and a couple of magazines. They were live rounds. My stomach turned.

"This isn't what we are," I said.

Hil shook his head. "You don't know what I am."

He had his shirtsleeves rolled down but I could still see the edge of the tattoo on his wrist. He saw me looking and pulled his sleeve down as he tucked one gun into the small of his back and picked up another.

"You want to know what it means?" he said, not looking at me, a set to his jaw.

I was guessing it was some kind of prison or gang tattoo. "Jem said you killed a cop."

He didn't deny it, taking his time to load the gun before

he turned and looked at me, leaning back against the cupboard, the gun in his hand. "I didn't know he was a cop. He was undercover. Just another guy who was beating the crap out of me." He looked like he was trying to gauge my response, like he was expecting me to be shocked. "I didn't exactly have anyone to vouch for my side of the story."

"Mendhel got you out of it?"

He nodded. "Looked like he got you out of some shit too."

It wasn't a question but I said quietly, "He did."

"And then they send us here…" He shook his head like he couldn't believe the mess we were in, scratching at the dressing on his neck.

I couldn't believe the mess we were in.

"I shouldn't have left Jem," he said vaguely.

"We didn't have much choice."

The rumbling of the DZs outside was getting louder.

I left the gun on the floor and went and opened the door a crack.

It looked like the sun was setting, dusk moving in. They'd established a perimeter about a hundred metres out, auto-sentry guns, infantry in full-on powered armour, DZs swinging their turrets round to point at us in our little hut.

"I don't know about you," he said, "but I'm not sitting in here waiting for them to storm in and kill me."

As I watched, the Commandant, McIntyre or whatever his real name was, climbed out of a jeep directly in front of us and stood there, hands on his hips, glowering, as his entourage buzzed around him, setting up mobile comms and ops like they were facing an enemy army.

I closed the door and turned to Hilyer.

"I'm not going to surrender."

My stomach was cold as he said it. I looked down at the kid who was lying there, still unconscious. I didn't know why they wanted the Emperor dead. It felt like we were caught up in stuff that was way bigger than we'd ever know.

Hil picked the gun up from the floor and threw it to me. "I don't think you'll get much chance to fire it."

He came and stood next to me at the door.

"You ready?"

I nodded.

We flung the door open and ran out.

The wave of intense pressure that hit us was immense. I stopped in my tracks, skidding to a halt, aware that Hil was doing the same, both of us ducking instinctively, the hairs on the back of my neck bristling and my skin crawling.

All around the cordon surrounding us, there was the clatter of guns as the soldiers dropped their weapons, putting their hands in the air, the tanks powering down, the barrels of the auto-sentry guns flopping to point at the ground.

The Commandant was staring at me, eyes narrow, mouth taut.

I wanted to crawl back into the hut, flinching from the

oppressive mass above us, but I glanced across at Hil, and we both looked up.

It was huge. Unbelievably huge and even more intimidating this close up. Silent. Big as a city block. Just hovering there. There was no downdraft, no heat, no noise, just this incredible feeling of mass so close it was worse than uncomfortable, it was painful.

Hil laughed. He spun around, arms flung out, head upturned, and yelled, "Holy shit."

I backed away, throat so dry I couldn't swallow and a pressure pushing against my chest so bad it was hard to breathe.

"How did it know we were here?" I mumbled.

Hil turned, a huge grin on his face. "Because I told her. You're not the only one that can hack into a comms system." He looked up and shouted, "Holy shit, Skye." He made this overly theatrical gesture of shrugging as he looked back at me. "What the hell do we do now?"

I had no idea. We didn't know how the guild operated. There's something awesome about being valued. And knowing that I'd never be left behind is what kept me going. Too many times to count.

They came for us. Sienna was with the Security forces that landed, descending out of nowhere, supporting a bunch of extraction teams, and blitzing the place, sending the Spearhead contingent scattering. They pulled us out, told us the Emperor would be fine, and took us back to the Alsatia. We never really found out what happened once we'd been extracted. I heard someone say McIntyre got away. I don't know what happened to Jem.

Sienna told me afterwards that they thought they'd lost us when we were taken from Redemption. We sat in the mess, way after everyone else had disappeared off to bed, and she gave me the biggest hug anyone ever has. I didn't tell her about Arianne. I've never told anyone. And now Mendhel is gone, I guess none of it matters anyway.

Luka closes his eyes and says quietly, "Incoming."

I don't know when I snuggled up next to him, but I have tight hold of his hand.

"They're ours," he says.

I don't want to move but I look up to see Hil, followed by people I recognise, people I feel I know even though I've never met them, Sean O'Brien and Hal Duncan, all of them breathing heavily like they've been running, and not just running, worrying, beyond relieved to see us and to see that he's still alive.

Just.

"I can't stop the bleeding," I say, feeling very small.

Hil offers me his hand. "Come with me."

I let him lead me away as the others sit by Luka and start to fuss. I glance back over. Sean has her hand on his shoulder, rubbing gently, reassuring him as Duncan tries to patch him up. I can't hear all of what they're saying, but I catch mention of them needing NG, that something's not right, and I know it's bad.

I must be staring because Hil sits himself down in front of me, blocking my view of them, a grin on his face like he knows what I'm thinking.

"He'll be fine," he says and puts his gun on the floor between us, starting to strip it, laying out the pieces and wiping each one carefully.

It takes him a minute to look up. "What's he been telling you this time?"

"Your first tab."

"Ah," he says. "You want to know what really happened?"

I nod, stupidly. I want to know everything.

"LC was a little shit. Seriously. But he was a runt of a kid when he turned up and he could do no wrong. He had these big puppy dog eyes and he'd pull this little face that made everyone melt. He got away with whatever shit he wanted."

He pauses, adding a drop more oil to the gun's mechanism.

I can't help asking, "What about you?"

"Me? You want to know what he didn't tell you? I didn't hate him. It was the only way I knew I could keep him alive. He was naïve as hell. My orders were to watch his back, keep him out of trouble. He was just a kid after all. Hell, we both were. I figured the easiest and safest way to keep us both alive was simply to take over. I'd been in prison, I knew how it worked possibly better than anyone, so I became the daddy, the head honcho, the big kahuna…" He smiles. "If anyone in that prison had found out I was

protecting him, we both would've been as good as dead. As it was, no one dared do anything unless I gave the order. He got roughed up a little but nothing to spoil those damn good looks of his." This time Hil grins.

"He said you tried to leave."

"He told you that, huh? Well he wasn't lying, but the truth was way more complicated than that. But isn't it always?" That quiet smile again. "I was running, Spacey, like I had been all my life. I always thought I was running towards something. Something bigger, better. But the truth was I was running away. I'd always been running away. LC gave me a reason to stop running."

I look at him, the unspoken question on my lips.

"The reason?" The grin is back but this time there's a thoughtful look in his eyes. "He believed in me. He was the first person to actually believe in me. He didn't want anything from me, he didn't need anything from me." He pauses again. "LC wears his heart on his sleeve. As much as he pretends to be cold and indifferent, he cares. Sometimes I think he cares too much. But that's how we need him to be. He believes in all of us. You need to believe in him."

I watch as he starts to reassemble the gun, leaning slightly to see if I can see Luka, see that he's okay. Except he's not. And from the look on Sean's face, I don't know if he's going to be.

Hil looks up. "It was when we got back that things got really cool. Next time you're caught behind enemy lines, you need to ask him about Temerity."

Next time? I can't help the shiver. "Are we clear now…? Are they gone?"

He glances back over towards the others and looks back at me, giving a small shake of his head.

"They won't ever be gone, will they?" I say.

"No, they won't. But, Spacey, what did LC tell you? In all of this… what was the one thing he told you that matters more than anything?"

I lift my chin defiantly. "That no one messes with the Thieves' Guild."

"Damn right," he says. "Don't forget that. Don't ever forget that."

———————————

DEFYING WINTER
LC BOOK THREE

LC Anderton, raw recruit and thief-in-training, is struggling at the Thieves' Guild.

Screwing up is second nature for LC and when he gets into trouble yet again, he's sent off on a minor assignment to get him out of the way. Only this time he's got his eye on a different mission, a mission no other field-op in the guild will touch. Because it's impossible. And to LC, that's a challenge he can't resist. But it's impossible for a reason, and LC isn't the only one after it. As the odds stack up against him, he can walk away or go all in... but even he can't imagine what will be asked of him and the price he'll have to pay.

"A story that defines LC as a field op, a story that at times had me on the edge of my seat and other times in tears as he beats the odds stacked against him."

"Fast-paced sci fi at its best. Written with passion and flair, this is a book that's hard to put down once you start reading because every chapter hangs you over a cliff."

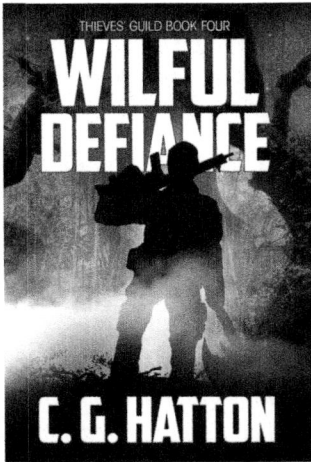

Also by C.G. Hatton
available from Sixth Element Publishing
in paperback and eBook

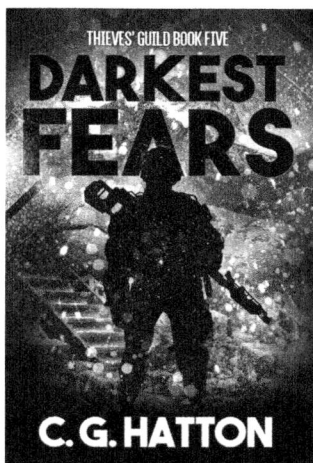

DARKEST FEARS
THIEVES' GUILD BOOK FIVE

The galaxy is at war… it's just not the war anyone expected.

Faced with an onslaught the like of which has never been seen before, only the remnants of the mythical Thieves' Guild stand between survival and extinction at the hands of an alien horde.

Taken captive by the ruthless invaders, thief turned reluctant soldier LC Anderton has only one priority – survive long enough to rescue NG, head of the Thieves' Guild who is missing in action and their only chance to turn the tide. But LC is fighting his own war, and it's one he's not sure he can win.

"WOW! Just WOW! The writing is fast-paced, which is characteristic of this universe of books (yes this is now a universe, not a trilogy - yay!)"

"Awesome twists, non-stop action, really cool characters and the world completely absorbs you! Great addition to the series! "

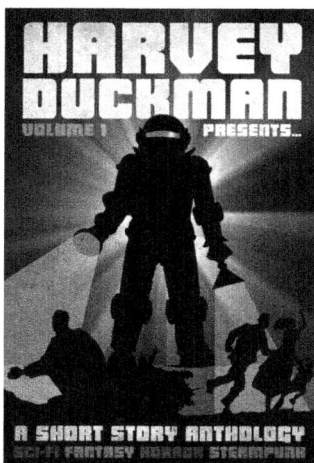

FIND OUT MORE AT
WWW.CGHATTON.COM

Printed in Great Britain
by Amazon

78311573R00174